"YOU CAN'T SCARE ME."

"I thought you said this afternoon that I did frighten you. Make up your mind, Mrs. Ellington."

"I'm not afraid of you," she said in a low, breathy whisper. "I'm afraid of the way you make me feel."

It was a tough admission for her to make. She was so open, he saw the pain on her face, the hurt and indecision that flickered there.

He lowered his face until his lips were almost on hers. "Don't feel anything for me," he whispered.

"What if I can't help it?"

He had started this, trying to scare her, but the ploy wasn't working. In fact, he could not have failed more miserably. She wasn't scared, but he sure as hell was. Nothing frightened him anymore. Nothing. It was hard to scare a man who didn't have anything to lose.

His mouth touched hers, his hands rose up to remove the pins from her hair. The warm dark strands fell—over her shoulders, down her back—and he threaded his fingers through those strands with an aching hunger.

Her body molded against his, and he felt her response to the lingering kiss. She quivered, her lips parted and her hands . . . reached around. Pale, delicate fingers danced over his back. She drew him in closer, deeper, with every tender second that passed.

Knowing he had no choice, he took his mouth from hers. God, he couldn't do this anymore. He couldn't dance to the edge of something he wanted more than anything and then walk away with a smile on his face.

In the low light he could see too well the hunger in Nadine's eyes. The trepidation and the curiosity and the love. At least, he could fool himself into thinking that it was love. . . .

Dear Romance Reader,

In July of 1999, we launched the Ballad line with four new series, and each month we present both new and continuing stories set everywhere from medieval England to the American West—the kind of passionate, romantic stories you love best, written by the most gifted authors. At the back of each book, we tell you when you can find subsequent books in the series that have captured your heart.

Getting this month off to a dazzling start is **Outcast**, the debut story in the passionate new series *The Vikings,* from longtime reader-favorite Kathryn Hockett. When a woman proud of her Viking heritage meets the Nordic warrior in search of her father's oldest son, she proves a woman's strength—in battle and in love. Next, ever-imaginative Alice Duncan takes us to the 1893 World's Fair in Chicago with her new trilogy, *Meet Me at the Fair.* Everything's **Coming Up Roses** for a trick rider in Buffalo Bill's Wild West Show—until she meets the man who threatens to steal her heart.

Linda Devlin returns this month with **Cash**, the long-awaited sixth installment in the *Rock Creek Six* series, in which a legendary ladies' man—and gunslinger—must face up to his past, and the future he glimpses in the smile of a certain woman. Finally, Corinne Everett ends *Daughters of Liberty* with **Sweet Violet**, as a young Virginia woman determined to find adventure in England discovers danger instead—along with a surprising chance at love.

What a fabulous selection to choose from! Why not read them all? Enjoy!

Kate Duffy
Editorial Director

The Rock Creek Six

CASH

Linda Devlin

ZEBRA BOOKS
Kensington Publishing Corp.
http://www.kensingtonbooks.com

This book is dedicated to Lori Handeland, who has been such a joy to work with. Thanks to e-mail, Wisconsin and Alabama just got a little bit closer.

Prologue

Webberville, Texas
March 1876

"Can I touch it?" Henrietta whispered.

"No."

"Please, Cash," she purred.

They lounged, naked and relaxed, across a canted and creaking bed in a small room above the Webberville saloon. Henrietta, a pretty enough calico gal for these parts, smiled widely. Of course the redhead was happy. She'd been well satisfied and well paid, and Cash wasn't finished with her. He just wished she wouldn't talk so damned much.

"No," he said again, setting his eyes on her in a way that made her bright smile fade.

Her own eyes landed on the fancy six-shooter that rested on the bedside table, close at hand, and she sighed deeply. Her ponderous breasts rose and fell. "But it's so pretty, and shiny, and . . . and I know what you can do with it."

Cash didn't understand the fascination. He killed with that six-shooter. He was fast, he was accurate, and he was deadly. Henrietta practically salivated over that damned gun. She wanted to caress it the same way she'd caressed him, with curious fingers.

The sick fascination annoyed him, but not enough to make him kick her out of his bed. He was on his way to Rock Creek, and once he arrived there, women available for bedding would be few and far between. There were too damn many respectable, meddlesome women in that town.

"Cash, darlin'," Henrietta began, rolling seductively toward him. Her eyes were no longer on his six-shooter. "How long will you be here?"

"Just until tomorrow morning."

"Take me with you when you go."

It was a tempting prospect for the span of a half second. "No."

She pouted, jutting out her bottom lip. "That's all you can say tonight. No, no, no. I don't like it here. I know you have your own saloon in Rock Creek. I could work there, or . . ." Her eyes got big. Wide and hopeful. "Or I could just be with you. I don't ask for much. I'm real easy to get along with."

"Honey, you wouldn't be in Rock Creek a week before the good women of that fine town had you opening a bakery or married to the closest single rancher," he teased.

"You don't think *good women* have tried to save me before?" she countered with a wicked smile. "I don't want to be saved. It would take an army of good women to drag me away from you."

"Unfortunately Rock Creek has that very army."

The shuffle of a shoe in the hallway registered in

his brain, in that small corner that was always on alert and kept him alive. He noted the shuffle as he continued his conversation with the woman who had decided to make her argument with her body. She could argue all she wanted, she could *argue* all night, but when he headed out of here in the morning, she'd be staying behind.

"You'll be lonely there," she whispered.

"Yes, I will."

"Then why are you going?"

It's home. He wasn't foolish enough to admit that, not even to a prostitute he'd likely never see again.

The muted snick outside the door made Cash sit up straight and shove Henrietta aside as he reached for the six-shooter on the bedside table. He kicked her off the bed and onto the floor as the door burst open. In the same smooth motion he swung the pistol forward, taking aim and firing in an instinctive and deadly accurate fashion. The man in the doorway got off a single shot, but it went wide and the bullet smacked into the wall above Cash's head.

Blood bloomed on the dingy white shirt of the attacker in the doorway. The moron looked surprised. Stunned, even, as he glanced down at his fatal wound. His six-shooter dropped from numbed fingers as he fell forward, slamming down face first onto the plank floor.

Henrietta screamed loud and long. Cash cursed as he reached for his trousers, leaping from the bed to pull them on. He was almost decent by the time a bald head peeked around the doorjamb. Again, his arm reacted and the gun snapped up.

But it was the bartender. Pale and shaking, the old man looked from Cash to the body on the floor. "Who . . . who is that?"

"I don't know," Cash said as he lowered his weapon. "You tell me."

Henrietta took a deep breath and started to scream again.

"Shut up," Cash ordered in a low voice. She did.

"He's not from around here," the bartender said. "Showed up an hour or so back and started asking questions. I reckon someone told him you were up here."

"I reckon," Cash whispered, stepping around the bed to glance down at the body. The man had landed nose down on the floor, so it was impossible to get a decent look at his face from a standing position.

Since the war had ended, he'd hired his gun out on numerous occasions. Killing people was Cash's gift, and he embraced his talent the way other people embraced their own chosen professions. Between jobs he stopped in Rock Creek for the closest thing to real rest he knew. In the past couple of years he'd often found himself talking and thinking about staying there, making his saloon, Rogue's Palace, home for good. Putting down roots of a sort. But he always got restless and changed his mind after a few weeks or a few months. Sometimes he didn't last more than a couple of days. There had been a time when Nate was always there to watch his back, and he'd returned the favor. For the past year, though, Cash had been on his own, more often than not.

Some days a real anger boiled up inside him, when

he thought of the way Nate had let Jo reform him. But
when he realized that his old friend would probably
be dead by now without that wife's interference, the
anger receded. That didn't mean Cash had forgiven
Nate for turning his back on the life the two of them
had led for so long, though. Who would have thought
he'd actually miss the companionship of a drunk who
was given to passing out at the most inopportune moments, and who quoted Scripture and occasionally
spouted incoherent words of wisdom when he was
awake?

Cash dropped to his haunches and lifted a mass of
stringy hair away from the gunman's face. It might
have been a relief to see an enemy, a face he recognized . . . but this man was a stranger. A stranger who
had tracked Daniel Cash down and tried to ambush
him. For revenge or to make a name for himself? No
one would ever know. This man's secrets would be buried with him in a Webberville grave.

He no longer had any desire to sleep in this bed, to
lie with this woman. Rock Creek was calling him.
Calling him home. He didn't know how long he'd stay
this time, but it was becoming increasingly clear that
he was not safe or welcome anywhere else.

He wasn't even sure he'd be safe or welcomed there.

One

"Marry me, dammit."

Cash grinned as he watched Jed chase after his very pregnant wife. Hannah had no reservations about bursting into Rogue's Palace with her husband on her trail.

"We're already married," she said with strained patience. "We have been for more than two years."

Jed let loose a long string of profanity. Her back to her husband, Hannah just smiled. Cash had never seen the quarrelsome woman so unnaturally serene. No one loved an argument as much as Hannah, and she normally had a most direct way of sharing her opinion. Jed swore his wife had been the very picture of gentleness since becoming pregnant. Cash found it downright unnatural.

"We were married in Italian," Jed argued. "I don't even know if that's legal in Texas or not!"

"Of course it is, darling."

Cash pulled out a chair at his table, bowed in a gentlemanly fashion, and offered Hannah a seat. Good

Lord, she really was huge. It wasn't like he hadn't seen expectant mothers before, but Hannah apparently did pregnancy the same way she did everything else: to excess.

Jed sat down beside Hannah and took her hand. After all this time, they remained a most unlikely couple. Jed's wavy dark blond hair was getting long again, and while he managed to shave now and then, he didn't get around to the chore every day. He was still given to leather and buckskins, though denim and cotton ran a close second. He was rough, he was crude . . . and he was accustomed to getting what he asked for. Hannah always looked like a lady, proper and refined. Regal and well bred. Her dark red hair was normally perfectly fashioned, and her clothes were always expensive, a fact Cash noticed and appreciated. You didn't usually see the toughness in her until she opened her mouth.

"Nate can just marry us again," Jed all but pleaded. "We'll have our family and friends with us this time. And the ceremony can be performed in a language I understand so I'm absolutely sure it's legal and our baby is legitimate."

Hannah leaned over and planted a kiss on Jed's roughly bearded cheek. "You are so incredibly sweet."

Cash lifted his eyebrows. Sweet? No one had ever dared to call Jed Rourke *sweet.*

It was distressing to see how marriage had ruined five perfectly capable men. Amusing, at times, but also depressing. There were babies everywhere, children, families, and at the center of it were those interfering good women. Sex was one thing. Complete surrender was another.

Cash had always felt like he lived on the outside, looking in. As an orphaned boy in Marianna, Texas, making his way however he could. As a soldier who had the ability to separate himself from everything and everyone else. As a gunman who could kill without compunction.

These days he really was the odd man out. His friends, former soldiers who'd always been better at war than at peace, were all married. Tamed and comfortable. Five of the desperadoes once known as the Rock Creek Six reproduced regularly or took in orphans or did both. They and their wives tolerated Cash and his ways, for old time's sake he was certain, but he no longer felt like one of them.

Nor did he want to. No woman would lead him around by his nose *or* his pecker, and he had no desire to reproduce.

There had been a time when Jed would have picked Hannah up, carried her to the church, and held her still while the ceremony he desired was performed. Hannah was enormous at the moment, but if any man could carry her, it would be Jed. Instead, the big man sat beside her, all but begging her to do as he wished.

Cash had a feeling Jed would get his second wedding, but only after Hannah had strung him along for a while. Women. At times like this, Cash was doubly grateful that he'd sidestepped the seemingly sweet trap his friends had fallen into.

"Tell me," Cash said, sitting down at Hannah's other side to join the conversation. "Why not just agree to the ceremony Jed wants and be done with it? Unless, of course, you're sorry you ever married . . ."

"No!" Hannah said sharply, lifting her head to pin her strong gray eyes on him. She immediately turned to her husband and raised a soft hand to touch his cheek. "Oh, you don't think that's why . . . You know I love you, and marrying you was the best thing that ever happened to me. But . . . our wedding was so perfect." She turned back to Cash and smiled, but tears sprouted in her eyes. "You should have seen the cathedral where we were married. It was ancient and majestic, the most gorgeous building I have ever seen in my life. The sun slanted through the stained-glass windows in a way that was certainly heavenly, and Jed looked so beautiful."

Jed Rourke, beautiful *and* sweet. Cash shook his head.

"The words were lovely—" she whispered.

"And in a language I couldn't understand," Jed interrupted.

"The day was magical," Hannah finished. "I don't need another wedding. I am already married in every possible way."

Jed sighed in what might have been capitulation. Cash suspected this surrender was nothing more than a temporary truce.

Cash laid his eyes on redheaded Hannah. "You have no idea how it distresses me to watch you ruin a perfectly good man this way."

Hannah pursed her lips. "Jed is not *ruined,* you imbecile."

"Imbecile?" Cash repeated with a lift of his eyebrows.

"Now, you two . . ." Jed began.

Hannah silenced her husband with a lift of a single finger, and Cash stifled a grin as she stated her case. "You remain in this dark, cheerless saloon all day and all night, leaving only because Eden won't deliver your meals."

"Rogue's Palace is *quite* cheery," Cash argued.

"You should be able to find yourself a woman somewhere," she said, the tone of her voice suggesting that Cash had tried to find one who would have him but could not. "You're relatively good-looking when the light hits you just so, and you can be charming when you set your mind to it." She made every word sound like a very friendly insult. "If you could just get a handle on that mouth of yours—"

"My mouth?" Cash interrupted with a bark of a laugh. "Oh, this is definitely the pot calling the kettle black."

"You two, cut it out," Jed said, his voice low and threatening.

Hannah turned a softening gaze to her husband. "Sorry, darling. It's just that Cash can be so exasperating. He needs a good woman—"

"I'd rather be shot," Cash interrupted. "I'd rather be hanged. I'd rather be drawn and quartered. God save me from the *good women* of this world."

"If divine intervention is called for," Hannah countered, "it would be on behalf of the women you try so diligently to avoid."

"Enough," Jed said softly. "Can we talk about the wedding some more?"

Hannah's smile brightened. "What wedding?" She turned sparkling eyes to Cash. Good heavens, the woman loved a good argument more than he did. "Can I have a small whiskey, please?"

"No," Jed and Cash answered at the same time.

She tried to pout. "Some saloon this is."

Jed assisted Hannah to her feet and led her toward the bat-wing doors. "We'll head back to the hotel and I'll have Eden fix you some tea."

"Tea is a poor excuse for a small shot of whiskey," Hannah complained. "Just a teensy-weensy—"

"No," Jed said as he held the swinging door open. "Eden said it's not good for the baby. You'll just have to wait another couple of months or so."

"You're right, of course," Hannah said demurely. "I want only what's best for the baby."

"I'm just trying to take good care of you both."

Hannah sighed. "Yes, dear."

Cash leaned back in his chair and shook his head. *Yes, dear?*

The saloon was empty, a condition that did not bother Cash at the moment. It was early afternoon, and besides, he never exactly did a rousing business. Most people looking for entertainment went to Lily's place, down the road. Three Queens. She had music in her fancy entertainment house, singing and dancing every night of the week. The last man who had tried to sing and dance in Rogue's Palace had been tossed out on his ear, the drunken, tone-deaf bastard.

Cash's saloon offered whiskey and the occasional

game of poker. It catered to men who were looking for the simple things. Booze and a way to lose their hard-earned money. Most days it was quite late before business picked up.

So he was surprised when, just minutes after Jed and Hannah left, the doors swung open again. With the sunlight bright behind the newcomer, it was impossible to tell who it was. A small man or a boy in baggy trousers and an ill-fitting shirt, boots that clipped on the wooden floor, a wide-brimmed hat, and no gun belt. There was no sign of a weapon at all, and still a shiver of warning crept up Cash's spine. Strangers, no matter how small and innocent-looking they might be, were usually trouble.

"Can I help you?" Cash asked in a tone that was purposely unwelcoming.

He came to his feet and laid his hand over the six-shooter at his right hip as the stranger removed his— *her* hat, and a wealth of dark hair came tumbling down around her shoulders. She shook out that warm brown hair and clutched the hat in pale, small hands.

Cash's heart damn near burst through his chest.

"Danny?" she whispered in a voice he still recognized too well. That softly spoken single word cut right through him, sharp as any knife.

She was the only good woman he had ever cared for, the only woman he had ever loved. They had been together a lifetime ago, so long ago that the man who had known her was nothing at all like the man Daniel Cash was today.

Taking tiny, uncertain steps, she walked into the saloon, her hat in her hand, her eyes wide with fear. And

her face . . . her face was as beautiful as ever. Creamy
pale, every feature delicately carved. The lips tempt-
ingly full, the cheeks a little leaner than he remembered, the green eyes . . . sadder. The years had been
kind to her; she looked almost exactly like she did in
his dreams. Her lips parted, as if she tried to speak but
could not.

He had faced more guns than he could count, but
his heart had never threatened to pound through his
chest the way it did right now.

This was the woman who had created the Daniel
Cash who existed today. The Cash who didn't care
about anyone or anything. The Cash who could kill
without blinking an eye. She was the one who had
taught him about betrayal.

No matter what, he couldn't allow her to know that
she was such an important part of his life. Only one
thing mattered: getting her out of Rock Creek as soon
as possible.

"Nadine," he finally said, his heartbeat steady once
again, his voice calm and low. "What the hell are you
doing here?"

Well, what had she expected? A warm welcome? A
hearty hug and a friendly "How are you?"

"We need to talk."

She would have known Danny anywhere, and yet he
was not the man she remembered. He was harder. Cold
and distant in a way the boy she had loved could never
be. Fifteen years had aged him, as those same years
had aged her, but physically he carried the years well.

He was an unusually handsome man, just as he had once been an unusually beautiful boy.

But there was something within him that he did not carry well. She saw a quiet disturbance in his dark eyes, in the coiled tension that radiated from him. In his perfectly cut black suit and ruffled cuffs, with those six-shooters hanging so familiarly on his hips, he appeared sleek and polished. The mustache and well-trimmed beard hadn't been there fifteen years earlier, though she was not surprised to see them. In the drawings she saw in the newspapers, Daniel Cash always appeared the same. The dapper dress and perfectly trimmed facial hair. Black-eyed and unquestionably deadly.

Precisely cut black hair lay against skin too pale, as if he didn't leave this dark cave of a place and step into the sun often enough. And his hands . . . his hands were long-fingered and beautiful, a man's capable hands. Tension was coiled through his long, lean body, a tension she could sense more than she could see.

But she looked at him and saw more than the carefully crafted picture he presented for the world. She saw pain. Not a normal physical pain, but something so dark and deep, it made her shudder.

He took a step toward her, moving with a panther's grace. "What on earth could we possibly have to talk about?"

"I need your help," she whispered as he came closer, every step calculated, the gaze he shot her way intense and cutting.

Danny smiled, and a shiver ran through her. The man she had loved had been warm and kind. Young, but . . . good at heart and generous to a fault. But this smile was as cold as ice. It was not the smile of a kind man.

"Did you come all this way to hire me? How unexpected." He moved closer still, one step and then another, those dark eyes roving over her dusty, worn clothing and finally landing on her face. "I don't take many jobs these days, but for an old friend I might make an exception." He leaned toward her and whispered in her ear, "Want me to kill someone for you? Is that why you're here?"

"No!" she said, stepping quickly back. She was tempted to lift a hand to her ear where his breath had touched her and started a tingle that rippled through her body, still. She refrained. "I most certainly do not want you to kill anyone for me."

"For Joseph, then." He circled around her, and she felt like nothing more than defenseless prey. A wounded rabbit to his panther. "A gift for the husband?" She couldn't help but hear the bitterness in his voice.

"I didn't know you even realized I had married." How could he know? Danny had never stepped foot in Marianna after he'd left for the war. He didn't even care enough to visit, to let her know he was alive and well.

"Oh, I realized," he said. "How is Ellington? Is he with you? Waiting outside, perhaps, while you beg for a favor?"

He moved in closer, leaned down, and whispered in her ear again, "What is he willing to let you do for that favor, Nadine? I usually charge cold, hard cash, but for you I might make an exception."

He broke her heart, what little bit wasn't already in shreds. She'd come looking for an old friend and found a stranger. A stranger who was, it seemed, determined to hurt her. It didn't matter.

"Joseph is dead," she said simply. Something in Nadine wanted to reach out and touch the man who moved restlessly around her. Just a brush of her fingers on his black coat. Perhaps a caress of the unexpected frill at the cuff of his fine shirt. Her Danny had been wonderfully warm and alive, bright in every way. The Cash she confronted now seemed to have no fire at all. If she could touch him, however briefly, would she be relieved to discover the warmth she remembered? She kept her curious hands to herself.

"Am I supposed to avenge his death? Is that why you're here?" He continued to circle around her, staying too close, breathing on her, studying every inch until she wished she'd taken a bath and changed clothes before rushing to the saloon to see him. She'd been so eager to lay her eyes on him that she hadn't even bothered to shake off the road dust.

"Joseph died nine years ago," she said softly. "Pneumonia. There's no one to blame for his death. No need for revenge."

"Nine years," he breathed. "I imagine you have another husband by now. Maybe you've been through two or three. You were never much of one for . . . waiting."

Her heart leapt, but she ignored the response. "I

never remarried, and this visit has nothing to do with revenge or killing. I need your help, Danny."

He grabbed her arms, too tight, and she lifted her face to look him in the eye. So dark a brown they appeared to be black, those eyes bored into her. "Danny is gone, sweetheart. He's been dead a long time. You can call me Cash, like everyone else."

She swallowed hard. "All right. Cash, I need your help."

He released her. "Sorry. I'm not in the rescuing business anymore."

She sighed. This was so much more difficult than she'd imagined it would be! And she had not imagined for a moment that this would be easy. "I don't need to be rescued, Da—Cash."

"No one needs to be rescued, no one needs to be shot," he said with a touch of biting humor. "Sorry, honey, that's all I do, unless you have an urgent need for a poker player."

He wasn't going to make this easy, so she'd just have to blurt it out. "My son has decided he wants to be a gunslinger. I need you to talk him out of it."

Ah, at least she managed to surprise him. His eyebrows lifted, and he took a wary step back. His entire body stiffened. "Your son? And he wants to be a—" His eyes narrowed suspiciously. "How old is this kid?"

"Thirteen," she said, the word fighting to make it through her dry mouth. He'd be fourteen in the fall, a detail she didn't bother to add. Not yet.

"Thirteen. You didn't waste any time, did you," he said wryly. "How many kids did you and Ellington have?"

"I have only one child," she whispered. "And I can't just sit back and allow him to make this mistake. You know . . . you know what the life of a gunslinger is like. He's entranced by the glamour and excitement that's portrayed in the dime novels and the newspaper serializations, but you and I both know that's not what it's like."

"Glamour," he scoffed. "If you call learning to sleep with one eye open glamorous—"

"Tell JD that," she interrupted. "Tell him how horrible it is to live this way."

Again, his eyebrows. "I didn't say my life was horrible."

"He'll get killed," she argued. "I know he will."

"Is he any good?"

He finally managed to make her angry. "What difference does it make! He's a child, and he has no business—"

"I was on my own at thirteen, if you remember. I was a man. Maybe he is, too."

She clenched her jaw. "You can do this one thing for me," she whispered. "You owe me that much."

"I owe you?" He grinned. "Honey, what the hell makes you think I owe you any goddamn thing?"

She looked him in the eye. There was no way she'd lie to him, no way she'd hide something this important. She searched his dark eyes for a hint of the boy she had loved, prayed to see a trace of tenderness mixed in with the pain and the bitterness. For a moment, just for a moment, she thought she saw what she was searching for. Then again, maybe it was just wishful thinking that made her, for one split second, see the boy she'd loved with all her heart in this hard man.

"Don't do it for me, then. Do it for JD."

"Why should I?"

Cash stood very still and waited for her answer. Oh, this was a mistake. A horrible, horrible mistake. Had she really thought the man who had deserted her would help her now? That the heartless Daniel Cash she read about would have any regard for her or for JD?

In a disgustingly hopeful moment, she had. She'd ridden toward Rock Creek with such ridiculous notions. But she lifted her chin and answered his question. Like it or not, he had to know.

"Because he's your son."

Two

Cash practically dragged Nadine to the table in the corner, where he pulled out a chair and made sure she sat in it. That done, he dropped into the chair he usually occupied, back to the wall with a clear view of the door.

Although he wouldn't admit it to her, he had no choice but to sit down. His knees were shaking. A moment longer and he probably would have been forced to sit on the floor at her feet.

He grabbed her chair and swung it around so that she faced him, knee to knee, eye to eye. The sharp squeal of chair legs against the rough wooden floor reverberated in the air.

"I don't have a son," he insisted.

"Yes, you do."

How could she drop a bombshell like this and remain so damned calm? Her eyes were dreamy and easy, her soft lips relaxed and tempting. As far as he could tell, *her* knees didn't shake.

One night, one joining. He'd been heading off to war, and they'd said good-bye the way sweethearts sometimes do. Frantically. Not knowing what tomor-

row would bring. They'd lost their virginity together
that night, on a blanket spread beneath an oak tree half
a mile from her father's ranch house. It had been De-
cember cold, but neither of them had felt the chill. He'd
been eighteen years old. Nadine had been two weeks
from her seventeenth birthday. She'd sneaked out of
the house. He didn't have anyone to sneak away from.
She'd cried. He'd promised to come back for her.

"Does he know I'm his"—the word he couldn't say
stuck in his throat for a moment—"father?"

Nadine shook her head. "No."

"Good. Let's keep it that way."

The pain in her eyes was there for anyone to see,
but what choice did he have?

"Then how in hell did he get the notion to be a
gunslinger?"

The softening of Nadine's lips might have been the
prelude to a smile, but the smile never happened.
"You're quite infamous in Marianna. Local boy makes
a name for himself. The kid who used to sweep out
the general store has dime novels and newspaper arti-
cles written about his exploits. From the first time JD
read about you, he was fascinated."

Cash shook his head in horrified wonder. "Where
is he now?"

"We checked into the hotel, and I told him to stay
in the room until I'd had a chance to speak to you."

"So he knows why you're here."

Nadine shrugged her shoulders. Even in those
baggy, shapeless clothes, he could tell she had a
woman's body. Fuller than he remembered, softer. Un-
corseted and inviting and *not* for him.

"Not entirely," she said in a slightly husky voice that sent chills down his spine. "When he found out I knew you, he begged me to contact you, to . . . to ask you if you would take him on as an apprentice."

Cash's mouth broke into a wide, harsh smile. "An apprentice? The kid wants me to take him under my wing?"

"Yes."

He was still trying to absorb the news that he was a father, that he had a son. He didn't have the ability, at the moment, to think rationally about this predicament.

Nadine leaned slightly forward. The top button of her shirt, a very plain man's shirt, was unfastened, and dusty fabric fell apart to offer him a tantalizing view of the base of her slender throat. "Please," she whispered. "Help me. JD is all I have, and if I lose him to this . . . I don't know what I'll do. Save our son, Cash."

Taking a calming breath, he leaned back in his chair. He could refuse to accept her story that JD was his child. He could send Nadine on her way without taking so much as a glance at the kid.

But somehow he knew she was telling the truth. Their one and only time together had resulted in a child. The boy was thirteen years old, almost a man. What color was his hair? His eyes? Was he tall or short for his age? Was he smart?

Was he as fast as his father?

"First rule," Cash said. "No one here is to be told that he's my son. Not ever. Does anyone in Marianna know?"

Nadine shook her head. "Joseph suspected it was you, of course, but we never discussed it. My father knew, but he passed on not long after Joseph. I never told anyone else."

"Second rule," Cash continued. "You do whatever I say."

Her eyes widened, and for a moment she looked truly afraid of him. Smart woman.

"The only way to make sure JD leaves here determined not to follow in my less than illustrious footsteps is to scare the bejesus out of him. By the time you two leave Rock Creek he'll be dreaming of the safe life of a farmer or a rancher or a shopkeeper. Or whatever it is you have planned for him. I don't need you playing mommy and getting in the way."

She nodded once. "I understand."

"What's the JD stand for?"

"Joseph Daniel," she whispered.

Joseph Daniel, named for the kid's natural father and the man who had married his mother on a warm spring afternoon.

The wind had been blowing in from the west that day, the sky had been so bright a blue it hurt the eyes, Cash remembered with an unexpected lurch of his heart. The sun had shone down on Nadine in her white wedding dress as her new husband walked her out of the church while a wounded soldier with his heart in his throat and his own blood staining his uniform watched from the alley across the street. He had never suspected that she might be carrying his child. At the time he hadn't been able to think straight.

The fever had been on him for more days than he could count. The bleeding had stopped, but he'd lost a lot of blood. He'd made it to Marianna on sheer will. Will and the need to see Nadine.

He'd seen her, all right.

"Don't look at me like that," Nadine whispered hoarsely.

"Like what?" he asked coolly.

"I thought you were dead. Your name was on a list . . . that cursed list of soldiers who had been killed in battle . . . and I didn't know what else to do. It was years before I found out you were alive." Her eyes bored into him. "Years. What happened to you?"

Now, that was a question that would take far too long to answer. "It was a long time ago," he said as if none of it mattered. "We can't go back and undo what happened. Everything worked out for the best, anyway."

She ran an exasperated hand through her hair, a mass of warm brown that was as soft and thick as he remembered. "You're right, of course. When do you want to meet JD and get started?"

Now. Never. "Tomorrow morning."

"He won't like waiting."

Cash leaned forward and did what he'd been wanting to do since he'd seen Nadine shake out her hair. He reached out and touched her cheek. She flinched but didn't move away. God in heaven, her skin was like silk.

"If he complains, you tell him this is lesson number one. A gunfighter must have infinite patience." He trailed his fingers down to her throat, felt her quiver against his fingertips. "We wait, and we wait, and we wait."

"All right," she whispered.

He took most of his meals in the Paradise Hotel dining room, but not tonight. Tonight he would prepare himself for what was to come, and he didn't need the distraction of watching Nadine and her son . . . *his* son . . . munching on Eden's biscuits and whatever else she was serving to her family and guests. He needed solitude to prepare.

"Thank you." Nadine started to rise, but he stopped her with a hand on her arm. His fingers closed over her forearm, and he absorbed her body heat through dusty cotton. He felt her softness under the dirty, coarse fabric.

"Don't thank me yet. There's no guarantee that I can change his mind."

This time her hint of a smile blossomed into a half-grin. "You will," she said confidently. "Mr. Brubaker used to say you were the best salesman he ever had. Said you could talk a man into spending his last cent and make him feel privileged to do so. He also said you could charm a bear out of his honey."

"Charm is cheap, and I don't think talking a thirteen-year-old boy out of something he wants to do is anything like selling penny candy to a farmer."

"But you can do it," she assured him.

He didn't release her. Not yet. "If I agree, you have to promise to do anything I say."

Her smile faded. "Yes."

"Your first instruction is that you tell *no one* that I used to sweep out Brubaker's general store and sleep on a pallet by the potato bin."

Her eyes danced. "Everyone in Marianna knows."

"Well, no one in Rock Creek has a clue, and I'd like to keep it that way. I have a reputation to maintain."

He peeled his fingers away from Nadine's arm and she rose slowly, almost as if she were drunk. "I wouldn't dream of staining your spotless reputation. I will do my best to make sure everyone here thinks you were born with those six-shooters on your hips and that killer gleam in your eye." The sarcasm was unmistakable.

"It would be best if they don't know about us, either."

She stared at him boldly, braver now that she had his word he'd do as she asked. "What's to know?"

"Not a damn thing."

Nadine wanted to think the worst was over, but she knew better. The initial meeting with Danny . . . *Cash,* as he insisted upon . . . had been difficult, and she imagined the days to come wouldn't be any easier. Of course he had changed, everyone had changed. But she didn't like what the only man she had ever loved had become.

"What did he say?" JD asked brightly as she opened the door to their hotel room. She was a little surprised he had stayed put, as she'd ordered him to. Her threat of hauling him along the Rock Creek street by the ear while his idol, the gunman Daniel Cash, watched was enough to keep him in line. For now.

"I think he's agreeable. He'll meet with you tomorrow morning."

"Tomorrow?" JD placed his hands on narrow hips,

striking a pose of youthful indignation. "We came all this way—"

"Patience," Nadine interrupted as she dropped her hat onto a table by the window. "He said patience was to be your first lesson."

JD grinned widely. Heavens, there were moments when her son looked so much like his father, he grabbed her heart and wouldn't let go. He had her green eyes, but that smile reminded her of better days, when the young man she'd adored had let her call him Danny. When he'd smiled without a scornful edge. JD's dark brown hair fell the way Cash's black hair had when he'd been a boy, windblown and untamed, framing his beautiful face. More than that, there were moments when JD moved like the boy she remembered. JD was comfortable with himself, even at this age when he was all arms and legs. He was limber, lithe and strong. So much like his father.

If JD followed in Cash's footsteps, what would she do? Seeing what Cash had done with his life hurt her more acutely than she cared to admit. If JD took the same route, she would die. She would literally die.

"If patience is the first lesson, there has to be a second one, right?"

"I think you have to pass the first lesson before you move on."

"I can wait until tomorrow morning," JD said brightly. "No problem." He picked up his six-shooter from the bedside table and began to twirl it in his hand. Smoothly, easily, so effortlessly her heart clenched.

"Put that down," she insisted softly.

"I have to practice," he insisted.

"You put it down or I go to Cash right now and beg him not to so much as meet with you."

He knew she wasn't bluffing, so with a scowl on his face he did as she asked.

This was her fault. She had no one else to blame. Allowing JD to learn how to shoot hadn't struck her as a bad idea at the time. When he'd turned out to be such a natural, it had seemed only fair to allow him to compete in local marksmanship competitions. A man should know how to defend himself and his family, and there had been a time when she'd been so proud of him for finding such a talent.

But then he'd discovered the stories about Daniel Cash and become fascinated. He'd decided his life's work would be to hire out his gun, to make a name for himself the way Cash had. And the nightmares had begun. The very idea of JD taking a life or having his own taken away was a fear more intense than she'd imagined possible.

"We'll get cleaned up and have supper, then tonight we'll get a good night's sleep. Tomorrow will be here soon enough."

"I won't sleep a wink tonight," JD said.

Neither will I.

The crowd was small that night, which suited Cash just fine. He was in no mood for company. His customers recognized his foul disposition and steered clear of him as he sat at his usual table, in his usual chair, sipping at a glass of whiskey.

Evan Hopkins, the aging bartender who didn't take

any guff from anyone and didn't allow anybody to sing in Rogue's Palace, served up drinks and kept the polished bar clean. A smart man, he also kept the small crowd away from Cash's corner.

Cash allowed the noise around him to fade, a dangerous and unusual reaction to the day's events. He had too many things to think about, and he didn't much like where his mind was taking him. Memories he'd thought gone rose to the surface. He had the oddest compulsion to head down to the hotel and walk into Nadine's room and just look at her. At her and their son. He wanted to stand at the foot of the bed in awe at how beautiful and fine she was, at how much time had gone by . . . at the fact that she had given him a son.

Cash shuddered and took a long sip. The very idea of having a child terrified him.

It was late when Jed burst through the bat-wing doors. His eyes landed on Cash, and he smiled as if nothing had changed. The big man was unarmed, a foolish mistake in Cash's estimation. Being happily married apparently robbed a man of a good portion of his common sense. Armed or not, though, Jed Rourke was an intimidating man.

"Just the man I wanted to see," Jed drawled.

"What do you want?" Cash asked tersely.

Jed pulled out a chair and with a flick of his wrist spun it around. He sat down, straddling the seat and resting his arms over the back of the rustic chair. "I need your help."

Not again. "Have I sprouted a sign on my forehead that reads Good Samaritan? If not, it must be my past record of doing good deeds that has people coming to me for favors today."

Jed ignored the sharp tone of Cash's voice. "Who else asked you for a favor?"

Cash lifted his hand and waved off the question. "Never mind. I'll ask again. What do you want?"

There was a sparkle in Jed's eyes, something new and rather frightening. The man was disgustingly *happy.* "Hannah's being difficult about getting married again because the first wedding was perfect for her and she doesn't want to spoil that image with anything common."

"So it seems."

"So," Jed said in a lowered voice, "we put on a wedding that's even better than the first one *and* performed in English. Everybody gets what they want. I figured you'd know how to make it special."

"You want me to help you plan a wedding," Cash said incredulously.

"Yeah." Jed flashed a wide grin.

"Me." Cash raised a hand to his chest. "This really sounds like a job for Eden. Or Mary or Lily or Jo. Any one of them—"

"Any one of them would tell," Jed interrupted. "They wouldn't shout it from the rooftops, not at first, but they'd whisper it to one of the other gals, and then that one would tell someone else, and before you know it they're all standing around Hannah with these goofy smiles on their faces and she'll know everything. This has to be a surprise or it won't work."

Cash opened his mouth to continue his argument, but Jed wouldn't allow it.

"And if I ask any of the other guys, they'll tell their wives and here we go. It'll be all over town before sunset."

True enough. "What makes you think I know a damned thing about weddings?"

"You have class, Cash."

He imagined it was supposed to be a compliment.

"You'll know what to do to make the wedding special."

His first instinct was to refuse. To utter an absolute, unequivocal *no*. But of course if Jed planned the surprise wedding himself, it would be a disaster. He'd end up dragging Hannah down the street to the church, issuing demands along the way. Hannah, docile of late or not, would protest. And Hannah did know how to protest. The affair was not likely to turn out well.

"How long do we have?"

Jed relaxed visibly. "Hannah's due in seven weeks, but she's so huge, I can't see her going another month and a half. I think the doctor she saw in Dallas made a mistake, I really do."

"If her size is any indication of the time of arrival, the sooner the better."

"Not too soon," Jed said with a wave of his big hand. "Too soon is *not* good."

"I'll see what I can do."

Jed's answer was a wide smile.

In many ways, Jed Rourke had not changed at all. In a fight he would always be handy. He could instill fear with a fierce glare and a low growl. But in some ways he was different. There was a peacefulness in his eyes that had not been there when they'd first come to Rock Creek.

"What's it like?" Cash asked in a low voice.

"What's what like?"

Marriage. Complete trust. Being able to sleep at night. "Impending fatherhood."

Jed's smile faded. "To be honest, I'm a little scared."

"You are?"

"No, I'm a lot scared." Jed ran a hand through his hair and mumbled a foul word. "I haven't said anything to anybody, but . . . Hannah is thirty-two years old and just now having her first child. She's so big, and I can't help but wonder if the baby is *too* big."

A logical worry, given Jed's size. "I'm sure she'll be fine," Cash said, not knowing what else to say. "Alex was a good-sized baby."

"Eden is younger than Hannah, and Alex was not her first child."

True enough. "Will another wedding make any of this better?"

"Yes," Jed insisted. "I know it's not logical, but I keep thinking that if we're married in English, everything will turn out all right."

So how could he refuse? "All right. Let me give it some thought."

Jed grinned as if a load had been lifted from his shoulders. "Thanks. I knew I could count on you."

Too many people were counting on Cash these days, and he didn't like it. Maybe it was time to move on. Permanently this time. This was not the same town the six of them had ridden into and saved. It was growing, becoming more civilized with every passing year. The men Cash had once lived and fought with were not the same. Hell, even Nate was domesticated! Married and tending the Rock Creek flock and constantly sober. Cash didn't talk to Nate much these days. He told himself that since they no longer had anything in common, there was nothing to say. Nate was as obsessed with his new life—his wife, baby, and congregation—as he had once been with his liquor and his need to hide. Cash stayed here, in a place Nate was sure to avoid. In some dark place deep within the Rev's heart, the things Rogue's Palace offered had to call to him still. At least a little.

Cash stared at the whiskey in his own glass. Yeah, time to move on. But he wasn't leaving tonight, or tomorrow. He had good deeds to perform before he would be free to go. "I know we always said we'd be there for each other, but I never imagined wedding planning as one of my duties."

"Maybe this will be the start of a whole new career for you," Jed teased.

"Bite your tongue."

Three

Eden Sullivan, the sheriff's wife and hotel proprietor, served an excellent breakfast. Nadine played with her eggs, unable to choke down more than a bite or two of the delicious meal.

JD's appetite wasn't dampened by excitement. He ate like he always did, shoveling the food in as if he couldn't ever get enough. Normal enough for a growing boy.

His eyes were bright this morning; he was going to meet his hero. More important, he was going to meet his father. He would never know that, though. Cash had made his wishes on that subject clear enough.

Not that Nadine had thought seriously about telling JD that Joseph Ellington was not his real father. JD didn't remember Joseph, but the people of Marianna did. They had been telling him stories about his father for nine years so he wouldn't be completely robbed of the memory.

Joseph had been a good husband and father, accepting JD as his own, never once reminding Nadine that she had married him because she'd had no choice. He'd even been kind enough to leave her be on the nights she couldn't help but cry, knowing that some days she

simply needed to mourn quietly, and that she couldn't
do that with him, or anyone else, watching over her.
He had known her moods well, understood and respected them. She had always regretted that Joseph
also knew, so well, that she'd never loved him. He'd
been a good man and he'd deserved better.

Eden Sullivan moved briskly around the dining
room, making sure no one went hungry. A bright and
genuine smile was plastered on her face as she went
about her work. She checked on the man who was
seated in the far corner, a farmer or a rancher by the
looks of him, and then something caught her eye and
she spun around to face the dining room entrance.

"Daniel!" she said, her smile growing impossibly
wider as she crossed the room. "Why, what a surprise.
You're rarely up and about in time to join us for breakfast."

Nadine couldn't see Cash, but the sound of his voice
sent a shiver up her spine. That voice was low, and
more friendly than she had expected it would be. "Perhaps I'm attempting to mend my wicked ways."

"I doubt that," Eden said familiarly.

Nadine turned her head slowly to watch the warm
reunion, jealous that Cash mustered a friendly expression for Mrs. Sullivan when he had been able to manage only distaste and disappointment for her.

Like yesterday, he was dressed in a perfectly cut
black suit and a fancy white shirt. There were no ruffles on that shirt today, but to make up for the lack he
wore a silver-gray brocade vest.

How could a man dress like a dandy and still look
so dangerous? It was more than the matching six-

shooters hanging on his lean hips, more than his bloody reputation. The very air around him was charged. The sight of him might make the hair on the back of anyone's neck stand up.

And she was going to entrust him with their son's well-being. Good heavens, what had she done?

Cash's eyes landed on her briefly, and then they shifted. Nadine snapped her head around to see that JD stared in awe at his hero, breakfast forgotten. Her son thought he was so grown-up, but at the moment he looked like a child on Christmas morning.

She wanted to warn him then and there not to expect too much of Daniel Cash. He was a man who could, and would, break your heart without so much as blinking. He made promises he would not keep.

Cash made his way to the table with a step that was lazy and still brimming with tension. The click of his boot heel on the floor was steady and rhythmic.

Eden Sullivan stayed right beside him, her own step less uniform. She almost danced across the floor. "Oh, Daniel," she said, her voice only slightly tight with a tension of her own. "These are our newest guests. Mrs. Ellington and her son, JD."

"How very charming," Cash said with a half-smile and a dark twinkle in his eye.

"Mrs. Ellington," Mrs. Sullivan continued. "This is one of our Rock Creek residents. Well, he is usually a resident, though he does tend to come and go."

The friendly blonde seemed surprised that Cash had stayed put for so long. Nadine wondered if the hotel proprietor was trying to avoid mentioning the name of the local gunslinger. That name was too well known these days. "Daniel Cash," she finally finished.

"Mr. Cash," Nadine said lowly. "A pleasure."

He offered his hand as if for a handshake. Nadine hesitated, then lifted her own trembling hand. Cash took it in his, raised it, and leaned forward to kiss her knuckles. His fingers lingered just a moment too long. A tingle shimmied up her arm all the way to her neck.

"This is my son, JD," she said, her eyes pinned to Cash's.

He took a deep breath before turning his eyes to take his first good look at his son. Nadine wondered if he saw himself there, if he was, in some small way, pleased to know that he had a healthy, beautiful, wonderful child. If that were true, he hid the emotion well.

His only greeting to JD was a curt nod of his head.

JD was not disappointed by the cool response. "Would you have breakfast with us? Please?"

Mrs. Sullivan tried to rescue them all. "Well, isn't that sweet? But Daniel prefers to dine—"

"I'd be delighted," Cash interrupted, rounding the table and choosing a seat that placed him between Nadine and JD, and facing the doorway.

Eden Sullivan stood by the table, wide-eyed in surprise. "I'll bring you a plate," she said.

"Just coffee."

The blonde dismissed her surprise and smiled. "Do you really think I'm going to let you get away with that? Eggs and ham and biscuits, coming up."

"And *coffee*," Cash added as she walked away.

"Of course."

* * *

He kept his eyes on Nadine, because looking at the kid was unexpectedly painful. It was as if the image of his son went from his eyes to his throat to his heart, where it grabbed and squeezed too tight.

And besides, looking at Nadine was definitely not a chore. She'd cleaned the road dust from her skin, piled her abundant hair in a simple and gentle fashion atop her head, and wore a pale blue blouse that showed off her figure to perfection. No corset again today, he noted. The curves were soft and natural, and might be tempting to any man. Even him.

Eden made quick work of serving him breakfast, and brought a refill for JD's almost empty plate at the same time. She was so curious she was about to burst, but she didn't dare say a word. Not while Nadine and JD were present, anyway. He was definitely in for an inquisition later.

He ate part of the breakfast Eden had put before him, because he knew her feelings would be hurt if he didn't.   When he had consumed most of his breakfast and finished one cup of coffee and a refill, he leaned back in his chair and laid his eyes on JD again.

Good Lord, the kid was almost grown. He had Nadine's green eyes, curious and bright in a youthful way, and finely sculpted features that could not possibly have come from his father. Cash studied every detail. The long lashes. The ruffled strands of brown hair that were darker than Nadine's, not black like Cash's but close. Too close. The straight, proud nose and wide mouth that might be, if he allowed himself to see it, somewhat familiar. If the kid ever decided to grow a beard and mustache, they *might* be in trouble.

"So you want to be a gunfighter," Cash said. "Why?"

JD swallowed hard. The Adam's apple in his long, boyish neck bobbed up and down.

"I'm good with a gun," the kid said, his voice shaking slightly.

"A lot of people can say the same."

"No, I'm *really* good."

"All right," Cash conceded. "You're good. That's not enough of a reason. Give me another one."

"I . . . I . . ." His eyes lit up as he came to a decision. "You only take on jobs that have some purpose, right? You fight for the folks who need help. I want to do that, too. I want to fight the bad guys."

"If that's the case, you could be a lawman or a soldier. I need another reason." He laid his eyes on JD in a way that he usually reserved for men on the other side of a fight. "The real one."

JD swallowed again, and his green eyes went wide. "Marianna is a crummy little town, and I don't want to be stuck there all my life. I don't want to be a nobody like my father."

"JD!" Nadine chastised softly. The men at the table ignored her.

"When I ride into town I want people to know who I am. I want them to respect me." JD's shoulders went back slightly, and in that instant Cash saw the man his son would one day become.

"You want to be famous," he whispered.

"Yeah."

"You want dime novels written about JD Ellington."

"I do."

"You want normal folks to shudder in their boots when they hear your name."

JD's eyes flashed. "Yeah."

The conversation stalled when Eden came to the table again, refilling coffee cups and collecting empty plates, looking on with a curiosity that was about to burst from her chest. All was silent until she moved away again.

Cash turned his eyes to Nadine. "Have you given anyone a reason why you're here?"

She shook her head.

"We'll need one. This might take a while."

"Yes!" JD muttered in triumph.

Nadine sighed. There was no light of triumph in *her* eyes. "Does this town have a doctor?"

"Not really. The preacher fills in when he can, but these days the Rev has his hands full with other duties. He can take out a bullet or stitch a wound." Drunk or sober, Cash remembered. "But as for everyday doctoring, you're pretty much on your own around here. Why do you ask?"

"I was Marianna's only doctor for six years."

Nadine? A doctor? The confusion must have shown on his face, because she added angrily, "Yes, a woman doctor. Doc Stokes taught me a lot of what he knew before he passed on, and Winema, the old Comanche woman who married Yale Willowby, taught me a few things as well. Actually, I consider myself more of a healer than a doctor."

"Yeah, but when Allison Peters got married to that real doctor from back East and he set up practice in town, Mom didn't have much business left," JD said in a young, too-fast voice. "Most of her patients decided to try out the real doctor. She still has a few folks who'd rather come to her, but everyone wanted to see that real doctor who had been to school back East."

Nadine's eyes flashed angrily every time her son used the words "real doctor."

Cash turned to his son. "If you're going to work for me, the first thing you're going to have to learn is that gunfighters do not run off at the mouth. They do not ramble on, they listen. They do not prattle like little old ladies, they are still, and quiet, and always ready for whatever happens next."

Properly reprimanded, JD blushed. Hell, the kid was as close to being a gunfighter as Cash was to being a nursemaid.

"Go upstairs and pack your bags," Cash ordered. "You're moving in with me."

JD couldn't get out of the dining room and up the stairs fast enough.

"Is this really a good idea?" Nadine asked softly.

Cash leaned closer to her. Not because he needed to lower his voice, not because he couldn't hear her well, but because he wanted to take a deep breath and smell her. No matter how close he got, it wasn't close enough. He wanted to hold her, just once. He wanted to kiss her and shake her and . . . touch her.

"We do things my way, remember?"

Nadine closed her mouth tightly.

"You're in Rock Creek because you're scouting out towns that need a doctor. JD is going to do odd jobs for me, he's going to live above the saloon, and I'm going to rid him of the notion that becoming a gunslinger is an option." He sighed deeply, allowing his eyes to fall to her well-rounded bosom. Ah, his fingers itched to touch her, here and now. "As far as the people of Rock Creek are concerned, if I'm doing anything nice for JD, it's so I can work my way into his mother's bed."

"Cash!"

"Never fear, it's all for show."

And still, she blushed prettily.

"No one here will accept the notion that I've taken a child under my wing out of the goodness of my heart, you can trust me on that." He allowed himself to look at her hard. "But they will believe that I'd give the kid a place to sleep over the saloon so you'll be alone in your hotel room at night. And they will definitely believe that I'd use a child to worm my way into a beautiful woman's bed."

"Does everyone here think you to be so calculating?"

"The people in this town know me better than anyone else."

His memories of Nadine were a hazy, distorted muddle. Their one night as lovers had been something to hang on to when times got rough. He remembered the sensation of entering her tight body with what seemed like clarity. He could almost feel the cold air all around them and the heat of their bodies where they touched, the heavenly sensation of Nadine's arms around him, her mouth on his. He remembered loving her so much it hurt.

But he didn't trust his memories anymore. Had that one night been so different from all the rest? Was this one woman really any different from the prostitutes and lusty widows who had followed her?

When he remembered watching her and Joseph Ellington walk out of the church, man and wife, he always saw a smile on her face. Had that smile been real? He knew now why she'd married Ellington. She'd been not much more than a child herself, and she must have been terrified. Had she really smiled, or was that part of some old nightmare that stayed with him as if it were real?

If he had stepped out from between the buildings and made his presence known, where would they be now? How would his life be different?

They would never know, so it made no sense to ponder on it. What's done was done, the past was past, and he was not a man to dwell on what he could not, would not, have. And yet as he sat there watching Nadine, he did ponder.

Daniel was a constant in an ever-changing world. He could always be relied upon to be distant, vulgar, and suspicious of all but a few close friends. He did not have breakfast with total strangers and . . . and *chat* over coffee.

Eden counted the man as a good friend. He had saved her life and Sin's, and in spite of his devil-may-care attitude she knew he would do anything to protect those few he cared about. But he was up to something and she wanted to know what. She *had* to know.

The young man, JD, left the table and hurried through the lobby and to the stairs. A few minutes later, his mother followed. Eden made a beeline for Daniel's table.

"More coffee?" she asked as he came slowly to his feet. "Biscuits? Another slice of ham? You didn't eat all your eggs, but I could—"

"You are always trying to feed me," he interrupted. Ah, he knew she was curious. That twinkle in his eye gave him away.

Eden pulled out the chair JD had occupied earlier and sat down. "My feet hurt. Have a seat and talk to me while I rest a minute."

Daniel complied, a half-smile flitting across his face.

Placing her forearms on the table and leaning just slightly forward, Eden asked bluntly, "What is going on here?"

With his usual casual air, Daniel leaned back in his chair and grinned. "I've hired the young man to work for me."

"To *work* for you? Doing what?"

Daniel hesitated. His smile dimmed just a little. "Sweeping out the saloon. Doing some repairs around the place. Whatever else I can think of. He'll be staying there."

"You've always gotten along fine without help," she said, her curiosity unsatisfied. "And if you needed someone besides Evan to sweep out the saloon, you could have asked Teddy or Rafe to do it."

His eyebrows arched up. "You'd allow them in my place?"

Good point. "Early in the day when you're closed, I suppose I would."

He knew her too well. His smile bloomed wide. "Let's just say I have my reasons for taking the boy in. One, actually. My reason stands a good four inches taller than you. Has green eyes and silky skin and the most tempting pair of—"

"Daniel!" Eden chastised before he could say more. Oh, it made perfect sense. Nadine Ellington was an attractive lady, but . . . "She's not your type of woman."

He did not seem at all disturbed by this observation. "Every time *my type of woman* comes to town you and your cronies have her reformed in an amazingly short period of time. Perhaps I'm getting desperate." He shook his head once. "Maybe Mrs. Ellington is not as strait-laced as she looks. Only one way to find out. Getting the kid out of her room is just the first step."

"Daniel!"

"Well, you can hardly expect me to . . . proceed with a child on a pallet at her bedside."

"I don't think you should *proceed* at all!"

"So I should become a monk?" he asked, his smile dying. He wanted to say more. She saw that in his clenched jaw and his darkening eyes. But he wouldn't. And he didn't need to.

"You should marry a woman who will love you and care for you and feed you and . . . and . . ."

"And?" he urged with bitter humor. "Never mind. I will allow my imagination to wander beyond that last *and* on its own." He thrust his long legs forward.

"I only want to see you . . . happy."

"Happy?" he asked with a crooked smile. "I'm already happy. I'm perfectly satisfied with my life as it is."

"But . . ."

"Look, sweetheart, marriage and all that comes with it is fine for the others, but it's not for me and it never will be."

"It's not too late . . ."

"It has nothing to do with how old I am, Eden." His humor disappeared, and suddenly he looked deadly serious. There was no more light of teasing in his eyes. "You want to know the truth, meddling Eden? Fine. Listen up. I barely sleep at night as it is. What would my life be like if I had a wife? Kids? Do you know how many people out there would love to hurt anyone who made the mistake of getting that close to me? Do you realize what a burden the name Cash would be to a child of mine? How could I ever watch them closely enough? How could I protect anyone who was foolish enough to become a part of my life?"

"It wouldn't be like that," she whispered.

"God, Eden, you have no idea," he said, disgust coming through clearly on the soft waves of his lowered voice. "You and Sullivan are safe here. Your kids are safe. Your home is secure. But there are people out there *hunting* me. Most of them are not stupid enough to come here, but they're out there, biding their time until I leave this town so I'll be more vulnerable. They're just waiting for the chance to corner me, waiting for me to land in a strange place where I don't have anyone to watch my back." She had no idea how tough the last year had been. How little he'd slept. How close he'd come to getting killed. "These men are willing and able to shoot me in my bed or while I'm eating breakfast or as I'm spreading a winning hand across a poker table."

A shudder shimmied down her spine. "You're safer in Rock Creek than anywhere else in the world," she said. "Stay here, where there will always be someone to watch your back."

"I will," he said. "For a while. As long as you don't mention the 'M' word around me anymore."

"It wouldn't be so—"

He stopped her with nothing more than raised eyebrows.

Eden sighed. "All right. But be careful, Daniel."

"I always am."

It was her turn to raise her eyebrows in disbelief.

Four

The hotel garden was well kept, the perfect place to spend a restless morning. And Nadine was definitely restless.

Cash's plan made perfect sense, but she didn't like it. She wanted JD with her at night, sleeping nearby. How else could she be certain he was safe?

Cash wanted people to think he was being nice to JD in order to get into her bed. That made sense, she supposed, given that the gunslinger didn't exactly have a history of performing selfless acts. She was willing to play along as long as things didn't go too far. Cash had made it clear he expected her to do as he said. Did that include more than she was willing to give?

She knew there were women who enjoyed sex, but she was not one of them. Perhaps something within her was not built right, or maybe all those other women were lying. That one night with Cash had been warm and wonderful, right up until the moment he broke through her maidenhead. The pain had ruined the moment, though she did remember enjoying the way he held her after as much as she had enjoyed the kissing and touching before.

Her marriage bed had been cold, at best. Joseph had done his utmost to be a good husband and father. Most of the time, once she quit mourning Danny, she had been content. But the intimate moments of their married life had been lacking. There had never been any kissing and touching before or holding after, which left her with the only part of the marital embrace that she didn't enjoy; the act itself. There had been no more pain, not after that first night with Cash, but lying with her husband had never been anything to look forward to, either.

When she didn't get pregnant that first year after JD was born, they sadly accepted the fact that Joseph was most likely unable to father children. His first marriage had been childless, but he had hoped it was his late wife who'd been unable to conceive. After that first year, when they knew more children were not likely, they didn't even bother with sex very often. She had tried not to let on that she dreaded the nights Joseph would come to her, but she was not good at playing games. She had never been good at pretending.

But she had a feeling Cash would definitely bother if he got the chance. He wasn't an easygoing man like Joseph, and he would never be satisfied with less than everything she had to give. She wondered if he'd be satisfied with the explanation that she didn't have anything left.

"What does washing windows have to do with gunfighting?" JD asked testily.

Cash crossed his arms and glared at his son's defiantly rigid spine as the kid swiped carelessly at a dirty window that overlooked Rock Creek's main street.

"Perfection," Cash said simply.

JD dropped his arm and turned to face him. "I don't get it."

"There is no room in this profession for sloppiness of any kind. Whatever job you take on, it must be done thoroughly. Completely. If you can't clean a window properly, how can you ever expect to attain the precision required to be a respected gunfighter?"

JD accepted that explanation with a grumbled, "Yes, sir, Mr. Cash."

"Just Cash," he corrected the boy.

JD dipped his rag in the pail of vinegar water at his side and began again, paying more attention to details this time as he cleaned the window. The kid had good hands, long-fingered and youthfully slim. "When will we get to do some shooting?"

"Patience," Cash advised. "I didn't kill my first man until I was eighteen, and that was in battle. If you rush this process, you'll be dead inside a week. Your mother would never forgive me."

Never pausing in his chore, JD scoffed. "My mother still treats me like I'm a baby. I wish she'd gotten married after my pa died and had a couple more kids. Maybe then she wouldn't watch over me like a hawk."

He had seen the way the women of this town watched over their children. He assumed it didn't matter if there was one child or a dozen. Mothers always stood vigil. "She's an attractive woman. I'm surprised she never remarried."

"Said she wasn't interested," JD said with a sigh. "We had the house there in town, and with her doctoring we never had any problem getting by. She said she didn't need a man to take care of us, that we could take care of ourselves."

Didn't Nadine miss having a man in her bed at night? Didn't she ever get lonely? A woman like her, so beautiful and full of life, shouldn't be alone.

"I think she loved my pa too much to ever marry anyone else," JD said in a confidential voice. "I caught her crying one night, and when I asked her what was wrong, she told me she was thinking about my father and all the years they would never have together."

A shiver worked its way through Cash's body. Had she been talking about Ellington? Or him?

"Funny thing is," JD continued, "my pa had been dead for a really long time when I caught her crying. I don't know what got her thinking about him right at that moment. I never saw her so sad as she was that night, and it scared me a little. It's been a long time, and I still remember. . . ."

He didn't want to stand there and wonder if Nadine had cried over what they'd never have. "Hey, kid," he said sharply. "Remember that prattling thing I warned you about?"

"Yeah."

"You're doing it again."

And then he caught sight of a feminine figure walking down the street, hips swaying the way a woman's will, head high, uncovered dark hair catching the rays of the sun. Nadine glanced over to the saloon and up and tried, very hard, not to allow her gaze to linger on Rogue's Palace.

* * *

Rock Creek was a nice enough place, with all the amenities one might expect in a small city blending nicely with the rustic air of an isolated town. The view to the south was lovely, the way the vast expanses of Texas often were, and yet her heart clenched when she looked beyond Rock Creek. She was so far away from everything she knew.

Nadine had studied the quaint church and the school, Three Queens, the general store, and all the shops along the way before allowing herself to walk past and take a really good look at Cash's saloon. She saw the figure beyond a dirty window, recognizing it as JD's even though her view was indistinct. Just seeing him there, scrubbing windows, was a relief. He was safe for now.

"Well, well." Cash's low voice interrupted her tour, and before she knew what he was doing he sidled up beside her, taking her arm. No one looking on would know that his grip was just a little too tight. "Checking up on me?"

"Of course not," she said, her heart in her throat. "I was just . . . restless."

"I suppose you know Rock Creek from end to end by now."

"It's a lovely place."

"It's no different from any other small town."

Somehow she didn't think that was true. "I met several of the Sullivans' children, and Mary Reese, and the preacher's wife, Jo."

"Did you tell them you were a doctor looking for a place to practice?"

"Yes." And after an initial silent span that revealed their surprise, they had all been quite thrilled at the prospect. They had seemed to be thrilled, at least. As she'd left the ladies to their social gathering, politely declining their offer to join in, she passed a very pregnant woman waddling down the hotel stairway on the arm of a huge hulk of a man, and she'd almost run over an exotic beauty who was mumbling about her husband making her late. The five of them had probably had a good laugh about the woman doctor. Most people did, even her old friends in Marianna.

"Good," Cash said, pulling her too close. Her hip brushed his. "It's kind of ironic, don't you think?"

"What's that?" Heavens, he stole her breath when he held her this close.

"I shoot people, you heal them. I kill, you bring new life into the world. How different could our lives be?" He delivered this observation with a matter-of-fact tone. He might have been commenting on the weather.

"We weren't always so different."

He didn't respond but silently led her across the street and toward the hotel entrance. They walked through the door and, as they approached the dining room filled with chattering voices, he draped his arm over her shoulder.

Instead of leading her past the large open entrance to the dining room, he stopped and looked in, a wide smile breaking across his face. The preacher's wife held her baby boy in her arms. Eden and Mary each had an older baby on their laps. Two little girls played on the floor nearby, lost in their doll play. And five pairs of wide eyes watched a grinning Daniel Cash standing there with his arm tossed possessively over her shoulder.

"Ladies," he said.

Their responses were mumbled. Cash. Daniel. Good Lord. *Canaille*.

"Eden, is Teddy around?"

She licked her lips before answering, bouncing her dark-haired baby gently on her knee. "He and Jed are down by the river. Target practice."

"When he gets back, would you have him come see me? I think he's about the same age as my new employee, JD. Thirteen?"

Eden nodded. "Teddy's fourteen."

"Close enough. JD's scrubbing my place from top to bottom, and he might need some help."

One of the women, the beauty who had been late arriving and had muttered something in French when Cash and Nadine had arrived, said, "I do not suppose it ever occurred to you to help the new kid yourself."

"Of course not," Cash said, not at all offended by the suggestion or the condescending tone with which it had been delivered.

"If Teddy would like to earn a little spending money, have him come see me." Cash nodded to Eden. "Early in the afternoon, of course, before business gets under way."

With that he nodded to them all and turned around, Nadine still in his grasp, and headed for the back door. "The garden is very nice, even in the heat of the day," he said, plenty loud enough for all the ladies to hear.

When they were outside, the door closed behind them, Nadine tried to slip out of Cash's grasp. He held on and refused to allow her to escape.

"Now, now," he said softly. "You never know who might be watching." He led her to a bench situated among the flowering bushes, held her hand as she sat, and then lowered himself slowly to sit beside her. Once again, that familiar arm draped over her shoulder.

"Who on earth would be watching?"

Cash turned to look at her and he smiled brilliantly. "Eden, certainly," he said. He drifted toward her slowly and unerringly. "Jo, by now," he added as he placed his mouth on her neck. How could he be so hard, so unforgiving, and then turn around and touch her in such a tender way?

Nadine's heart kicked furiously. It didn't help matters any when Cash took her earlobe between his teeth, then sucked it into his mouth for a split second. "Mary's probably right behind Eden and Jo, telling them that they really shouldn't be spying." His breath touched her ear, and a shiver worked its way through her body. "Lily is disgusted with them all, and Hannah would really like to watch but getting out of her chair is no easy task these days. Those two should be along in another minute or so."

"How could you possibly . . ." About that time a curtain in the lobby window fluttered. Just slightly.

Cash trailed his lips down the side of her neck and raised a tender hand to her hair. His fingers threaded through the strands, brushed against her ear.

"Stop," she whispered.

"No. We have to make this look good."

"I just arrived yesterday. Surely they expect something a little . . ." Her heart hammered. "Slower. More seemly. You could court me. Walk me around town. Have dinner with me at the hotel. Bring . . . flowers or candy or . . . something." God, she couldn't breathe right!

"No," he whispered, and then he sucked on the side of her neck until she felt as though she would dissolve and melt through the slats in the weathered bench. "They'd never buy it."

"Why . . ." She swallowed hard as Cash's fingertips brushed the skin behind her ear. "Why not?"

"I might be teaching JD patience, but that doesn't mean I have much of my own. And I have *none* where women are concerned."

Cash was surely trying to devour her neck. He sucked, he nibbled. He kissed. Something about the way he worked his mouth on her flesh made her tremble all over. She felt the force of those gentle kisses everywhere, as if they seeped through her skin and wafted through her body on golden waves.

"Besides," he whispered between kisses. "I am not now, nor have I ever been, seemly."

"Surely they'd expect me to resist," she said weakly.

"They all know I'm irresistible," he muttered, his lips brushing lightly against her neck.

Ha! Of that she had no doubt. "But . . . how can I expect to doctor these people if they think I'm so weak, I can't even resist the advances of a man they believe I've barely known for one full day?"

He lifted his head and looked her in the eye. His lips were slightly swollen, his eyes heavily lidded. "You're not actually going to stay, Nadine. It's just a part of the ruse. Who cares what they think?"

Her heart sank a little. He was right, of course. "What am I supposed to do?"

"You could kiss me," he suggested. "On the lips, on the neck. Anywhere that strikes your fancy. You could throw your arms around me and hold on tight while you tell me what you want. Where do you ache, Nadine?" His eyes darkened, and he didn't wait for an answer. Surely he didn't expect one. "And you *will* open your door to me whenever I knock. Day or night."

Oh, pretending or not, she did not want this man in her hotel room! "I don't think that's such a good idea."

He grabbed the back of her head and forced her to look at him. "If the people who live here don't think I'm sleeping with you, they'll question my motives for taking JD in. Maybe they'll look at him too closely and wonder. Maybe if they look hard enough, they'll see the resemblance. Do we want that?"

Would it really be so bad? "I guess not."

"They know I'm not going to waste my time on any woman who won't spread her legs for me."

She couldn't stop the warm flush in her cheeks.

"So, while it doesn't matter what we do in that room once I'm there, you *will* let me in. I might show up in the middle of the night, at dawn, or in the afternoon. Don't you ever turn me away."

He brought his mouth toward hers, his lips parted, and his hand rose to cup her breast. His fingers swept up and brushed over a nipple that hardened at his touch. Unexpected sparks flashed through her.

She placed her hands on his chest before he could kiss her. He was like rock beneath her palms, hard and unyielding. But he was warm, human and male and real. The hand at her breast continued to move, boldly caressing.

The past few days had been too much for her, too emotionally charged. Her head was spinning, her knees shaking, her skin much too warm. It wasn't like her to feel so completely out of control. She couldn't do this. She couldn't be the kind of woman Cash wanted and expected her to be.

Cash's lips were just an inch or so from hers when she pushed at him with all her might, raised her hand, and slapped him. Hard.

He went still. Not only in his body but in his eyes. There was no more spark of humor, no passion, no hint at all of the boy she had once known.

The back door of the hotel burst open. "There you two are," Eden said too brightly and too fast. "I thought you might want some lemonade and cookies. Do come in and have some refreshments. It's so hot out here."

Cash rose to his feet. "No, thank you," he said, his eyes never leaving Nadine's face. "Perhaps Mrs. Ellington would care for some lemonade. I need to get back to the saloon."

The other ladies gathered in the open doorway. Cash had been right. They'd been watching all that time.

Nadine's heart beat so hard, she could feel it pounding against her chest. Cash said these people knew him better than anyone, and Eden obviously thought he might be tempted to harm a woman for slapping him. She'd been worried enough to come running out of the hotel with a blatantly obvious lemonade-and-cookie rescue.

Cash raised a hand to his red cheek and let his fingers trail over the skin she had slapped. Already she felt sorry. He'd touched her and she'd panicked. This is *not* why she'd traveled to Rock Creek! Would he send her and JD packing now? Worse, would he take his revenge by turning her son into a cold-blooded killer? She wanted to be so sure he was not a vindictive person.

What was she thinking? Daniel Cash not vindictive? Everything she had read, everything she had learned about his life since he'd left her, made it clear that he did not take insult lightly.

"Would you have dinner with me tonight, Mrs. Ellington?" he finally asked softly.

Eden's eyes almost popped out of her head.

"I'd be delighted," Nadine said, only a little surprised.

Cash leaned down toward her, and she did not flinch. No matter what he said, no matter what she'd learned, *she* knew him better than anyone. And she knew, more surely with every beat of her heart, that he would never hurt her.

"Perhaps," he whispered, "I'll even bring you some friggin' flowers."

Cash stepped into the lobby a few minutes early, wondering what the hell he was doing here. How had his perfectly ordered life gotten so out of hand in the span of a single day? Wedding planning, a child, and a woman who was determined to drive him crazy had already turned his life upside down.

He moved into the lobby and sat on the ratty green couch that had been there when the six of them had come to Rock Creek. Eden had cleaned the sofa, and was forever talking about having it replaced, but here it remained.

"Uncle Cash!" a frighteningly sweet voice called as

Fiona Sullivan ran around the couch and leapt toward him. "Are those flowers for me?"

Having no choice, he caught the four-year-old beauty as she landed in his lap and against his chest. "No," he said succinctly.

She pouted, sticking out her lower lip and dipping her chin.

"Not all of them," he amended, plucking out a pink rose and handing it to her. Immediately, her expression changed to one of pure joy. He didn't have the heart to tell her that the rose had been plucked from her own garden without Eden's knowledge.

"Thank you, Uncle Cash," Fiona said. Instead of climbing down from his lap, she settled against his chest and admired the rose.

Cash didn't like children and didn't mind letting them and everyone else know. Fiona didn't seem to care. The poor girl had her mother's soft spot for lost souls and her father's stubborn streak. Those qualities had all but driven the child to Cash and to Nate in years past, and from the age of two she had been their girl. Sheer determination and wide hazel eyes had won them over.

She rested against Cash's chest, admiring the rose.

"No drool on the jacket," Cash said in a lowered voice.

"I'm not a baby," Fiona argued. "I don't slobber like Alex does."

"Of course you don't." Cash studied the curve of Fiona's chubby cheek, the perfection of her mouth. What had JD looked like at four years old? Had he still had those baby cheeks like Fiona did? Had he trusted this way? Had he loved everyone around him and known no fear?

He touched Fiona's dark hair very briefly, brushing a curl away from her face. It was so soft.

"I like flowers," Fiona observed. "They're pretty."

"Yes, they are."

Fiona tipped her head back and looked into Cash's face. "You've been here a long time. Are you going to stay forever?"

Forever. The word itself made Cash shudder. "No."

"How come?"

"Nothing lasts forever, kid."

Fiona wrinkled her button nose, not liking that answer at all. "I think you should stay forever," she said, effectively dismissing his argument. "Millie and Carrie won't ever let me play with them, and Uncle Nate got married and had his own baby." She wrinkled her nose again. "Sometimes I play with Georgie, but her mommy and daddy make her study, since she's in school now, so sometimes I don't have anyone to play with. Daddy said I can go to school next year, but that's a very long time." She sighed and set big hazel eyes on his face. "When I'm all grown up, will you marry me, Uncle Cash?"

He was properly horrified. "Of course not."

Her little lower lip trembled.

"By the time you're old enough to get married, I'll be an old man and you won't want anything to do with me," he explained.

She answered with a tiny, childlike snort of disgust and pinned her gaze squarely on her pink rose.

Cash placed a finger beneath her chin and made her

look up. "You will have your pick of any man in the world," he said, meaning it. Fiona was going to be a rare prize. "I'm sure you'll be able to do better than an aging, wrinkled, stoop-backed, toothless, smelly old gambler."

Fiona giggled. "I don't want to marry you if you smell bad and don't have any teeth."

He wouldn't live long enough to see Fiona married, he knew it. Gunfighters didn't live to be wrinkled and toothless.

"What's this?" a new voice interrupted.

"Daddy!" Fiona flew off Cash's lap and into her father's waiting arms. She was, in spite of her dogged determination to win over every heart she met, Daddy's little girl. She rested her head on Sullivan's shoulder and stuck the rose in his face. "See what Uncle Cash gave me?"

"I see," Sullivan said with a smug smile as the rose petals brushed his nose.

Cash knew what kind of nauseating picture he must have made, sitting here with flowers in one hand and Fiona cuddled on his lap. "You see nothing," he said tersely.

Sullivan continued to smile.

"Wipe that grin off your face," Cash warned, shaking Nadine's bouquet at the half-breed, "before I take these flowers and stick them——" His eyes flitted quickly to Fiona. "In that vase Eden keeps in the kitchen," he finished.

Sullivan set Fiona on her feet and leaned down to place his face close to hers. "Why don't you go show Mommy that pretty flower."

"Okay." She skipped away and left the two men alone.

Sullivan crossed his arms over his chest. "What's going on?"

"Nothing." Where the hell was Nadine? If he'd ever needed to be saved . . .

Sullivan shook his head. "No, something's different."

"I'm in shock, because your daughter just asked me to marry her."

The sheriff nodded, not at all surprised. "Yeah, she's been a little fascinated with weddings lately." He laid narrowed eyes on Cash. "You did turn her down, right?"

"I tried. She doesn't take no for an answer very well, does she?"

Sullivan sighed. "No, she doesn't," he muttered.

Cash leaned back and studied his old friend. "You're letting your hair get long again."

"Yeah." That one word was Sullivan's idea of a detailed explanation.

"Why?" Cash pressed.

Sullivan shrugged.

"You're going to make me guess. All right. You like looking like the breed you are," Cash said tersely. "The barber pissed you off. You want the longest hair possible, so if we're ever staked to the ground by renegades again you'll have the best scalp to offer. You think it makes you look—"

"Eden likes it," Sullivan interrupted in a low, curt voice. "Satisfied?"

Cash grinned. "You are so incredibly whipped."

"I am not."

"If Eden said she liked you in pink calico, would you pin your sheriff's star to a shift that matches Fiona's?"

"You're the one who wears ruffles around here, not me."

Cash raised his eyebrows. "Perhaps, but you're the one who has the hair to go with those ruffles."

"It never bothered you before."

"It doesn't bother me now."

Sullivan sighed. "Now I remember why you and I never talk."

In truth, he didn't converse much with any of his old friends these days. They had nothing to talk about. Cash wanted to talk women, cards, and war. The men he had once fought with talked of other things. Babies, wives, plans for a better and bigger Rock Creek.

Cash didn't bother to respond. Nadine was coming down the stairs. Her step was soft, tentative . . . and he would have known it anywhere.

With a last despairing glance to Sullivan, Cash stood and circled around the couch to offer Nadine the pilfered flowers. She smiled shyly as she took them. If he allowed himself to be so foolish, he might be swept away by a smile like that.

But he was not like the others, and nothing swept him away. Not ever.

Five

The world was his kingdom, and he ruled with the arrogance and sense of immortality that only an eighteen-year-old can muster. He'd been a soldier for only three months, but he was good at it. In battle he was fearless, his aim flawless, his ability to tune out the noise and the ugliness around him a true gift. Before this war was over, he was going to be a goddamn general. He'd go home a hero, and Nadine's father would have no choice but to give them his blessing.

"Hey, Danny." Melvin, who was scouting with him on this fine morning, hurried to catch up. He stumbled through the dense Tennessee brush, making all kinds of racket.

The morning had been so quiet, Danny really didn't mind the noise. There were no Yankees about, no enemy lying in wait. He was king, and Nadine was waiting for him at home.

"How come my jacket is already in shreds and yours looks like you just joined up and got a new one?"

Danny glanced over his shoulder and grinned. "You're worried about your clothes? This is war,

Melvin. Nobody cares what kind of shape your jacket is in."

Melvin, who in Danny's opinion had no business in the army, glanced down at his stained and torn jacket. "I really hate to look so shabby. What would the girls back home think?"

Danny liked Melvin, but fearless the kid was not. "Here," he said, shrugging out of his own coat. His uniform looked almost untouched. It was as if he were protected when he went into battle. Protected from blood and dirt and the scrapes that left most of the others looking ragged. He tossed the jacket to a delighted Melvin. "When we get back to camp, scratch my name off the inside of the collar and put your own there."

Another skirmish and the jacket would look as bad as the one Melvin whipped off and tossed toward Danny. But if such a simple thing cheered him up for a few days, what difference did it make?

The jacket Danny caught easily was not befitting a king, so he tossed it over his shoulder and continued scouting, one finger hooked around Melvin's jacket, his own army-issue Colt six-shooter fitting nicely in the other hand.

Danny didn't hear a thing, not a single rustle of warning, but suddenly someone was there. The unexpected appearance of the small man in civilian clothes took both Danny and Melvin by surprise. At the sight of the shotgun clasped in the man's hands, Danny froze. So did Melvin.

"Hey," the stranger said in a soft voice. A boy, Danny

decided, not a man. The voice was too mellow to belong to a grown man. He relaxed.

"What are you doing, kid?" Danny asked, taking a step forward. "Don't you know it's dangerous to be out here all by yourself?"

"I can take care of myself," the boy mumbled, slightly hefting the shotgun.

Danny cocked his head to the side, trying to see beneath the wide brim of the boy's hat. "I'm sure you can," he said, trying not to hurt the kid's feelings. "But you need to run on home now, you hear?"

Without warning the shotgun popped up, and Danny instinctively dropped down, rolling forward. The kid fired, and Melvin didn't have a face anymore. For a very long second, Danny stared at the soldier on the ground. He had seen battle, he had seen soldiers killed. But not like this. And not a friend.

When Danny tore his gaze from what was left of Melvin and looked up, the innocent looking attacker took aim again. At him this time. The boy cocked the hammer on the double-barrel shotgun, and Danny propelled himself off the ground and up, taking the kid by surprise. Danny grabbed the barrel and forced it up, so when the trigger was pulled the shot fired aimlessly into the air.

Danny yanked the weapon from the boy's hands and threw it aside with a scream that was ripped from his gut. The shotgun broke through branches and landed in thick brush. He lifted his Colt smoothly and pointed it at the kid's midsection. At the moment, he didn't care that the boy was unarmed. Melvin was dead. God, he hoped Melvin was dead.

"Who are you?" Danny croaked. He wanted a name before he shot the boy who had killed Melvin. He got no answer. "Yankee?"

This time the shooter answered with a shake of his head.

"You live around here?"

A nod was his answer.

"What do you have against Confederate soldiers?" Danny shouted.

"This is my land," the boy said softly. "Since my pa died, it's mine. You're trespassing."

"You didn't have to shoot him!" Danny shook his gun. "We are Confederate soldiers and we have an army behind us. Do you hear that you moron? An army!"

Incredibly, the kid sniffled.

His urge to shoot the unarmed kid was gone. No matter that the boy had killed Melvin, it wasn't right. It wasn't why he was there. "You're coming with me," Danny reached out to grab the kid. "I'll let the captain hang you for murder."

The arm beneath his hand was soft, the cheek peeking out from beneath the wide-brimmed hat too pale. Something wasn't right. With an insistent hand, Danny forced the kid to look him square in the eye.

"You're a girl," he said incredulously.

She sniffled. "I'd rather you shoot me now than take me where there are any soldiers," she said softly. "I won't let another soldier touch me, you hear? I won't let that happen again."

Danny felt slightly ill. "Someone . . . hurt you?" His life had been hard at times, sometimes downright un-

fair. But still, he came from a world where women were protected, not abused.

The girl shook off his hand, nodded softly, and dipped her chin. "They broke into my house and . . . and . . ."

She didn't want to tell any more, and he didn't want to hear. "Come with me to camp, and we'll tell the captain what happened," he said.

"Can't you just . . . leave me here?" she begged, turning what had to be the bluest eyes in the world up to him. "I'm sorry, truly I am. I just panicked."

Danny turned around and glanced at what remained of his friend. Melvin in a fine jacket that was not his own. Melvin, who had been so worried about looking shabby. They'd hang the girl for sure when he told what she'd done. He really didn't want to be responsible for sending a girl who'd been so badly treated to her death. Maybe she had just panicked, like she said. Danny walked toward Melvin's body. But Melvin was still dead. He couldn't just . . .

Danny heard her movements while his eyes were still on Melvin. In a split second it all came together with heart-wrenching clarity. She had another weapon hidden on her somewhere. Stuck at her spine, under that baggy shirt, in a boot . . . somewhere. He heard the unmistakable sound of gun metal brushing against clothing. The snick of a trigger being cocked came next. Danny turned, and with a quick shifting of his weight saved himself from a belly wound. But the bullet she fired tore into and through his side, there near his waist.

He'd been in the army long enough to know how to

respond. His Colt popped up, he fired. The girl fell just seconds after he did.

The girl who'd killed Melvin and tried to kill him wasn't moving, but Danny was able to make his way to her on his hands and knees. When he reached her he placed a hand on the wound at his side. Damn, that was a lot of blood.

She wasn't dead, but she would be soon. The single bullet he'd fired had caught her in the chest.

"Why?" he asked, angry that she'd shot him, just as angry that she'd made him shoot her. "Just because one man hurt you . . ."

Amazingly, she laughed. "I have allowed an idiot to kill me," she said softly.

"What do you mean?"

She laid her blue eyes on him. Hard blue eyes with no hint of womanly softness. "If any man tried to lay his hands on me without an invitation, I'd rip off his privates and feed them to him."

Danny flinched. He had never heard a woman speak this way. "So you weren't— "

"No," she interrupted. A trickle of blood marred her mouth. "I'm just a thief, you idiot. I was after your weapons and your money. For God's sake, do you believe everything you're . . ."

She died without finishing her sentence.

Danny made a bandage using his own shirt and the old jacket Melvin had given him. It wasn't the best of doctoring, but the dressing did slow the flow of blood. He searched the thief's pockets, and found proof that she'd been telling the truth. Notes. Coins. Watches and rings. He took them all.

He had never thought he'd be called upon to kill a woman. But then, this one was unlike any female he had ever met. She shook his faith in everything he knew to be true.

The world was no longer his kingdom. He no longer felt like the fine soldier he'd thought himself to be. Blood loss robbed him of clarity of thought, and as he made his way through a dense copse of trees and found the bandit's tethered horse, he had only one clear thought. Getting to Nadine. She would make things right. When he saw her, his life would make sense again.

He climbed into the saddle and headed away from camp. He hadn't gone far before he passed out in the saddle.

Nadine had brought the dream with her, Cash decided as he rose from his bed with the sun. Damn her, he hadn't thought about Melvin and the thief who had shot him for more years than he could count.

He used to have a dream where everything was different. Instead of a female thief, it had been a Yankee soldier hiding behind that tree. Instead of being surprised, he had been expecting the shotgun-wielding soldier. He had not hesitated, but had raised his gun and fired without a second thought. Melvin lived. Danny wasn't shot. There had been no need to climb into a saddle and take off looking for something that didn't exist.

But the Cash in that dream was the man he had become, not the boy he had been more than fourteen years earlier.

JD slept in the room next door. By God, if he had to be up at the crack of dawn, so did the kid.

Cash allowed the door to slam against the wall as he threw it open. JD shot up in his bed. For an instant, one heart-stopping instant, JD looked an awful lot like the Danny who occasionally haunted Cash's dreams. Naive. Hopeful. Stupid.

"Rise and shine," Cash said too loudly.

JD rubbed at his eyes. "Are we going to shoot today?"

"No," Cash said abruptly. "First you're going to scrub the floors downstairs."

JD sighed but did not complain. "Then what?"

Cash smiled. "We have a wedding to plan."

Dinner with Cash last night had been interesting, Nadine thought as she entered the dining room for breakfast and her eyes landed on the table they'd shared. The table in the corner, where Cash sat with his back to the wall. They'd both been a little uncomfortable after the scene in the garden. Cash hadn't been quite sure what to do with his hands. She hadn't been quite sure what to say. They weren't strangers, but they didn't know each other, either.

There had been moments—brief, wonderful short spans of time when he looked at her and she looked at him and the years melted away. She knew and loved him; he knew and loved her. And then that feeling would disappear, and there would be nothing left but an uneasy queasiness and an urge to run.

She would endure a lifetime of discomfort if it

would help to rid JD of his ridiculous notion. Her son would *not* be a gunfighter!

This morning there was a crowd gathered for breakfast. There were couples and children everywhere. Sheriff Sullivan, Eden's husband, was surrounded by his family. A tall, slim young man who listened carefully, a younger boy who could not quite sit still. A young lady with blond curls and the happy child Fiona, a charmer Nadine had already met and come to adore. A baby, old enough to reach his father's ear and tug enthusiastically and occasionally yank on a handful of long dark hair, laughing all the while, sat on Sullivan's knee.

Such a scene made Nadine wish she'd had more children of her own. A daughter, perhaps, or a brother for JD.

Jed Rourke and his very pregnant wife, Hannah, sat at a table near the entrance. Hannah lifted her eyes and smiled when she saw Nadine. "Join us for breakfast?"

Nadine happily accepted, not eager to sit alone in a room filled with families.

"Be careful," Jed said as he rose and pulled out a chair for her. "Hannah has a tendency to steal food from other people's plates these days."

"I do not," Hannah protested with a grin. "Well, if I do, I steal only from *your* plate. Nadine's breakfast is perfectly safe."

As Nadine sat, her eyes fell to Hannah's stomach. "You must be due any day."

Hannah sighed, and her grin faded. "I have almost two months to go, according to the doctor I saw in Dallas on our way home, and by my own calculations. But I just don't see how that's possible."

There was a lot of stomach there. Nadine glanced around. Eden had her hands full, and the little girl with the blond curls had just joined her mother in helping with the crowded dining room. They were likely to be undisturbed for at least a few minutes.

"May I?" she asked, lifting her hand.

Jed looked skeptical, so she assured him. "I'm a doctor. I've lost count of how many babies I've delivered."

He seemed relieved, and Hannah moved her arms aside to give Nadine better access. Nadine laid one hand and then another on Hannah's midsection. After a moment, she closed her eyes. Her fingers explored expertly. Goodness, there was baby everywhere!

"Do either of you have a history of twins in your family?"

After a moment of silence, Jed muttered a foul word, and Hannah sighed in despair.

"Oh, dear," the mother-to-be said. "I never really considered . . . It did cross my mind early on, but I dismissed it as unlikely . . . Oh, my sister has the most dreadful twin boys!"

Jed muttered another foul word.

Nadine removed her hands and opened her eyes. "I can't be certain, but it's definitely a possibility. Twins often come early, and that can be a problem if the babies aren't fully developed. You really should stay in bed as much as possible."

"Stay in bed for more than a *month?*" Hannah said, her voice just a bit too sharp.

"Now, Hannah, I'm sure Nadine knows what she's talking about." The big man had gone very pale. "If she says it's best for you to stay in bed, then I think you should stay in bed."

"It likely won't be near two months," Nadine said calmly. Maybe she should have kept her mouth shut. Jed and Hannah were both terrified. "If it's twins, they will come a little early, no matter what you do."

"I suppose I could read," Hannah said. "It's not as if I'm able to get around and do anything, in any case."

"I'll sit with you," Jed said, still pale.

It was very sweet, Nadine decided, that Jed was so concerned about his wife. He loved her. It was so obvious, a blind man could have seen it.

"Will you still be here when the baby . . . or babies come?" Jed asked. "Eden and Mary both said they'd midwife, but they've never delivered twins before. Nate has some experience, but I'm pretty sure he's never delivered twins before, either."

"I can certainly plan to be here that long," Nadine said. "If I decide to locate my practice here, I'll most definitely be around."

But, of course, she wouldn't be setting up practice here. Cash would not allow it. As soon as JD was convinced that taking up gunfighting was not an option, Cash would probably escort them both to the edge of town.

Nadine took a deep breath. Well, he might make life difficult for her, but he couldn't force her to leave. At least, not before Hannah delivered.

"What kind of a gunslinger plans weddings?" JD asked in disgust as he stepped from Rogue's Palace onto the boardwalk.

Cash grinned at the kid's back. "A man should always be prepared for anything. No task is too ordinary, or too bizarre."

JD turned toward the south end of town, and Cash stayed close behind him. "Why can't I just call somebody out and get it over with?" he asked, so impatient he couldn't be still. His head turned as he looked over the town. His long, thin fingers danced. "This is the town where the Rock Creek Six live. I could call any one of them out, win, and my name is made."

Something in Cash's heart shriveled, making him shudder deep. He couldn't allow the fear the very idea of JD taking on one of his own caused to show. "Great plan," he said dryly. "Let's see, we have a bunch of aging family men to choose from. A schoolteacher, the sheriff, and the preacher. Not such a hot idea, kid."

"That's just three. What about the other two?"

"A rifle is Jed's weapon, and besides . . . he's about to become a father."

"So?"

Cash took a deep breath. "The whole idea doesn't sit well with me," he said in a tone that left no room for argument.

"And the other one?"

They were passing Lily's place, and Cash glanced toward the closed doors. "I tried to teach Rico to shoot, I really did. It was a hopeless cause. He might put a knife through your heart before you can draw your pistol, but you can't make a name for yourself taking out a man who can't hit the broad side of a barn."

JD sighed in disgust.

"That leaves me," Cash said.

JD whirled around, but he kept walking. Backward. "I would never call you out. You're my hero." The kid gave him a wide, true smile. "There's gotta be somebody else I can start with."

Cash caught and held the kid's green eyes. "There's always Teddy. He's damn good."

JD's smile faded. "He's just a kid."

"So are you."

JD glanced toward the hotel. "And he's my friend. I don't think I could shoot a friend."

"Glad to hear it." JD and Teddy had become friends quickly. Sweeping and scrubbing together, they'd had plenty of time to talk and get acquainted. Well, from what Cash had heard, JD did most of the talking and Teddy listened. It was eerily familiar. A little Cash and a little Sullivan, nearly twenty years younger and yet . . . so similar. Teddy wasn't really Sullivan's son, and no one but Nadine knew JD was a little Cash.

"There's the church." JD pointed ahead. "I guess if you're planning a wedding, you start there."

"Why?" Cash said softly.

"Because that's where people get married."

Cash shook his head. "First of all, the Rock Creek church is nothing special. It's small, it's old, and it's disgustingly plain. Second of all, I haven't set foot in a church in several years, and that was under duress."

"How come?" JD asked, wide-eyed with curiosity.

Cash stared at the church. Nate's church now. On Sunday morning most of the townspeople went into that church and listened to Nate Lang preach. It was a concept Cash could not quite imagine, and one he would never see if he had any say in the matter. "If you're going to enter my profession, you might as well get used to it. The people who hire you to clean up their messes don't want you sitting next to them while they pray for their souls. They don't want the blood on your hands to rub off on them."

Besides, it was damned difficult to take a man's life and then sit down in a quiet church and sing hymns, like it was going to make a difference.

JD put his hands on his hips. "Well, if you don't get married in a church, what other choice is there?"

Cash glanced around the town. It was a hell of a lot better than it had been when he'd first seen it, but Rock Creek was still . . . plain. "New Orleans would be nice, but that's out of the question."

"How come?"

JD didn't know who this wedding was for. Jed wanted it to be a secret, and Cash was pretty sure JD didn't know how to keep one. "Never you mind."

"Is it for you?" JD asked brightly.

"Good Lord, no."

JD nodded his head slowly. "Well, what else is there to plan besides the place?"

"The time, the flowers, the candles, the music, and the words."

"You can pick your own words?" JD was apparently confused. "I thought all weddings were pretty much the same."

"Pretty much." The last thing he wanted to do was stand in the middle of the street and plan Jed and Hannah's second wedding. He was thinking of advising Jed to toss his wife over his shoulder, carry her to Nate, and have it done. If he did this while Hannah was pregnant and unusually agreeable, there shouldn't be too high a price to pay.

Cash shook his head as he looked up and down the street. Most dreams faded quickly, leaving nothing but a vague recollection behind. But now, as he and JD planned another Rourke wedding, last night's dream remained too damn clear. He could still taste the fear, still feel the burning path of the bullet. He could still see what was left of Melvin.

Even worse, considering the current situation, the dream had him remembering what a fool he'd been about Nadine. What had he been thinking? That he could go home, marry her, and buy old man Brubaker's general store? Daniel Cash, a shopkeeper? What a ridiculous notion.

She'd done him a favor by marrying Joseph Ellington. It was the best thing that could have happened, given the circumstances.

"You could have a wedding in your place," JD suggested as he studied the plain town around him.

Cash slapped his son lightly on the back of the head, and they both laughed.

Six

Cash hadn't asked her to dine with him again, and he hadn't so much as shown his face all day. Nadine didn't like it. She wanted to know what progress he was making with JD, and she needed to see her son.

It had taken all her will to stay away from Rogue's Palace today, as Cash had ordered her to do before he left last night, but she'd managed to stay busy. Taking care of Hannah had consumed a good portion of the day, and baby Alex had a tummyache she'd treated with a mild mint tea she carried in her medical bag. Eden had been full of questions, and over tea during a quiet part of the afternoon they'd had a long conversation about natural remedies. The mother of five had been quite interested, and had even asked Nadine to help her put in a useful herb garden.

But the night was so lonely. She'd never wished for a man in the house after Joseph's death, and JD was always there. They talked in the evening, sometimes they read or played a game. She missed him now. She did not, she silently chastised herself, wish for even one minute to see Daniel Cash!

She paced the room long after dark. The lamp on

her bedside table was turned low, and she'd donned her nightgown and wrapper hours before, right after she'd had dinner with the Sullivan family. She had hoped to fall asleep early, but that was not to be. She paced, and she worried.

The soft knock on her door took her by surprise, so much so that she jumped. Ah, word was out that she was a healer, and everyone would be coming to her with questions now. At all times of the day and night.

She opened the door, and quit breathing when she saw Cash standing there. His eyes raked over her, taking in the plain calico dressing gown and her loosened hair.

"Invite me in," he whispered, even though there was no one else in the hallway to hear.

She shook her head. He raised his eyebrows.

With a sigh, Nadine stepped back and invited Cash in with a wave of her hand.

He stepped into the room and closed the door behind him, slamming it so forcefully, everyone in the hotel was sure to hear.

"What are you doing here?" she whispered.

"It's part of the plan, remember?"

"But no one knows . . ."

"Sullivan was in the lobby and so was Rico. They saw me and I'm sure they knew exactly where I was headed, with a grin on my face." He was not grinning now.

She couldn't care less what the people of Rock Creek thought of her, she told herself forcefully. As Cash had reminded her more than once, she wouldn't be here long. "How's JD?"

"Fine."

"Does he still want to be a gunfighter?"

Cash gave her a smile. Even in the low light she could see the festering anger there. "Afraid so. You didn't think I could do this overnight, did you?"

"No," she admitted softly.

Cash's eyes fell to her lips and lingered there, and his hand came up to caress the strand of hair that fell over her shoulder. The back of his hand barely touched her, high on her breast. The light contact stole her breath away.

"You are just as beautiful as you were at sixteen," he said in a low voice.

"A pretty lie," she whispered.

His eyes snapped up to hers. "I don't lie."

"You're lying to JD. You're lying to everyone in this town *about* JD."

"That's a lie of omission," he said. "And it's for the kid's own good."

"Why?" She wanted to know why he refused to accept his own son.

He winced just slightly. "Think about it, Nadine. The kid already wants to hire his gun out. Stick him with the name Cash and he won't last a week."

She shuddered, and he responded by laying a comforting hand on her cheek.

"I never thought of it that way."

"I haven't thought of anything else."

Her heart broke for him, for the boy she had known and for the man he had become. "How do you live like that?"

"It's all I know."

She had the strongest, strangest urge to rise up on her toes and kiss him. A comforting kiss, that's all it would be. Something to tell him she was so sorry that he couldn't claim his son. Something to tell him she wished their lives had worked out differently.

But she didn't. Cash was not the kind of man to whom one offered a kiss of comfort.

"You should go now," she whispered.

His eyebrows shot up. "I told you, Sullivan and Rico saw me come up."

"Well, you've been here long enough to . . . to . . ." She felt herself blush warmly. "Do whatever it is you want them to think you're doing."

"I most certainly have not," he said, sounding utterly horrified.

Their first and only time together had been fast and furious, an uncontrolled frenzy. Her nights with her husband had been mercifully quick. She could not imagine what might take Cash so long. He'd been in her room for a good five minutes!

"Don't tell me Ellington never—"

"I don't want to talk to you about Joseph," she interrupted.

His curious eyes devoured her, and he saw too much. The uneasiness in her rigid body, the fear in her eyes. "Has no one ever made proper love to you, Nadine Ellington?"

"That's none of your business!"

"Is that why you never remarried? Nothing to miss? Nothing to crave on cold, lonely nights?"

"What I crave or don't crave is none of—"

"None of my business," he finished for her. "I

know." His hand caressed her neck, and the soft touch was unexpectedly agreeable. Warm and intimate, that gentle caress made her relax. "Why do I feel like it is very much my business?"

Agreeable or not, this had to stop. "I don't know, but that's your problem, not mine." She tried to sound cool, but it wasn't easy with those fingers caressing her throat, with those dark eyes looking at her so hungrily.

"You said you would do anything I say," he reminded her.

Nadine's heart skipped a beat. "That doesn't include allowing you to—"

"Kiss you," he interrupted. "Surely there's nothing wrong with a kiss."

Oh, she did remember the way he kissed, the butterflies that had fluttered in her stomach and the way she had never been able to get enough of his mouth. Joseph had never kissed her that way. Usually, he hadn't bothered to kiss her at all.

"A kiss," she whispered huskily. "I don't suppose there would be anything wrong with that." Suddenly she wanted the kiss more than anything. It was as if she were starving for the touch of Cash's lips. Her heart beat too hard. She trembled down deep.

But Cash didn't quickly lay his lips over hers, as she expected. He threaded the fingers of both hands through her hair. He stared at her so hard, she felt the force of his gaze. He licked his lips and tilted his head and pulled her body up against his. And held her there. She was helpless. Completely and totally *helpless*.

The hands in her hair moved subtly, caressing her

scalp, pulling her just a little bit closer and tilting her head back. Had she really thought Cash was a cold man? There was heat here. An undeniable, sensual heat. His body, which was pressed so closely to hers, was wonderfully warm.

His nose brushed against hers, and she closed her eyes. Warm lips brushed her cheek, the place just beneath her ear, and then came back to touch her mouth.

Her entire body responded, shuddered and burned. She lifted her arms to wrap them around Cash's waist, needing something solid to hold on to. And he was solid. Wonderfully, warmly solid.

He parted her lips with a slight shift of pressure and she allowed her mouth to drift open. She felt his breath, his very heartbeat, and when he flicked the tip of his tongue into her mouth, she began to melt.

She didn't want the kiss to end, not ever. The world shifted, everything changed, and all because he moved his mouth over hers. The years rolled away and he was her Danny again. She was madly in love. Nothing would ever come between them. She wanted to slip beneath his skin, to be with him always.

Her entire body throbbed, and an unexpected heat pooled low within her. Something tugged at that heat, made it swirl and dance.

Cash took his mouth from hers as slowly as he had brought it to her. She could taste his reluctance, and her own. Her brain was fuzzy. Her dogged determination was fading rapidly. "Why didn't you come home?" she whispered. "Why didn't you come back to me?"

"I did," he whispered against her neck, where he laid his wonderful lips.

"When?"

He was silent as he kissed her throat. "It doesn't matter," he said. "The only thing that matters is now. Right now, Nadine."

He dropped one of the hands that had been lost in her hair to her breast, caressing her through the thin wrapper and nightgown, raking his fingers over the pebbled nipple. It felt good, and she wanted him to touch and kiss her again and again. But she also knew where this would lead if she didn't put a stop to it now. She didn't want Cash, or any man, in her bed.

"Stop," she whispered.

"Why?" His exploring hand trailed from her breast to her waist, where it stopped and held on.

"You can go now," she said quickly. "Surely you've been here long enough to maintain your reputation and satisfy your friends."

He lifted his head from her neck and stared down at her. "I am not at all concerned about satisfying my *friends.*"

"I don't think you should stay here," she insisted.

He gave her a crooked grin. "I can't possibly leave in this condition and expect to maintain my reputation." He pressed his body closer to hers and she felt his arousal, hard and insistent, pressing into her flesh.

She had gone too far with that one kiss. Cash would insist that she do whatever he demanded, and if the kiss was any indication, he would not be quick.

"Wipe that worried expression off your face," he growled. "I don't force myself on women who don't want me."

"What about your . . . condition?"

He let her go so abruptly, she felt a wave of dizziness. "Talk to me of other things. Boring things," he suggested as he turned his back on her, ran a hand through his hair, and laughed harshly.

"No," he said, whirling around on her without warning. "Tell me about JD. Before he decided to become a gunfighter, was he a good kid? Has he given you much trouble?"

Nadine smiled. "He's so much like you."

"Sorry about that."

He sat in the single chair in the room, and she crawled into the bed and sat there with her back against the headboard. She talked about JD until the middle of the night, and he listened intently. There were no more kisses, which was just as well considering the effect of the last one, but Cash didn't seem to mind. When he nodded off in his chair, she covered him with the extra blanket from JD's pallet, slipped beneath her own covers, and turned out the light.

His neck hurt, his arm was asleep, and he was more out of the damned chair than in it. Coming awake slowly, Cash clutched at the blanket and tried to work out the kinks that had his body in knots.

The sun was coming up, lighting the hotel room with a soft glow, and suddenly he remembered where he was and how he'd gotten there.

Nadine slept on, curled beneath the covers with her dark hair spread across the pillow. Cash came to his feet to see her more clearly. She was so beautiful, so much a woman. And she was so very terrified of him.

He'd seen her fear last night, in her eyes, in a tremble that had nothing to do with passion. She was afraid of him, and he couldn't blame her. Because what he wanted right now was the same thing he'd wanted last night. To crawl into the bed with her and make her his again.

But it was too late for that. He didn't cry about the past, he didn't wallow in self-pity over what he didn't have. The woman who had once been his wasn't his anymore. They'd gone in different directions. Hell, they couldn't possibly live their lives any differently!

Besides, Nadine wasn't a woman a man could bed and walk away from.

He slipped quietly out of the room, grateful that no one else was in the hallway at this ungodly early hour. With any luck, he could make it back to Rogue's Palace without being seen.

Why the hell did that thought even cross his mind? He wanted everyone to think he and Nadine were sleeping together. Why did he have this urge to protect her reputation now?

Because she was a good woman. Because she deserved so much better.

The lobby was deserted as well. He had almost made it to the doorway, when a cheerful voice called out.

"Daniel!"

Cash spun about to face Eden, who exited the dining room wearing a flour-covered apron and wiping her hands on a linen towel.

"I thought I heard someone in here. It's a little early for breakfast, but I'll have something ready in just a few minutes." She glanced at the closed door behind him, then raked her eyes over his wrinkled suit. "Wait a minute. Are you coming in or going out?"

"Coming in, of course," he said coolly. "I . . . couldn't sleep and wanted some decent coffee, but the dining room was empty and I decided I'd just slip out and try again in a little while."

Eden's eyes narrowed suspiciously. "That's the same suit you were wearing yesterday, and it's rumpled."

"I had a long night," he explained.

"Your hair is . . . mussed."

He quickly ran a hand through the short strands. "Better?"

"Yes."

Cash took a step toward Eden. Actually, coffee sounded pretty good right about now.

"You're limping," she said in an accusing voice.

Well, you try sleeping in a damned chair all night! He bit that comment back. "I'm feeling incredibly old this morning."

Eden was no fool. She looked him over, glanced toward the stairway, and sighed.

"I wish I could believe you, Daniel, but you see, the door is still bolted from the inside."

He spun around to glance at the door. "It is not."

"Yes," she sighed. "But you did bother to look. For goodness' sake, Daniel, I told you already. Nadine Ellington is not the woman for you."

How well he knew that. "Who put you in charge of my love life?"

"Obviously someone needs to take charge," she said with a lift of her pert nose. She took his arm and they walked into the dining room. "Actually, I like her very much."

"So do I," Cash muttered.

"She's not the kind of woman you trifle with."

"No, she's not."

Eden walked with him to his favorite table and stood there as he lowered himself into a hard chair. "If I thought that you'd commit yourself to a fine woman and settle down, I'd do everything in my power to make it happen."

"I will never settle down."

"I know," Eden said sadly. "So don't break Nadine's heart. She seems very capable; she's a strong woman. But she's also vulnerable. I don't think she would admit that to anyone, but if she falls in love with you and things end badly . . . it would really hurt her, Daniel. You just don't understand how a woman's heart functions."

"You have never learned to mind your own damned business, have you?"

Eden shook her head. "No."

"Well, don't worry," he said, leaning back in his chair. "Nadine's heart is perfectly safe."

He wondered what Eden would say if he confessed that the only heart in mortal danger was his own.

This was definitely not what he'd had in mind when he'd decided to become a gunfighter. JD scrubbed at a stubborn stain on the wall of Rogue's Palace, putting everything he had into the chore. He didn't really want to know what the stain was.

"Hey, Teddy," he called, glancing over his shoulder to watch his friend attack a similar stain on yet another wall. "When I'm famous, don't you be telling nobody that I had to scrub down this ramshackle saloon."

Teddy might have smiled, but the curve of his lips was subtle. "Don't worry. Your secret is safe with me."

He believed, no, he *knew* that Teddy would keep his word. It hadn't taken them five minutes to become friends, and already he liked the boy better than any of the kids back home. He would almost hate to leave his new friend behind when the time came.

"Maybe you could . . . come with me."

Teddy shook his head. "I don't think gunfighters travel in pairs, do they? I mean, Nate and Cash used to go off together a lot, but mostly Cash is on his own. Nate was never actually a gunfighter, I don't think. Besides," he added with a subtle note of cheer in his voice, "I'm going to work for Uncle Jed as soon as I'm old enough."

"Doing what?" JD returned his attention to the stubborn stain.

"He and Aunt Hannah are going to start an investigation agency. Like Pinkerton's, only smaller. He said when Eden gives her okay, I can go to work for him."

"That wouldn't be too bad."

"If you wanted," Teddy suggested, "maybe you could work for Uncle Jed, too, instead of being a gunfighter."

JD shook his head. His mind was made up. Nothing less than what Daniel Cash had would satisfy him. "They don't write dime novels about detectives."

"Maybe they do," Teddy said in a low voice. "And even if they don't, maybe you could be the first."

JD considered the proposition for a moment, then shook off the fleeting indecision. "Nah. Sounds like a good job for you, though. At least it'll get you out of this little town. Rock Creek is worse than Marianna!"

Teddy scrubbed for a moment before responding. "It's not so bad."

JD scoffed. Loudly.

"Sometimes it's an exciting place, not boring at all," Teddy continued. "There are lots of celebrations, like the one for Fourth of July that's coming up. The ladies around here, they do their best to make things nice."

"Nice isn't exciting," JD grumbled.

For a second Teddy looked like he was going to argue, but he didn't. He scrubbed some more before saying, "Things will really get exciting around here if anyone ever finds the gold."

JD dropped his arm and turned around slowly. "The *gold?*"

Teddy didn't lift his eyes from his chore. "Most folks don't believe the legend, but I think it might be true."

JD waited for Teddy to continue, and when he didn't, he prodded, "What legend?"

"The old man who owned the hotel before Ma, he used to be a bandit. There was some gold that never turned up." Teddy shrugged. "That's all."

"He would've hidden it in the hotel," JD speculated. "Some secret hiding place no one would ever find unless they looked really hard."

"Maybe," Teddy said, uninterested.

JD dropped his rag into a pail of water. He was damned tired of scrubbing. "We could look for it," he suggested.

"I don't know," Teddy answered, less than enthusiastic. "People have looked before. What makes you think we could find it?"

"What makes you think we couldn't? Just imagine it, Teddy. Your uncle would really be impressed with your detecting skills if you were the one to discover where the gold was hidden."

Teddy didn't answer, but he did look interested. *Very* interested.

JD grinned. A little treasure hunt would take the edge off the indignity of being turned into a housekeeper.

Seven

It was time. The saloon had been scrubbed from top to bottom, and JD was getting restless. The kid scurried over small, grassy hills with real excitement in his step as they headed for the river and a little target practice.

JD owned his own gun, a plain but serviceable six-shooter that had once belonged to Joseph Ellington. The kid kept it clean and well oiled, and wore it on his hip with more ease than Cash was comfortable with. A thirteen-year-old shouldn't strap on a holster with such deftness; he shouldn't wear a weapon with such obvious comfort. But then, JD had likely never seen what that well-oiled gun could do to a human being. There was never any blood in those pen-and-ink drawings that graced the dime novels JD loved to read.

"Here?" JD called, spinning around as they reached the river.

"This will do."

Cash handed the burlap sack he carried to JD, and told the boy to set up six of the empty whiskey bottles inside the sack on a flat rock that jutted over the water. The kid quickly did as he was told.

With a grin on his face, JD posed a good distance away from the bottles. Long legs spread, feet planted steadily on the ground, he stared at the targets.

"Go," Cash said.

JD settled the palm of his hand over the butt of his six-shooter and rotated his head as if he had a crick in his neck.

"You're dead," Cash said, crossing his arms over his chest.

"What?" JD's head snapped around.

"I said"—Cash took a couple of slow steps toward the kid—"you're *dead*. While you were getting ready to fire, preening for the crowd like a popinjay, your opponent drew and pulled the trigger and shot you dead."

"They're bottles," JD said, disgust in his voice.

"No, they're your opponents. They want the same thing you do. To survive another day." Cash drew his own six-shooter smoothly, aimed with habitual precision, and began to fire. He fired without thought, without emotion. One by one the six bottles exploded.

"Set 'em up again," he ordered as he flipped open the chamber and began to reload.

JD did as he was told, moving quickly, not smiling this time. As soon as he was back in place, before he had a chance to plant his feet or study the target, Cash yelled, "Go!"

The kid reached for his six-shooter and found it, but not without some difficulty. His nervous fingers fumbled just a little, but he did draw fairly quickly. Cash pointed to the sky and pulled the trigger. JD jumped and spun around as Cash fired again.

"You're dead again," Cash said.

JD sighed with youthful indignation. "Why did you shoot into the air like that? Are you trying to ruin my aim?"

Cash slipped his weapon into the holster and stalked toward JD. "Anyone can do well when they're having a leisurely target practice, where there's no noise, no pressure, nothing on the line. But what are you going to do when you have gunfire all around, bullets whizzing in your direction, people trying to *kill* you?" He glared into JD's wide eyes. "Now!"

The kid spun around and fired. Three of the bottles exploded. Three shots went wide.

"Not bad," Cash said when the echo of the explosions faded away. "But you're still dead."

"I'll do better this time." JD headed toward the rock to set up another six bottles.

"No, we're done for today," Cash said.

"What?" JD spun around. "We just got started!"

"Clean up all that glass," Cash instructed with a wave of his hand. "Kids come down here to play."

"So?" JD muttered sullenly. "That's not my problem."

Cash set his darkest glare on his son. "Clean up your own mess, and get used to it."

JD grumbled, but he did as he was told. Cash watched, amazed by the way the kid moved, by the way there were moments when the sunlight hit the boy's face just so and he looked like the Nadine he remembered. When he allowed it, he saw himself there, too. Why did watching this kid do something so ordinary as pick up broken glass hurt so damned much?

Shaking off the unexpected pain, Cash stepped to the bank to look over the river. The water flowed steadily, with purpose and inevitability and beauty. Sun sparkled on the flowing water; wildflowers grew on the bank. The pain of knowing what he'd missed faded slowly, not quite leaving him but finding a safe place in his heart and easing in.

There was a rare peacefulness here. Peace. He hadn't known any for so long, he was surprised he knew what it was when he found it.

"Here," he said.

"Here what?" JD asked as he picked up scattered slivers of glass.

"The wedding. Sunset . . . or sunrise."

"You're still planning that wedding?"

"Did we finish yesterday?" Cash snapped.

JD grumbled but continued with his chore. "Do I have to do any more cleaning this afternoon?"

"I don't know. I haven't decided."

"I was just thinking, I might go over to the hotel and play with Teddy if we're finished for the day."

Cash set steady eyes on the kid. "Gunfighters—do—not—play."

"Not play, really," JD corrected himself. "Just talk, you know? About . . . weapons and women."

Cash raised his eyebrows, but the kid, who was picking up glass, didn't see. "Women?"

"Yeah. I'm going to be a ladies' man, like you. Heck, nobody's going to tie me down with a dowdy wife and a bunch of babies."

"So you like the ladies?"

JD was still such a child. On the cusp of becoming a man, perhaps, but still a child.

"Sure," JD said, deepening his voice a bit.

His son had a lot to learn that had nothing to do with gunfighting. And Cash knew he wouldn't be around to do the teaching.

Nadine stepped cautiously into the saloon, feeling like a thief sneaking about as she glanced around the empty room.

"What do you want?" a gruff voiced snapped, and Nadine jumped as her eyes flew to the gray-haired man entering the main room through a rear door, three bottles of whiskey balanced comfortably in two large hands.

"I'm looking for Cash," she said softly.

The old man smirked as he set the bottles on the long, polished bar. "Upstairs," he croaked. "Second door on the left."

Nadine gave the crude man a prim smile. "Thank you." She walked through the saloon with her head high. It didn't matter what the unshaven ruffian thought of her. She climbed the stairs cautiously, taking silent steps, going over the questions in her mind. She needed to talk to Cash, and she couldn't possibly wait until the next time he decided to knock on her door. That knock might come tonight, but it might not come for days. It might not ever come again.

Standing outside the second door on the left, she took a deep breath. Last night she had let her emotions get the best of her; she'd allowed a kiss to make her question everything she knew to be true. Cash was right. As much as she hated to admit it, JD could never know the gunslinger he admired was his father.

She laid her hand on the doorknob and took another deep breath, for courage to face the man who had the power to turn her tidy world upside down.

A gentle push of her hand was all she managed before the door flew open. Since she gripped the doorknob tight, she was jerked inside. She gasped as a strong hand closed over her wrist and yanked her around so hard that her head spun. The door slammed behind her; Cash cursed.

"What the hell are you doing?" he seethed, not releasing his hold on her wrist.

She glanced up into piercing dark eyes. Cash had discarded his jacket and vest and boots, and his dark hair was slightly mussed. The bed behind him, a bed decadent with red silk and more pillows than any one man would ever need, was wrinkled. He'd been napping.

"We need to talk."

He placed his face close to hers. "Don't ever sneak up on me like that. It's a good way to end up dead."

It was then that she noticed the gun in his hand. "You heard me coming," she whispered.

"Friends don't skulk," he said, releasing his grip on her at last.

"I was not . . ." she began, and then she realized what her cautious steps and silent pauses might have seemed like to a man who was constantly on alert. "Well, I didn't mean to skulk."

Cash walked away from her, raked a restless hand through his hair, and carefully placed his weapon on the bedside table near a silver flask, a deck of cards, and a fancy lamp. He sat on the edge of the bed, on red satin that dipped and wrinkled beneath his weight.

"You were sleeping?" she asked needlessly.

"Yeah. I didn't sleep much last night, and I can't be sure that tonight will be any better. By the way, you'll be pleased to know that Eden caught me trying to sneak out of the hotel at dawn. Our fabrication is secure."

The mention of Eden gave her an opportunity to pursue a line of questioning she had been unable to broach until then. "She seems very sweet."

"Uh-huh," he said sleepily.

"And you seem to be very close to her."

"I suppose."

"Were you two ever—" She took a deep breath, searching for the right word.

"Good Lord, no," Cash interrupted, seeing too clearly where she was heading with her questions. "Eden is a friend's wife and another friend's sister. I like her, she's as close to a little sister as I ever had, but for God's sake . . . Is that why you're here? To interrogate me about Eden?"

"No."

"Then what do you want?"

Nadine had an answer she was satisfied with, and for some reason breathed easier. "I saw JD at the hotel," she said, taking a few steps around the bed so she could see Cash's face. "He said you finally got in some shooting practice." She shuddered. "Is that really a good idea? Should you be encouraging him?"

Cash lifted his head and stared at her. "We do things my way, remember? Trust me."

She didn't mean to, but she shook her head very slightly.

A hand, lightning-fast and deadly accurate, snaked out and grabbed her skirt. With a tug from that capable hand she stumbled toward Cash. He grabbed her arm and pulled her down to the bed, where she landed with a squeal.

Before she could even think of sitting up and moving away, Cash was there. Hovering over her, his body close but not actually touching hers as he pinned her to the bed. He took a deep breath she felt, licked his lips, and tilted his head as he stared at her.

"You must trust me," he whispered.

He hung above her, hard and long, muscles taut. For a second Nadine didn't know whether she wanted most to push him away or pull him down.

"Why should I?" she argued, her heart hammering in her chest. "What have you ever done to make me *trust* you?"

He realigned his body so he was lying against her, so lightly it was almost as if he weren't touching her at all. "I've never lied to you, I've never broken a single promise . . ."

"You broke every promise you ever made," she snapped angrily. In this position, nothing else seemed important. He reached inside her so easily, stirred up emotions she'd be better off ignoring. She'd been able to ignore them for a very long time. "You promised you'd come back."

"I did," he whispered.

"When?"

"Too late."

"You could've come to me," she said softly.

"And interrupt the happy bride on her wedding day?"

Her heart lurched. "No," she breathed. "Oh, no, tell me you weren't there . . . that day."

"Yes."

Suddenly she was cold. Cold to the bone and shivering with the chill. "They said you were dead; just the day before we received a list of names—"

"Is that why you smiled so brilliantly?" Cash interrupted caustically. "The blissful bride, with flowers and a wedding ring and a smile bright enough to light up the night sky."

Nadine looked deep into his eyes. She didn't know what he'd seen, but he believed what he said. Even after all these years, she wanted him to know the truth. It was important that he know. "I didn't smile on my wedding day. I cried like my heart was broken, because it was. I didn't smile for a very long time."

"I saw you with my own eyes," he whispered darkly. "Why should I believe you now?"

"Because I never lied to you, and I never will."

His hand settled familiarly at her hip. "So I can ask any question I want and be assured of a true answer."

"Yes." Her heart hammered.

His hand stroked her hip. "Did you ever love me?"

"Yes," she answered quickly.

"If I had shown myself to you that day, would you have left your husband and your father and come with me?"

Again, there was no hesitation in her answer. "Yes."

His body settled more snugly to hers. A hand rose to stroke her hair. "Do you still love me?"

She swallowed hard. His question stole her breath away, and while he waited for an answer, he touched her. Fingers through her hair, a hand at her waist. "No," she finally whispered. Heaven help her, she could not love him!

He didn't seem at all disturbed at her answer. "Do you want me?"

"No."

He actually smiled, but his eyes did not meet hers. "Liar," he whispered.

"I am *not* . . ."

"Your body is shaking."

"You're scaring me, of course I'm shaking."

"That's not fear I feel," he argued lightly. "Are you lying? Or do you just not know what to make of . . . this."

"I came here to talk about JD . . ."

"We could've talked about JD tonight."

"I didn't know if you would come to my room again or not." She tried to push against his body with hers, but it didn't do any good. "And I didn't want to wait."

Cash lowered his head and kissed the side of her neck. "I've never been very good at waiting, either," he whispered against her neck, his voice low and warm. "But don't worry," he added as he moved his lips to the other side of her neck. "I won't ever do anything you don't want, and I won't make love to you until you ask."

Just a few days ago, she would have sworn that he was in for a very long wait, but right now . . . something was happening and she didn't understand. She understood only that the weight of Cash's body and the warmth of his mouth were different from anything she'd ever known, and they made her want . . . something more. It was that wanting that scared her, she realized. More than any threat from the man Daniel Cash had become, it was her own response that frightened her.

"Yes," she said breathlessly. "That's very gentlemanly of you, I suppose."

"Gentlemanly," he muttered. "I'm trying to be nice, and you insult me."

"This is your idea of nice?"

"Sweetheart, this is as close as I get to nice." He kissed her one last time and raked his body against hers as he left the bed.

He was gone; she had no reason to be afraid, and still she trembled.

JD slunk down the third-floor hallway, Teddy at his back. "If I had something to hide in this hotel, I'd find a safe place on the top floor," he whispered. "It might be under a floorboard, or in the wall, or even in a secret compartment in a piece of furniture."

"A secret compartment?" Teddy asked skeptically.

"Sure," JD hissed. "If I had gold to hide, I'd definitely have a secret compartment."

"Why are you whispering?" Teddy asked. "No one's up here but us."

JD cast a narrow-eyed glance over his shoulder. Teddy didn't know anything about treasure hunting.

At the far end of the hallway, JD came to a halt and

turned around slowly. "We'll start here," he said, "work our way across the third floor, and then, if we don't find anything, we'll move down to the second floor."

"Okay."

JD tapped a knuckle against the wall, listening for a telltale echo. The wall seemed solid enough.

Teddy got down on his knees and tested floorboards, searching for a loose plank as JD worked his way down the hall. He kept his ear close to the wall, listening intently as he crept along the hallway. He continued this systematic search until his progress was impeded by a very tall, very wide, very unhappy man.

"What the hell are you doing?" the man growled.

"Uncle Jed," Teddy said, jumping to his feet and dusting off his trousers. "We were just—"

JD stepped between Teddy and his uncle. "None of your business," he interrupted.

Teddy muttered a low "uh-oh."

This was Jed Rourke, JD thought with just a little seedling of respect and fear. He'd seen him from a distance, but up close he was rough-looking and hairy and . . . *big*. He could get a crick in his neck looking up at the man.

But JD wasn't afraid. Gunfighters had to be fearless. "We're not doing anything important," he said calmly and sternly. There was no hint, in his steady voice, that his heart was about to pound through his chest. "So get lost, old man."

Jed Rourke leaned down slowly, placing his face close to JD's. A muscle in his beard-roughened cheek twitched. "You're a mouthy kid. You belong to the new doctor?"

"I don't *belong* to her," JD said tersely. "But she is my mother."

"Then I won't kill you," the hairy man said in a low growl.

JD straightened his spine. "Are you calling me out?"

The big man straightened, a look of horror on his face. "Of course not. You're just a kid."

"I might be just a kid, but I could take you on if I had to." Jed Rourke might be big and tough, but he was also *old*. Over thirty, for sure.

The old man tried to step around JD, but JD was quick. He placed himself in Rourke's path, eyes lifted challengingly.

With a sigh the big man reached out and placed his hands under JD's arms.

"Hey!" JD shouted as Rourke lifted him, swung him around, and deposited him where he was out of the way.

Rourke glared down at Teddy. "What are y'all doing?"

"Looking for the gold."

"Okay," Rourke said, not at all concerned by the news. "Do it quietly, you hear? Hannah sent me up here to look for a wayward woodpecker."

"JD was tapping on the wall," Teddy explained.

Rourke glanced back to JD and grinned. "So you're the little woodpecker."

JD narrowed his eyes in a glare he hoped would be threatening. Rourke did not appear to be at all moved.

"Tear up Eden's hotel and she will have your hide."

"We'll be careful," Teddy promised.

Jed stepped around JD. "A word of advice, little

woodpecker. Grow a couple of feet before you go around running that mouth of yours. It's going to get you in trouble one of these days."

JD glared at the man who didn't bother to so much as glance back. When he was ready to start his new career, Jed Rourke would be the first man he called out, no matter what Cash said.

It was late when he walked into the dimly lit lobby of the Paradise Hotel. There would be no children running around at this hour, and Eden, who usually started her day early, was probably already in bed. Which meant Sullivan would be in bed, too.

If he wanted people to think he was sleeping with Nadine, why hadn't he come earlier, when there would be plenty of witnesses?

The place was not deserted, though. Cash heard lowered voices from the dining room, and stopped in the entrance to peek inside. Sullivan and Reese sat at a table near the middle of the room. Quiet as he was, he didn't surprise the two men. It wasn't easy to surprise Rock Creek's sheriff. Sullivan nodded and waved Cash into the room.

"What's going on?" Cash asked as he ambled toward the table.

"One of my students who lives outside town reported that her father saw an Indian the other day."

"Just one?" Cash asked, pulling out a chair and spinning it around to straddle the seat.

"Yeah," Sullivan answered. "But that doesn't mean there aren't more waiting over the next hill."

"Think this Indian might be one of our old friends?" Cash leaned slightly forward.

"After a year that's unlikely," Reese said, but Cash could tell he had considered the possibility.

Those renegades had staked four of them, the three sitting at this table and Rico, to the ground. Only the appearance of Nate, a man the Indians thought was a crazy warrior, had saved them from being scalped.

"What are we going to do?" Cash asked.

"Renegades have always stayed away from town," Sullivan said. "But we're going to add a nightly patrol anyway."

"We'll take turns riding the perimeter, once in the morning and once at night, for a while," Reese said. "If we see anything, we'll up the patrols."

"One-man patrols or two?"

"One, for now."

"Count me in," Cash said with a smile. He was always ready for a little action, and something like this might actually take his mind off Nadine for a while.

Reese set all-knowing eyes on Cash. "What are you doing here?"

Cash gave his former captain a wide smile. "I have a lady friend."

"Don't you always?" Sullivan muttered.

"Upstairs," Cash added.

"I think I heard something about that." Reese remained calm, casual, but Cash could only imagine what Mary had told her husband about Nadine. Did the entire town know that he'd been caught sneaking out of the hotel at dawn that morning? No, not the whole town, just the ones who counted most.

"Should I take the first patrol?" Cash offered.

"No," Reese said. "Sullivan and I have tonight and tomorrow morning covered. You can take tomorrow night," he added. "Since we know your idea of a morning patrol would be riding the perimeter at noon."

"I'll be going, then." Cash stood and returned his chair to its proper place. "Tomorrow night, Captain."

Reese looked a little uncomfortable with the designation of leader, as he always had. Still, it's who he was and would always be.

Cash turned around and headed for the lobby and the stairway. Why was the prospect of facing Nadine tonight and not touching her more frightening that the idea of running into those renegades again?

Eight

He didn't kiss her, not tonight. Cash stood by the window that overlooked the garden and stared into utter darkness.

If he could go back and do things differently, he would, but there was no going back. The past fourteen years could not be undone. He wished he didn't know that Nadine had thought him dead when she'd married Ellington. He wished he didn't know she had married a man she didn't love because she was carrying the child they had made on their one and only night together.

If he didn't know, he could put the past back where it belonged. He wouldn't be plagued with these annoying what-ifs.

Tonight she had been prepared for his arrival. Instead of wearing a nightgown and a thin wrapper, she still wore her clothes. A plain linen blouse, a blue calico skirt, those sensible boots. She hadn't even taken her hair down. Did she think that if she kept herself all tied up and proper he wouldn't want her? Foolish woman.

"Is JD safe sleeping in the saloon?" Nadine asked nervously.

Cash turned around to watch her fidget. "Of course he's safe." Did she think he would leave the kid there if he weren't safe? "He falls asleep as soon as his head hits the pillow, and everyone knows better than to go upstairs. Evan makes sure of that."

She wrinkled her nose. "I don't like him," she said softly.

"Evan?"

"He . . . he smirked at me when I stopped by the saloon this afternoon, and when I left he snorted and laughed!"

Of course Evan had snorted when he'd seen Nadine. When she'd left his room, her silky hair had been tousled, her blouse hung slightly askew, and her face had blushed a pretty pink. He had barely touched her, and still she'd left his room looking well-tumbled. And like everyone else in this town, Evan knew Nadine Ellington was not the kind of woman who normally made trips to Daniel Cash's room.

She'd reshaped her hair and straightened her blouse, and looked as strait-laced and prim as ever. And he wanted her in a way he'd never wanted anything else.

Best to move the conversation in a direction that would take his mind off what he so foolishly wanted. "Where will you go when you leave here?" he asked. "Back to Marianna?"

She looked at the tips of her boots. "I suppose. I don't have much of a practice left, since Marianna now has a *real* doctor, but . . . it's home, I guess."

That "I guess" was so uncertain.

Nadine lifted her head and looked him square in the eye. Ah, she might be afraid, but she could be strong when she needed to be. "I won't leave until Hannah has her baby. Or babies."

"Babies?" Cash asked with a lift of his eyebrows.

She told him about her suspicion that Hannah was going to have twins, and that she'd ordered the very pregnant woman to bed.

"That's why I haven't seen Jed in a couple of days." So much for planning a wedding. If Hannah was confined to bed, she definitely wasn't going to drag herself to the river's edge for a second ceremony she'd never wanted in the first place.

"He's staying with her," Nadine said. "He's very worried," she added softly.

"I know," Cash whispered, turning to look down on the garden at night once more. Behind him, Nadine took slow, deep breaths he felt to his bones.

"Didn't you ever want that?" she whispered. "A wife, a family."

"No."

"I see." She sounded vaguely disappointed.

"I suppose I might have taken that route," he added. "Years ago. It's too late now."

"Why is it too late?"

Was she going to make him say it out loud? That no one he took into his life would ever be safe. That even if he did want such normal things, they were not for him. And, by God, he did not want anything so drab and ordinary as a family that would tie him down.

"A man can't go back and undo the things he's done."

"You could go somewhere where no one knows you," she suggested softly. "Shave off the beard, change your name, start a whole new—"

"Maybe I can get a job sweeping the general store in some little backwater town," he snapped. "I'll change my name to Bob Smith and marry a farmer's daughter and pray every day that no one who knows my face rides into town."

He heard her coming. Surely she wouldn't make this worse by touching him. He had so little control where Nadine was concerned.

His eyes closed when she laid her hand against his back. A hand so gentle it reached through and grabbed his heart. He couldn't allow that to happen.

With a stony expression in place, he turned and looked down into her dreamy green eyes. He knew how to scare her away, how to yank her notions of saving him right out of her tender heart.

"Maybe I'm perfectly happy with my life as it stands," he whispered. "I have my own place, money, and there are plenty of women out there who like to brag that they've slept with Daniel Cash."

She flinched, as he had known she would.

"Maybe in the beginning they like the reputation more than the man, but by the time I'm finished with them . . ."

"I really don't need the details," she said primly.

"Maybe you do." He gripped her chin so she couldn't look away. "I'm a better lover now than I was when I screwed you. That shouldn't be a surprise. What do you expect of a couple of virgins?"

"Cash, don't . . ."

"I'm older now. Wiser. Slower," he whispered darkly. "Maybe I owe you one good lay for old time's sake, something to make up for my inexperience the first round."

She should be angry right now. She should lift her hand and slap him again. But the eyes she laid on him remained soft and tender. "You can't scare me," she whispered.

"I thought you said this afternoon that I did frighten you. Make up your mind, Mrs. Ellington."

"I'm not afraid of you," she said in a low, breathy whisper. "I'm afraid of the way you make me feel."

It was a tough admission for her to make. She was so open, he saw the pain on her face, the hurt and indecision that flickered there.

He lowered his face until his lips were almost on hers. "Don't feel anything for me," he whispered.

"What if I can't help it?"

He had started this, trying to scare her, but the ploy wasn't working. In fact, he could not have failed more miserably. She wasn't scared, but he sure as hell was. Nothing frightened him anymore. Nothing. It was hard to scare a man who didn't have anything to lose.

His mouth touched hers, his hands rose up to remove the pins from her hair. The warm dark strands fell—over her shoulders, down her back—and he threaded his fingers through those strands with an aching hunger.

Her body molded against his, and he felt her response to the lingering kiss. She quivered, her lips parted, and her hands . . . reached. Pale, delicate fingers danced over his back. She drew him in closer, deeper, with every tender second that passed.

Knowing he had no choice, he took his mouth from hers. God, he couldn't do this anymore. He couldn't dance to the edge of something he wanted more than anything and then walk away with a smile on his face.

In the low light he could see, too well, the hunger in Nadine's eyes. The trepidation and the curiosity and the love. At least, he could fool himself into thinking that it was love.

He dropped his hands, but Nadine held on. "Make love to me, Cash," she whispered.

He shook his head. "You don't want—"

"Just once," she interrupted. "Just tonight. I know we aren't right for each other anymore, but I think we deserve one night together. For what we used to have. For what we missed. Tomorrow you can be Cash the gunslinger again." Her eyes filled with tears that didn't fall. "But tonight I want my Danny back," she whispered hoarsely. "One night is not too much to ask for, is it?"

He didn't think he could be her Danny again, didn't think he could even pretend.

But when she laid her mouth over his, he wanted nothing more than to try to give her everything she wanted.

Cash unbuttoned her blouse, taking his time, lingering over every button as if it were somehow important. He kept his eyes on the task, and trailed his fingers over the flesh beneath her blouse after every successful unfastening. The touch of those fingers, in an almost innocent way, made her heart beat too fast.

What had she been thinking, to ask him to make love to her? It was unlike her to be so bold.

But she wanted more of the kissing, and she wanted to feel his body against hers. She didn't understand why she wanted this so much, but she did. Knowing that he had come home for her, that he had seen her on her wedding day, softened her heart for him. She tried to imagine what it had been like for him to come home and find her married, and she couldn't.

And like it or not, she did love him. She loved the boy he had been and the man he had become. She loved him because he was the father of her child and because no matter how hard he tried not to care, he couldn't quite pull it off.

His hands found and released the buttons at the side of her skirt, and the plain garment dropped to the floor and pooled at her feet.

He would lay her on the bed now. Lift her petticoat and pull down her drawers and push inside her. It had been so long since a man had touched her. Cash thought it had been nine years, since Joseph's death, but in truth it had been longer than that. In the last year of his life, Joseph hadn't bothered to come to her bed.

She didn't expect pain like she'd experienced the first time, but it had been more than ten years since a man had touched her. That alone was enough to make her question her decision to ask Cash to make love to her.

It didn't matter. She wanted the kissing first; that was what she craved so much, she hurt. She took Cash's face in her hands and laid her mouth over his, parting her lips, flicking her tongue into his mouth and reveling in the unexpected sensation of heat pooling deep inside her.

While she kissed Cash he kissed her back and deftly untied the ribbons of her chemise. Her heart kicked once as he peeled the loosened fabric away from her breasts. No one had ever seen her completely bare, and it wasn't necessary that she discard *all* her clothes, not for what they were going to do.

She trembled as he loosened the tapes of her petticoat, and it fell to the floor. Apparently he planned to completely undress her. *Completely.* She wasn't sure it was such a good idea. She was a mother, a grown woman. Cash was sure to see all her imperfections.

Soon she wore nothing but the chemise. When Cash took the linen in his hands and bunched it in his fist, intending to lift the undergarment over her head, she placed her hands over his.

"Is it really necessary that I take off . . . everything?"

Already his eyes were heavily lidded, dark with desire. "Necessary? No." He did not try to pull the material out of her hands. "Desired?" he whispered. "Yes." He laid his mouth on her shoulder and sucked lightly at her flesh. "Trust me, Nadine. Just for tonight."

After a moment's hesitation, she dropped her hands and Cash pulled the chemise over her head. With a flick of his wrist, he tossed it to the floor.

A moment ago she had been worried, but Cash didn't look at her as if he saw any imperfections. He cupped one breast with a tender hand, and placed his other hand on her hip, where it rested, warm and possessive.

"You are so beautiful," he whispered. "So beautiful, it hurts to look at you."

She closed her eyes as he flicked his thumb over her nipple. Heavens, the sensation shot right through her. When he dipped his head and took that nipple in his mouth, she sucked in her breath and grabbed his head, surprised, and shocked, and . . . delighted. Good heavens, she felt the tug of his mouth all through her body.

He lifted her from the floor and carried her to the bed, where he deposited her gently. Nadine took a deep breath and held it, waiting anxiously for what would come next. Oh, she hoped he would hold her afterward, like he had more than fourteen years ago. He might not whisper that he loved her, he might not whisper promises he would not be able to keep, but she did want him to cradle her in his arms.

"You can douse the light," she whispered.

He smiled down at her. "And miss the sight of you lying there, naked and open? No." He drifted down to join her on the bed, still fully clothed.

Nadine closed her eyes. She had said she could trust him, just for tonight. And she would. No matter what, she *would* trust him completely.

His mouth covered hers and he kissed her deep. So deep she felt like he reached inside her with that kiss.

She slipped her hands beneath his jacket and pushed it off, her movements slow, as if she moved through molasses. Her fingers found and unfastened the buttons of his ruffled shirt, thinking it only fair that she get to see him if he was going to look at her so hungrily.

When the shirt was unfastened, he assisted her in her efforts, pulling the garment over his head and tossing it aside, then laying atop her with his chest pressing against hers. Oh, it was such a warm, tender feeling, intimate and heartbreakingly wonderful, to have him so close.

She could lie like this all night, Cash kissing her, his body against hers.

He moved his mouth to her breasts again, kissing one and then the other, taking a nipple deep into his mouth while he caressed another still damp from his attentions. She had never felt anything like this, had never expected that such a sensation was possible. She felt Cash everywhere. Touching her, above her, inside her in ribbons of raw pleasure that made her quiver to her bones.

And she ached. An unexpected throbbing between her thighs beat in time with her heart.

Cash's palm slipped over her ribs, down to her hip, and between her legs. He spread her thighs and ran that palm up from her knees to caress the tender skin of her inner thigh. A new tremble shimmered through her body, making her shake.

When he touched her intimately she sucked in her breath and twitched before settling easily into his embrace. He stroked her, and she felt herself grow wet. He caressed her in rhythm with the movement of his mouth against her breast, and she let her thighs fall farther apart.

She had not expected it, but she wanted him inside

her. Now. *He* was what she ached for, *he* was the reason for the increasingly insistent throb that made everything else in the world unimportant. She was losing control, she, who had never lost control before.

Cash lowered his head, kissing her stomach, her belly button, the sensitive skin beneath. He placed himself between her thighs and laid his mouth on her.

"What . . . what on earth . . ."

"Shhhh," he said, taking his mouth from her, flicking his tongue over her in a way she had not imagined possible. "Relax."

Relax? Was he insane? Nadine gripped the sheet as Cash made love to her with his mouth. He was relentless, and she found herself rocking against him, shuddering deep, losing herself a little more with every flutter of his tongue. It felt . . . wonderful and torturous at the same time. A powerful need forced a low moan from her throat, and a moment later she cried out loud as an intense pleasure washed through her, like a flash of lightning on a stormy summer night.

When the lightning faded, she melted into the bed. Shuddering still, but with boneless satisfaction this time.

Cash left the bed slowly, and she reached out to touch his arm. She didn't want him to go. She wanted him there beside her.

"I never . . . felt anything like that before," she said breathlessly.

He smiled down at her, and for an instant he was Danny again.

"Don't go," she whispered.

"I'm not going anywhere." He unfastened his trousers and kicked off his boots. "Hell, darling, we're not finished. We've just gotten started."

Cash crawled into the bed, raking his body along Nadine's as he aligned himself above her. Never in his life had he experienced anything as tender as this. Never in his life had he felt like he was a real part of another person. Not just with his body, but with something so deep he couldn't give it a name.

Nadine wrapped her arms around him, and he buried his head against her neck, trailing soft kisses there. She smelled so good, all heat and woman.

All heat and all woman. She had a shape any woman would kill for, with rounded breasts and hips and a tiny waist to accentuate those attributes. Everything about her, from her soft, husky voice to the way she lifted her hand, was feminine in a way that might call to a man.

If tonight was all they had, he wanted it to be special. He wanted to stay up all night, loving her. He wanted to watch her come apart beneath him by lamplight, and moonlight, and morning's sun.

He rested between her spread legs, ready to bury himself inside her, and yet he hesitated. He kissed her deep and cupped her breasts, fine breasts creamy pale with delicate blue veins just beneath the sensitive flesh. He kissed the veins, the pebbled nipple, the valley between her breasts.

Her hips rocked, bringing her wet entrance closer to his erection, as if she couldn't wait to have him inside her. Her breath caught in her throat, a soft quiver shot through her, and he felt it. Her eyes drifted closed, and the sound that broke from her throat was enough to make any man lose control.

But Cash didn't lose control. Not ever.

Her head tilted back, her hair spilled across the pillow. "I never knew I could feel like this," she whispered. "I never knew I could . . . *want* this way."

He guided himself to her, pushed inside, and she arched against him. He pushed deep and she gasped, throwing back her head and wrapping her legs around his.

"Open your eyes," he demanded softly.

She complied, laying hungry, heavy-lidded eyes on his face, licking her lips as he stroked her long and slow and deep. He sheathed himself inside her, got so lost in the sensations of loving her that he forgot who he was. Where he was. *When* he was.

He moved faster, filling her with every thrust. When she closed her eyes again he didn't demand that she open them. He watched her face, savored the wonder there as her desire grew.

"Oh, Danny," she whispered.

He didn't correct her.

Her hips rocked against him and she cried out, emitting a husky sound that spoke of sex and surrender. Her inner muscles contracted around him, and Nadine, his beautiful, magnificent Nadine, shuddered and held on tight as the waves of her release cracked through her. His own completion came on the soft ebb of her own. He buried himself deep as with a powerful, shattering surge he emptied himself inside her.

They lay there for a while, trembling together, surprised by the power of their encounter. Unable to breathe properly.

Cash rose up to look down at Nadine, and she gave him a tender, easy smile. "Oh, my," she said softly.

Nadine might have been another man's wife, but she was the mother of his child and she was *his* woman.

For tonight.

The room was completely dark when she opened her eyes, but she suffered not a single second of disorientation. Her breasts pressed against Danny's back, her bare leg was caught between his.

With a tender hand she touched the scar low on his side, the ugliest of all his scars. And he had a few. A puckered flaw marred the perfection of his thigh, a long, thin mark on his back had been barely visible by lamplight. Other smaller scars marked his body here and there. They were all reminders that he'd lived a hard life.

Her heart broke for the man who lay beside her, but she didn't know if her soul cried for the Danny she had loved or the Cash he had become. Did it really matter? No one should be hurt and scarred this way. She wanted to go back, change things, heal these wounds before they ever hurt him.

But that was impossible, so she closed her eyes and thought of the here and now. She thought of the dilemma that had brought her here, and the man she had found.

She still could not believe what had happened to her tonight, the way this man had made her feel. His hands, his mouth, his body joined to hers and the incredible pleasure that followed. Just thinking about it made her ready again, made her ache for him.

Her arm encircled his waist, and she rested the flat of her hand low on his belly. Her fingers rocked as she laid her lips against his spine.

"Danny?" she whispered. "Are you awake?"

He rolled to face her and took her in his arms.

Morning light lit the room, and that meant he needed to go. Last night had been great, but it had been only one night. That had been her offer. One night to make up for everything they'd missed.

But one night was not nearly enough to make up for what they'd missed. If he'd had any doubts about that, spending the night loving Nadine had wiped them away.

Sufficient or not, one night was all they had.

He looked at her and got hard again. He touched her, and knew it was too soon to leave. She opened her eyes and smiled at him, and he surrendered.

He made love to her, slow and easy. He took his time, because he did not want this to end. Heaven help him, he could stay inside her forever; he could stay in this bed for the rest of his life and never miss anything outside this room.

Nadine made love with artless abandon, surprised by the pleasure they gave each other. Hungry for more. There was nothing so arousing as the expression on her face as he touched her. Nothing so erotic as the way she touched him with curious fingers.

They climaxed together, and Nadine cried out hoarsely. She clasped him tight, held him close, and when he lowered his head to rest it on her shoulder, she placed her hand in his hair and sighed deeply.

"I love you, Danny," she whispered. "I never stopped loving you."

He closed his eyes and wished with all his heart that she hadn't said that. Nadine couldn't possibly love him. She couldn't expect that they had anything beyond this room.

He kissed her neck and raised his mouth to her ear. "Cash," he reminded her. After all, the night was over.

Nine

"It's all right, Jed," Hannah said in a soothing voice. "You go downstairs and have a big lunch, visit with Eden and the kids, and I'll be just fine." She gave her large and very worried husband a big smile from the bed where she sat with her back against the headboard.

Nadine watched the big man back toward the open door, uneasy about leaving his wife for even a few minutes. "Call if you need anything," he said as he stepped into the hallway.

"I will," Hannah promised.

Nadine closed the door and breathed a sigh of relief. Jed Rourke hovering over her while she examined her patient was a little unnerving.

"How are you feeling?" she asked with a soft smile.

"I'm tired of staying in bed," Hannah confessed without any real frustration, "but of course I'm willing to do anything for my baby."

"Or babies," Nadine corrected Hannah with a lift of her eyebrows.

Hannah sighed as she moved carefully and slowly into a horizontal position. "Do you really think it's possible I'm having *twins?"* She sounded a little distressed by the prospect.

Nadine laid her hands over Hannah's huge stomach, closing her eyes as she gently explored. "Very possible."

"I have been so looking forward to being a mother," Hannah said, "to holding a child that Jed and I created. I didn't even know how much I wanted a baby until I found out I was going to have one, and then . . . I was ecstatic and so was Jed. But two! How will I manage with two babies?"

"I have a feeling you'll manage just fine."

The babies would be small, if there were indeed two of them. Twins always were. She could only hope they would not be *too* small.

The first time Danny . . . *Cash,* she corrected herself caustically, since he insisted . . . had made love to her, they'd created JD. What if last night had left her carrying his child again? If it happened, it happened. She wouldn't be sorry, no matter how scandalous it would be. She had survived scandal before.

She ached in ways she had never ached before but didn't mind the reminder of the times he'd been inside her. It had been more wonderful than she'd imagined possible. More exciting and pleasurable and *important* than anything she could have imagined. She'd never known lying with a man could be like that, powerful and beautiful.

One night, they'd said. Would Cash still be satisfied with that single night now that he knew what they were like together? She hoped not. She could not imagine seeing Cash and not touching him, wanting Cash and not having him. Oh, this craving was so unlike her!

"Is everything all right?" Hannah asked.

Nadine gave the woman a wide smile. "You're healthy and you're strong. I'm confident that you're going to do very well."

"I hope so. Jed is just beside himself. He's so worried that . . . something will happen. He hasn't actually told me he's concerned about the delivery, but I know him too well. He can't hide anything from me."

Nadine couldn't deny that childbirth was dangerous, that every woman who bore a child put her life at risk. But most deliveries were uneventful, and even those that weren't usually worked out fine.

"I'm so grateful that you'll be here when I deliver," Hannah confided in a low voice. "Eden and Mary are quite capable, but . . . if something goes wrong, it will be nice to have a doctor present."

"Nothing will go wrong," Nadine assured her patient.

Hannah nodded in acceptance, but she didn't quite believe that assurance. Her eyes remained skeptical, her smile halfhearted.

"I'll check in on you often." Nadine smiled. "I'm right across the hall, after all. If you feel unwell, or if you think you might be going into labor, call me and I'll be here."

"Thank you."

Nadine opened the door to find Jed standing in the hallway, impatiently waiting for her to finish the examination. He snapped to attention as the door swung open.

"Is everything okay? Do you still think it's twins? What can I do?"

Nadine smiled at the big man, who was becoming quite unnerved. His devotion was so open, so apparent for all to see, she felt a little jealous. To be the object of such devotion would be wonderful . . . and it was something she would never know.

"Hannah's fine. Yes, I still think it's twins. And you need to calm down so I don't end up with two patients in this room instead of one."

Jed swept into the room as she left it, closing the door as he rejoined his wife.

And Nadine needed, more than anything, to see the man who had left her bed just a few hours ago. She craved the sight of Cash in a way she couldn't explain. And she wanted him to love her.

"I thought the darn wedding was called off," JD mumbled.

"No," Cash said. "It has been postponed, not canceled. We proceed with our plans."

JD bent over a table in the deserted saloon, pen in hand as he carefully composed an invitation. *You are cordially invited to a wedding ceremony celebrating the marriage of Jed Rourke and Hannah Winters Rourke, to be held at sunrise tomorrow on the jutting rock over the river.*

Two invitations had been completed and set aside. Three others had been discarded after Cash declared them unworthy.

"There's still the matter of food," Cash mused. God,

anything to take his mind off last night and this morning! "Picnic style, I suppose, unless we decide to trek back to Eden's for the reception. What do you think?"

JD was bent studiously over his chore, but he did answer. "I like the picnic idea. But what do you eat at sunrise?"

"Cake, of course."

"Cake for breakfast," JD said with a smile. "My ma would *never* let me have cake for breakfast."

"Of course not. I'm sure it's not . . . healthy." Cash squirmed uncomfortably in his chair. When you had a child, you had to think of all those things, he imagined. You had to make sure they were warm in the winter, well fed all year round. That they were cared for when they were sick, and well schooled. Nadine had done such a good job with JD. How could he possibly thank her for that? He couldn't. To do so would reveal more than was wise. Still . . . she'd done so well.

So why did the kid want to become a gunslinger?

The question nagged at Cash. JD wanted to be famous, but why? Did the desire come from somewhere deep inside, or was he trying to impress someone else? The people of Marianna, his mother . . . The most likely explanation came to Cash in a flash. When he was JD's age, what would have made him want to make a name for himself? The answer was crystal clear. *A girl.*

"You know," he said, "if you plan to be a gunfighter, you will have to resign yourself to a life without such ordinary things as a wife."

JD scoffed. "So? What would I want a wife for?"

Not a girl, then, Cash thought with a sigh.

"Women are fickle," JD added after a long pause. Cash couldn't help but detect the hint of bitterness in his son's voice. Maybe he'd been right after all.

"Are they now?" he asked, his voice nonchalant so as not to reveal his interest in the subject.

JD set the latest invitation aside and pulled another piece of paper toward him. "Yep." He set the pen down and flexed his fingers. "There was this girl back home, Becky Rogers. We're the same age, and we've been friends for as long as I can remember." He tried, too hard, to remain aloof. "I used to pull her pigtails, but she didn't mind. And then this new boy came to town. Billy Sanders." JD curled his lip. "He's a couple years older than I am, and his pa bought the sawmill and built a big house just south of town. And all of a sudden Becky didn't even look at me anymore. And if I pulled her pigtails, she got all . . . snippy. Said I was a child; can you believe that?"

"How dare she," Cash said, his heart pounding too hard. JD wanted to become famous to impress a thirteen-year-old girl? He was tempted to box the kid's ears.

But even though JD was a child, the hurt he'd been hiding was very real.

This complicated matters. It was impossible to reason with a man where a woman was involved. Even a little one. He knew that too well.

If reason wouldn't work, he'd have to scare the kid out of his notions. And soon. He couldn't bear to look at Nadine day after day knowing he couldn't have her. The sooner she got out of Rock Creek, the better.

And if she didn't leave, he would.

* * *

"We've looked everywhere," Teddy whispered.

JD and Teddy were both on their hands and knees, searching a vacant room for loose floorboards.

"Not everywhere," he said softly. "We can't search the room your uncle Jed is in, because your aunt and uncle are always there." In the past couple of days they had covered a lot of ground in their frustrating search.

He should've known this would not be easy. "What about the garden?"

Teddy lifted his head and placed wary eyes on JD. "You want to tear up Ma's garden?"

"Not tear it up, exactly," JD explained. "Just poke around a little."

Teddy shook his head. "I don't know . . ."

The door flew open and Rafe, Teddy's younger brother, walked in and looked around. A kid with pale brown hair who stood every bit as tall as JD, Rafe was always poking his nose where it didn't belong. "What are y'all doing in here? Still looking for the gold?"

"You told him?" JD asked angrily, his accusing eyes on Teddy.

"No. Uncle Jed told," Rafe answered. "Can I help?"

"No," JD said. "We're not sharing the gold with you. We're not splitting it three ways." He'd go back to Marianna and build a house twice as big as Billy Sanders. After he'd made a name for himself, of course.

"He can have half of my half," Teddy said softly.

JD conceded with a nod of his head. "All right, but he'd better stay out of my way." All this waiting was making him anxious, and when he got anxious he tended to lose his temper easily.

"Millie could help, too," Rafe suggested. "I'd give her half of my half of Teddy's half."

"No," JD said firmly. "No girls."

"Okay," Rafe conceded without a fight. He dropped to the floor and began tugging at floorboards.

JD was sound asleep. Nadine was no doubt pacing in her room, wondering if Cash would be so foolish as to call on her again tonight, and his patrol of the edge of town had proven to be too damned peaceful.

Cash approached the noisy saloon across from the hotel with dread in his step. Lily's place, Three Queens, was lively, bright in a way his saloon was not. People laughed, danced, and sang.

He hated it.

But that was where he'd find Rico, and he was sure Rico was the one to help him with his newest plan. Reese would never agree, Sullivan would probably find something illegal about the scheme, and Nate would surely think it . . . ungodly. Besides, he didn't talk to Nate any more than he had to these days. He was afraid if they actually spoke in a more than casual way they'd end up having one of their arguments. He suspected that this time there would be no mending fences afterward. Jed was completely preoccupied with his pregnant wife, rendering him all but useless. That left Rico.

Cash pushed through the bat-wing doors and his eyes swept the room. No danger here, unless you counted the drunken cowboy who was trying to sing a lullaby to his equally drunken companion. Johnny glanced toward the door and smiled widely, but continued playing his piano. A few other, less friendly glances were thrown his way. Lily glowered. Rico grinned.

Cash nodded his head and turned around to walk back into the night, where he belonged.

He waited on the boardwalk only a moment before Rico joined him.

"What is wrong?" the kid asked.

Cash laid his eyes on Rico. There had been a time when he'd known he could go to any one of his five friends for assistance, but right now Rico was the only one. If he refused . . .

"I need your help," Cash said.

Rico grinned. "You shall have it."

She waited as long as she could. Cash had insisted that they appear to be lovers. Now that they really were lovers, she waited anxiously for him to knock on her door, and he was mysteriously absent.

He wasn't coming. She had been the one to mention that they could have only one night, but . . . she'd changed her mind. She had decided to tell Cash just that when he arrived at her room for appearance's sake, but he wasn't going to give her the chance. He wasn't coming back.

Nadine whipped off her nightgown and slipped into a yellow calico skirt and white blouse. If Cash wouldn't come to her, she'd go to him. Heaven help her, she had no pride where Daniel Cash was concerned.

It was so late, no one roamed the halls of the hotel. A light still burning on the third floor shot pale rays down the second-floor hallway, just enough to light her way. By the time she reached the lobby, though, she was lost in darkness.

When her eyes adjusted to the dark, she saw the door before her. She found her way there and swung it open, holding her breath as it creaked.

The deserted Rock Creek street was brighter than the hotel had been. The moon shone down, and the saloon across the street was well lit. A little bit of light spilled from Cash's saloon, too. She headed in that direction.

A few feet away from the swinging doors, she hesitated. This was not going to be easy. Cash was determined to remain as he was. Alone. Bitter. Slightly decadent. But last night she had seen that her Danny was not dead. No matter what Cash said, there was some of that idealistic boy left inside him. It was a part of who he was. A hidden part, perhaps, but it was there.

And she still loved him. She had not expected to, she had not thought it possible. But she did love him. And love would fix anything. Oh, she had never been so starry-eyed and fanciful before.

She walked toward the Rogue's Palace entrance, and when she reached it she peeked over the tops of the swinging doors. Cash sat in the far corner, five cards in his hand, a glass of whiskey at his elbow, a trio of plainly dressed poker players sitting across from him. A small stack of bills sat next to his glass. The other players had been reduced to a few coins.

As she watched, Cash laid his hand on the table.

One of the other players groaned and threw his cards down. The other two folded more calmly. Cash grinned and raked in his winnings. The other players, busted, pushed their chairs back and left unhappy.

Alone at the table, Cash became suddenly still. He lifted his head and laid his eyes on her in a way that made her shiver. It was as if he had sensed her there, as if he had felt her eyes on him.

He gathered up his cash and stuffed it in a deep pocket of his black jacket, drained his whiskey, and then stood, taking the time to yank on his brocade vest, straightening it with that tug before heading for the door. He told the bartender, the surly Evan, that he needed a breath of fresh air, and headed toward the exit, his eyes pinned to her.

She couldn't breathe.

She backed up as Cash pushed through the doors. "What are you doing here?" he whispered.

"Looking for you," she said simply.

Cash spread his arms wide as he bore down on her. "Well, here I am." His expression remained cool, his voice just short of biting. "What do you want?"

She realized she had been backing away from him, so she stopped. So did he. He came no closer. "I was worried about you," she whispered.

He flashed a crooked grin. "Why?"

"You didn't knock on my door tonight. I expected you would."

"Not a good idea," he said simply.

"I thought you wanted everyone to think we were . . ." She couldn't say the word aloud.

"They do," he said. "In a day or two I'll be finished

with JD, everyone will think I lost interest in you, and you two can get out of town."

"Did you?" she whispered.

"Did I what?"

"Lose interest in me." She hadn't even considered the possibility that last night had not been as wonderful for him as it had been for her. The very idea made her more than sad.

He took a moment to consider his answer. Not a good sign. "No," he finally sighed. "But it's not a good idea to let this continue. Once you're away from here—"

"I can't leave yet," she interrupted. "I have things to finish here before I go."

"Hannah?"

She nodded her head. "I told you, I promised her I'd stay."

"I can go. . . ."

"No." Nadine stepped forward and laid her hand on Cash's chest. Heavens, he was hard. Unyielding and so damn stubborn. "Don't leave. Surely we can survive a few more weeks of living in the same town." She wanted so much more but was afraid to say so at the moment. If he would ride away from her and JD without so much as looking back, her heart really would break.

"A few more weeks," he hissed. "How am I supposed to look at you every day and smile and pretend I don't want you."

"You don't have to pretend."

"Great. I should allow you and everyone else to watch me suffer."

"You don't have to suffer, either." She moved a step closer, raked the hand at his chest down and around his waist. "I know I was the one who said we could have only one night, but I was wrong. I'm not ready to let you go."

She rested her forehead against his chest and sighed; the hand at his back rocked lightly. Couldn't he see how much she needed him? Couldn't he see how difficult this was for her?

"I can't become the man you want me to be," he said, still inflexible. His arms did not wrap around her; he did not smile.

"I want you as you are."

"You don't even know me as I am."

"Show me," she whispered. She pressed herself tightly against him. He might not admit it, but he did want her. She felt the evidence of his arousal pressing against her. Whether he liked it or not, he did want her. Maybe he even loved her a little. "Introduce me to the real Daniel Cash."

"You have no idea what you're asking for," he muttered.

She kissed his jaw, her tender lips trailing over the dark stubble of his short beard. "Last night was wonderful." She kissed the side of his neck. "I never knew anything could be so wonderful." His arms finally wrapped around her. "I want more," she whispered. "We can have that, at least, until it's time for me to leave."

"And you'd be happy with that?" he asked.

"Yes."

"No romance, no sweet talk, no future. Just sex."

"Yes," she breathed.

He walked her into the deepest shadows of the

boardwalk and cupped her bottom in his hands. "Be careful what you wish for," he whispered.

Cash brought his mouth to hers with a hunger he couldn't hide. He might try to stay cool and calm and distant, but he couldn't disguise his physical response to her. He devoured her with his mouth, pulled her body up against his, and rocked his hips against hers. His erection brushed against her mound, and she felt herself grow damp.

The bat-wing door swung open, and as two cowboys left, Cash swung Nadine off the boardwalk and into a narrow alley where the darkness was complete. The cowboys passed, unaware that anyone stood so close.

Cash untucked her blouse and slipped his hand beneath to caress bare skin, his fingers burning a tender trail across her flesh. She cupped his head in her hands and kissed him deep as he fondled her breasts. The kiss was tempestuous and complete, a thrilling sex act all its own.

Her body throbbed. She didn't need to be led as she had last night. She knew where they were going, she knew what it felt like to have Cash inside her. She had been thinking about that sensation all day, and she was ready to experience it again.

He reached beneath her skirt and touched her, and she almost fell apart then and there. Her knees were like warm butter; her heart pounded so hard she was sure he must feel it beating against his.

Feeling bolder than she ever had before, she reached out to caress the ridge beneath Cash's black trousers. He groaned as she stroked, and she caught that groan between parted lips.

She unfastened his buttons blindly, until she was able to free his manhood and stroke it again, uncovered this time. Her fingers explored and teased, stroked hard and easy. Heavens, she loved the way he felt in her hand, hot and steely hard.

With a growl Cash lifted her, and she anxiously guided him inside her. With her back against the wall of the deserted building next to the saloon and her arms wrapped securely around his neck, she surged against him in a frantic rhythm that was theirs. Only theirs. He impaled her, he drove himself deep inside her body, and she relished every stroke, every ribbon of pure pleasure that wound through her body.

She wanted to cry and scream and laugh all at once, but a muted moan, half caught in her throat, was the only sound she made. Cash pounded into her, his own moan a growl from low in his throat.

Completion came quickly, sparking through her body and making her shudder deep, and as she trembled in Cash's arms he found his own release.

They were silent for a moment, silent and still and breathlessly satisfied. She had never known such complete fulfillment was possible.

Cash slowly put her back on her feet, but she didn't drop her arms. She held on as if for dear life.

"I fully intended to invite you back to my room," she said breathlessly. "I didn't know—"

"Anywhere will do," Cash interrupted caustically.

She was not dismayed. Her fingers raked through his hair. "You can still come back to my room," she whispered.

"No." He removed her arms from around his neck

and quickly righted his clothes. "We're not going to take any more chances. No one will know about this but us."

She felt a little . . . cheated. "I thought you wanted everyone to know we were . . ." Again, she could not make herself say the word *lovers* aloud.

"I changed my mind," he said succinctly. "Evan suspects. Eden, Sullivan, Rico, and Reese know I spent one night with you, which means all the guys and their wives know. They'll assume that one night was the price you had to pay for me to work with JD, but they won't blab it all over town."

"Do you want your friends to think you'd be so heartless?"

"My friends already know I'm that heartless."

He didn't want anyone to know they were truly together, no matter how briefly, no matter how insignificantly. He didn't want to claim her in any way. Not publicly, at least. Most of all, she realized, he didn't want anyone to know that he cared for her.

And he did care for her. She had seen it in his eyes, felt it in his touch. "If that's what you want."

"What I want has nothing to do with it," he hissed, and then he turned his back on her and walked away. "Go back to your room, Nadine," he said as he stepped onto the boardwalk. "Dream sweet dreams."

"Aren't you coming with me?"

He turned to her and offered his hand. She took it. "No," he whispered.

Ten

Cash sat back in his chair, exhausted after another sleepless night, and watched as JD grumbled and scrubbed the floor. Sunlight streamed in over the doors, lighting the wet slats of worn wood and a surly JD.

He had to get this chore over and done with as soon as possible so he could get JD and Nadine out of his life before this went too far. He couldn't afford to feel like they were his. His to protect and to love. His to claim. It was a trap, one he had carefully avoided since leaving Marianna for the last time.

Rico came bursting through the doors, a scowl on a face that was almost always smiling, an ominous thud in his step.

He nodded to Cash and started toward the table, kicking over the bucket of soapy water at JD's side as he passed. Water splashed everywhere, rolling over the floor, soaking JD's knees and feet.

"Goddammit!" JD said, shooting to his feet.

Cash raised his eyebrows slightly. "Language, JD," he reprimanded gently.

JD was not at all chastened. "This greaser splashed

dirty water all over a floor I already washed and all over me!" With his hands on his hips, JD glared at Rico's back.

Rico turned around slowly, his hand falling to the handle of the knife he wore at his waist. "Greaser?" he repeated softly.

JD did not back down. "Apologize," he commanded, "and then clean up this mess."

God in heaven, Cash thought in dismay, his kid wouldn't last a week on his own.

Rico looked JD up and down. "Big talk for a *niño tonto*," he said lowly. There was an unmistakable threat in Rico's voice, a hint of warning most men would take seriously.

JD didn't budge. "What did you call me?"

Rico leaned slightly closer to JD. "I called you a foolish child."

"Don't call me a child," JD seethed. "And you're the one who's foolish. Clumsy, too! Can't you watch where you're going?"

Cash didn't know whether to be proud or terrified that this fearless child was his son.

With a move so fast it was a blur to the eye, Rico drew his knife. In the same motion he grabbed JD by the shirt collar and pulled the kid close. The tip of the knife touched JD's throat, and the boy went deathly white.

Without conscious thought, Cash's hand fell to his six-shooter. His heart threatened to pound through his chest. This confrontation was his idea, his latest plan, but the sight of that knife touching JD's throat was enough to make him do something rash. His hand stilled over the butt of the weapon.

"I do not scrub floors, *niño tonto*," Rico said in a low voice. "And I do not take any lip from errand boys who do not know when to shut their whiny mouths. And I do not apologize. Not to the likes of you."

JD trembled. Cash could see it, and it made him a little crazy. "Enough," he muttered in a low, dark voice.

Rico released JD, and the kid stepped back. Yes, that was terror in his eyes, the kind of terror you experience only when your own death is imminent. A knife at the throat, a gun barrel in the gut . . . Any man who didn't respond with fear was dead inside. He didn't have anything left to lose.

Cash had not felt real fear in a very long time.

"Go upstairs and change your clothes," Cash ordered. "You're soaking wet." JD quickly complied, bounding up the stairs without looking back.

Rico smiled wanly as he sat at Cash's table. *"Dios!* What a kid. I thought he was going to challenge me to a gunfight."

"You'd better hope he never does."

"He is that good?"

"No, you're that bad."

Not at all offended, Rico placed his forearms on the table and leaned forward. "Think I scared him out of his ambition to be a gunslinger?"

Having come face-to-face with possible death, surely JD would think differently about his plan now. Fear wasn't pretty. It didn't make you feel powerful and important.

"Hell, Rico, I think you scared me out of my ambitions," Cash said lightly, not revealing how important this moment was. Not letting Rico know that if he had actually cut JD, he'd be bleeding himself.

Oh, hell, this was a sad state of affairs. It was bad enough that he liked the kid, but to get protective and possessive was not a good idea. First Nadine and now this. How much worse could things get?

Nadine came down the stairs for lunch to find Eden in a tizzy. Eden was always so calm, so sweetly in control, the sight took Nadine aback a little. The pretty blonde leaned down to place her nose next to Millie's. "What do you mean you don't know where she is? She was with you."

"No," Millie said, frowning. "Carrie and I were talking. One minute Fiona was there, and the next she was gone. I thought she was in the kitchen with you."

Teddy came running down the stairs, and Nadine deftly moved out of the way as the young man hurried past. "She's not upstairs."

Rafe burst through the back door. "She's not in the garden."

Eden stood tall and took a deep breath. "Teddy, go fetch your father. Now." The kid ran to do as he was told.

Nadine approached Eden cautiously. "Fiona's missing?" she asked, heart in her throat.

"She's wandered off," Eden said, trying to remain calm and not doing a very good job of it. "I thought she was with Millie, and Millie thought she was with me . . . and . . . and . . ."

"How long?" Nadine asked.

"About an hour, we think."

Not so long, Nadine tried to convince herself. And yet, if JD had gone missing at the age of four, five minutes would have been too long.

Word spread quickly in a town like Rock Creek. Sullivan arrived, angry and looking a little scared. Rico and Lily, who had seen the commotion, were on hand moments later. Jed came bounding down the stairs, having heard the news from Teddy as the kid searched the hotel. It wasn't long before Cash walked into the hotel lobby, cold-eyed and tense.

They split into groups, determined to search the town from one end to the other. Lily and Rico went off together, to start at the north end of town and work their way down the street. Jed was going to start at the south and meet them in the middle, unless one of them found Fiona before that happened. The kids went to call on all of their friends, and Eden remained in the lobby in case Fiona should return on her own. Sullivan headed out to the street.

"What should I do?" Cash asked the sheriff as he followed.

"Check with Nate," Sullivan said tersely. "Fiona might have wandered down to the church."

"You got it," Cash said without hesitation, and the two men stepped out of the hotel.

Nadine decided to remain with Eden, who was much too pale and agitated. She definitely shouldn't be left alone. "I'm sure everything will be fine," Nadine said with a half-smile. "Children do this sort of thing. They wander off and turn up in the oddest places."

Eden nodded her head, trying to agree. "I should have checked with Millie earlier," she said, blaming herself. "I shouldn't have just assumed that Fiona had stayed where she was told to stay. She usually does," she said softly. "But she has that stubborn streak, and . . . and . . ." She lifted tear-filled blue eyes to Nadine. "Everything's going to be fine," she said softly.

"I know," Nadine agreed, even though she could see very clearly that Eden didn't believe what she said.

Cash knocked on the rectory door, his eyes peeled as he searched every corner, every alley, for a little girl with dark hair and a devastating smile. He had always known kids were trouble, but he hadn't realized a single little girl could turn an entire town upside down so quickly.

A surprised Nate answered the door. He certainly hadn't expected his old friend to come calling. Cash didn't waste any time with niceties. "Is Fiona here?"

The Rev shook his head. "No. Why?"

"She's missing," Cash said succinctly. "Sullivan thought she might have come here."

Nate joined Cash on the porch, and together their eyes scanned the street, searching windows and doorways. "She wouldn't have gone far," Nate said. "Right?"

"Who knows?" Cash said curtly.

Since the others were working their way up and down the street, Nate and Cash rounded the church and headed for the edge of town. There was nothing out there, no good place to hide or exciting place to play, but with a kid . . . who knew where they went when they wandered? Not far. Cash knew that. Fiona would never go too far.

Who was he kidding? Sullivan's daughter was much too bold for four years old.

At first he and Nate didn't talk as they searched for Fiona, each of them taking his turn calling the little girl's name as they checked in every ditch, each patch of tall grass, and around every woodpile they passed. With every passing minute Cash got more anxious. Where the hell was that kid?

"So," Nate said as they turned over a discarded door that had been propped against a rock, making a Fiona sized cave. "How have you been?"

"Fine."

"Glad to hear it."

Cash glanced at his old friend, took a good long look. Nate's hair hung over his ears now, and an awful lot of it was white. "How about you?"

"Good," Nate answered with a smile that showed he meant it. "Really good. You should come by one evening," he suggested. "Have dinner with the family . . ."

"Talk about old times," Cash interrupted caustically. "I'm sure Jo would like to hear about those whores in Dallas. The sisters, remember them?"

"No," Nate grumbled.

"There was the gunfight that next morning, and the girls were so excited they . . . never mind. Maybe you'd rather have me tell the tale about that shoot-out in Laredo and the four-day celebration that followed."

He expected Nate to get either riled or indignant, but instead the Rev answered calmly. "I'm sorry. I know you feel betrayed, the way things happened. We can talk about it sometime if you want."

"Betrayed?" He cast Nate a wide smile. "The way you talk, you'd think we were married. You went your way and I went mine. No hard feelings." Hell, if this was what Nate wanted, he should have it.

"I understand you've been seeing Mrs. Ellington."

Cash snorted, turned his back on the Rev, and headed down the trail they'd found, a narrow beaten path through the long grass. "If I'm going to get a sermon while we search, I'd just as soon you shoot me now and get it over with. Fiona," he called in his sweetest voice. "Come on out and give Uncle Cash and Uncle Nate a big hug." He listened carefully, hoping to hear something. The sound of little feet running across the ground, a familiar giggle. There was nothing. "She probably crawled into a hiding place somewhere and is taking a nap while the entire town searches for her."

"Could be," Nate agreed, letting their unpleasant conversation die.

After a good hour of searching, they headed back for the center of town and gathered in the street with the others. Reese and Mary were there, too, having gone to the homes of a few friends just on the outskirts of town. Jo was there, baby in her arms, doing her best to keep Eden calm.

Sullivan paced in the street, steps long and angry,

hair whipping behind him. "Fiona!" he shouted, lifting his head and calling his daughter's name. "If you're hiding, you come out right this minute! Game's over!"

Cash stepped forward and matched his step to the stalking Sullivan, laying a stilling hand on the frantic man's arm. "If she is hiding, you're going to scare the crap out of her, yelling that way."

"You got a better idea?"

Cash lifted his head and took a deep breath. "Come on out, Fiona," he called in a calm, friendly voice. "Let's play another game now, sweetheart." He stopped and listened, again for those little feet, that giggle. All was silent. Nothing moved. Even the children were still and quiet as everyone awaited some kind of answer. "You win," he called. "Come on out and find out what your prize is." A spanking followed by a big hug, he imagined.

He was getting a bad feeling about this, and he didn't like it. He didn't like it at all. The uneasiness grew as he stood in the street and waited for an answer. Cash turned around and stalked back toward the crowd. "We've looked all over town. Would she go down to the river?"

Eden went even paler than she already was. "No. I've told her a thousand times . . . She wouldn't go there alone."

"Maybe I should ride down there and check, just in case," Cash offered calmly.

"I'm going with you," Sullivan said through clenched teeth.

Cash nodded, and Teddy went off to fetch their horses.

Reese stepped up. "The rest of us will ride the perimeter, widening out as we go. A single shot in the air when you find her, and then we all meet back here."

As everyone headed for their homes and horses, Eden made her way through the crowd to find Cash. "You keep an eye on Sin, you hear me?" she said softly.

"Of course I will." He gave her his most charming smile. "It's what we do."

"You don't understand," she whispered. "If anything happens to Fiona, it'll kill him." Tears filled her eyes.

"Nothing is going to happen to Fiona," Cash insisted. The renegade who had been spotted in the area was on everyone's mind, but no one mentioned it aloud. The possibilities were too horrible, too frightening to bear. For any of them. Cash found that oddly enough his knees were weak and what was left of his heart threatened to climb into his throat. What must this be like for Sullivan and Eden?

Teddy quickly led Cash's horse and Sullivan's to the front of the hotel. Most everyone else had dispersed, getting ready to widen the search. Sullivan's head popped around, and one at a time those who remained gathered in front of the Paradise Hotel turned their eyes south.

Cash squinted in that direction. Dust rose around the hooves of a horse that lumbered down the middle of the street, just entering town. The next thing he noticed was the headdress on the rider. Buffalo scalp.

The sight that stopped his heart was a flash of yellow calico and a head of dark curls.

Sullivan shooed everyone back onto the boardwalk

and into the businesses that lined the street, and walked boldly down the center of the street. Cash joined him. Eden, who had been warned to stay back, shook off the order and kept pace with them. She did have the good sense to stay on the boardwalk, in the shadows.

"I can take him from here," Cash said, hand on the butt of his six-shooter.

"No."

"You know damn well I won't miss," Cash argued.

"You are not shooting that Indian while he's got my daughter in his lap, do you hear me, Cash? I don't want that renegade's blood and brains splattered all over my little girl." Sullivan swallowed hard. He'd gone pasty white. "You shoot as a last resort," he said in a lowered voice. "He might want to trade her for food or something." They were close enough now to see that Fiona was fine, smiling and waving when she saw her daddy and Uncle Cash in the street.

"And once you get her out of his lap?"

"He's all yours."

The horse coming toward them moved slowly, but soon they got a good look the rider's face. "Is that who I think it is?" Cash asked through clenched teeth.

"I'm afraid so," Sullivan answered, his eyes unerringly forward.

The Comanche who had Fiona in his arms was the same one who had staked four of them to the ground last year.

"Well, shit," Cash drawled. "I wonder where his pals are."

Sullivan didn't break his stride or take his eyes from Fiona. "The others will find them if they're out there."

"You heard them leave?"

Sullivan grunted what seemed like an affirmative answer.

Apparently Reese, Rico, Jed, and Nate had seen the Comanche and Fiona and had taken off to look for the other Indians. On occasion a renegade rode alone, but this one didn't. They knew that too well.

Finally they met. The horse came to a halt, and so did the two men who met the Comanche warrior face-to-face.

"Daddy!" Fiona cried with a wide smile.

Cash waited to see what would happen next, hand on his gun, eyes on a spot in the middle of the renegade's forehead. Sullivan stepped to the horse's side and raised his arms. Without argument, the renegade lifted Fiona and handed her to her father.

"I got lost," Fiona said, throwing her arms around Sullivan's neck. "Just a little bit. My new friend Issy found me. He has hair like yours, and doesn't he have a pretty hat?"

"Yes, he does, sugar," Sullivan said in a lowered voice. He turned around, presenting his back to the Indian. "Eden, come get Fiona." Eden rushed from the shadows of the boardwalk to scoop her little girl out of Sullivan's arms.

Cash kept his eyes on the renegade's forehead for a moment, then his eyes dropped to the heart. Since Fiona was safe, that would be a better shot. He waited for the Comanche to make a threatening move. A twitch would do at this point.

Sullivan looked up at the renegade. "I don't suppose

you speak any more English than you did last time we met."

The man on the horse said nothing.

Jo spoke a little of the Comanche language, but she wasn't here. She was back at the hotel minding a passel of babies.

From the boardwalk Cash heard Fiona say loudly, "We're hungry. We missed lunch."

The Comanche turned his black eyes toward Fiona. Cash tried to see a threat there, a reason to draw and fire, but he couldn't. If the renegade had wanted to hurt Fiona, he wouldn't have brought her back to town this way.

A firm, soft voice coming from behind Cash shocked him. Surprised Sullivan, too, by the look on his face.

Cash glanced quickly over his shoulder. Apparently Nadine spoke the Comanche language quite well.

The man who said his name was Isatekwa told the story simply, and Nadine translated. He said he'd found the little girl by the river and brought her home, to the town where the crazy warrior lived.

That done, he turned his horse around and started riding back the way he'd come.

"Wait," Eden said, stepping into the street with Fiona in her arms.

Isatekwa halted his horse and turned to look down at Eden. And he waited.

"Are you hungry?" she asked.

Cash groaned lowly as Nadine translated. From the

look on the renegade's face, no translation was necessary. Surely he spoke some English, and *hungry* was a word he might well know.

The man on the horse looked pointedly at Cash and asked if that one was going to shoot him.

"Not if he doesn't give me a reason," Cash muttered, after Nadine translated.

Isatekwa's hunger won out over his worry about Cash's trigger finger. He turned his horse around and headed toward the hotel, following Eden. Cash stayed at his side like an armed guard. He wasn't too happy about this recent turn of events, Nadine could see that too well.

Fiona reached for her father when Sullivan walked by, and he took her with a sigh. As they all walked down the street, Fiona talked.

"I didn't mean to get lost. Millie and Carrie wouldn't play with me, and I was just going to catch a lizard, like the one Carrie used to have. I thought if I had a lizard, they would play with me." She took a deep breath. "But I couldn't find one. I walked and looked and still I couldn't find one. Then I found a snake."

Eden sighed. "Fiona, you didn't."

"Well, I figured that a snake would be almost as good as a lizard," she reasoned. "Maybe better. I was sneaking up on my snake so he wouldn't be scared, and then a knife just came out of nowhere and stuck my snake in the neck." She made a face. "Well, snakes don't have necks but if a snake had a neck this is where it would be." She shook her head. "I cried and cried, and then Issy came up to get his knife back. I was mad, so I kicked him in the leg."

Sullivan groaned. Cash shook his head and sidled a little closer to Fiona and her father. "Your kid won't live to see seven with that kind of common sense working for her," he mumbled. And then, in an unexpectedly tender move, he reached out and brushed a strand of hair away from Fiona's face.

"But I didn't stay mad very long. Issy picked up the snake and opened its mouth, and it had teeth. Big ones!" She demonstrated by lifting both hands to her mouth, one finger of each pointing down to fashion a pretty good imitation of fangs. "I didn't know snakes had teeth."

"How many times have I told you to stay away from snakes?" Eden said breathlessly.

"Lots, but you didn't tell me they had *teeth.*"

By the time they arrived at the hotel entrance, everyone present stared at Isatekwa with a new respect. They didn't trust him, and probably never would, but they weren't ready to shoot him anymore, either. Even Cash had relaxed a little.

"Come on, Issy," Fiona said brightly. "Let's eat. My mommy is a really good cook."

Cash sat back and watched the renegade eat. He ate well, cautiously, while Fiona told the story about the snake again and all the women coddled her. It wasn't long before the others returned. A shake of Reese's head told that no other renegades had been found. Isatekwa was alone.

As the others walked into the room, armed to the teeth, the Indian almost smiled. It was probably as close to a grin as the man ever got. He nodded to Nate. *"Pukutsi,"* he said. Nate, the crazy warrior.

The Indian studied all of them closely, intently. He looked hard at Reese. "Me first," he said, his English strained and awkward.

"Me first what?" Eden asked.

None of the guys said a word as the Indian looked at Rico. *"Yo primero."* In turn, he looked to Sullivan and Cash. "Me first, me first."

Eden looked at her husband. Since Fiona was safe and she was getting the opportunity to feed a lost soul, the color had returned to her face. "Sin, what is he talking about?"

"Nothing," Sullivan grumbled.

Eden didn't give up. "Nadine, Jo, you both speak some Comanche. Y'all ask Isatekwa what he's talking about."

They did, and Cash could only imagine, as the old Indian rambled on, that he was telling the whole ugly story. What Jo or Nadine couldn't translate, Isatekwa managed to provide in English. Cash had an idea the warrior spoke better English than he let on, as he pointed to each of the four who had been there that day. When he was finished, Nadine glared at Cash. Jo shook her head.

"Eden," Nadine said calmly, "why don't you have Teddy and JD take all the children upstairs and put them to bed."

Eden didn't question the suggestion but did as

Nadine suggested. When all the kids were gone, Nadine translated.

"Apparently there was a time when Isatekwa and some of his, uh, friends, had Sullivan, Rico, Reese, and Cash staked to the ground. They were planning to"—she stopped to lick her lips and swallow—"scalp them."

Eden sat down hard. "Oh, I remember when that happened." She turned accusing eyes to the man she had just fed. "That was *you?*"

"Oh, that's not the best part," Nadine said softly. "Apparently they all begged to die first. *All* of them. One after another. No, no, kill me first."

The women didn't like what they heard . . . which is why they had never heard this part of the story. Cash watched as the other three were confronted by their wives. They were married men with children. How could they beg to be killed?

Isatekwa added another short statement, and Jo translated. "He thinks they're all very brave," she said.

Nadine turned her eyes to Cash, and he knew how the others felt. She accused him with those eyes, asked him why he would throw his life away. If he'd died that day, he would never have seen JD, he would never have held her again. Was he glad he'd survived? Yes. Could he tell her that? No.

Would he still give his life for these men? Now and always, yes.

"Ask him if his friends will be calling," Cash commanded.

Nadine asked, and the renegade shook his head.

"He said two are dead, and the others have returned

to the reservation." The harsh expression on her face softened. "And he isn't ready to do either."

When it was well past dark and time for Isatekwa to go, Eden packed him a sack full of food. He tried to refuse, until she said it was a gift to thank him for saving her daughter. He wouldn't take charity, but a gift of thanks was another matter. The renegade left, and everyone watched him go. Afraid he would spin around and turn into the warrior who had almost scalped them? Whatever the reason, they were all happy to see him go.

When Isatekwa was gone and Eden turned from the doorway, her brother confronted her. "I can't believe you wasted all that food on a damn Injun."

She looked up at Jed defiantly. Since he was more than a foot taller than she was, she had to crane her neck. "We have plenty."

"Yeah, but he's . . ."

The day had been too much for Eden. She lost her temper. "A renegade. An Indian. A warrior. I know. Tell me something." Her eyes swept the room. "If when the war was over, the Yankees had tried to stick the six of you on the lousiest piece of land they could find, if they took away your weapons and penned you in and ordered you to remain there for the rest of your lives, would you have stayed? Any one of you?" She got no answer. She shook her finger in Jed's face. "So don't say anything ugly about the man who saved my little girl's life." Tears filled her eyes. "Not a word."

The crowd dispersed, all but Cash, who sat in the dining room, savoring the quiet for a few moments.

He wasn't there long before Nadine joined him. She crossed the room, angry, tired, confused.

When she stood beside him, looking down, Cash wondered if she planned to hit him. She sure enough looked like she wanted to, and if anyone could get away with it . . .

Her expression softened. "I don't want to know how many times you've come so near death, do I?"

He shook his head.

She took his hand and gently pulled him to his feet. "Come on. Take me to bed before I remember what you did and change my mind. Begging to go first," she muttered.

"I'd do it again," he said. She had to know. "The others, they all have families, a future, women who would die a little if they didn't come home."

"So do you."

He shook his head, thought about arguing but didn't. "Where did you learn to speak Comanche?"

"From Winema, the Comanche woman who taught me about healing with herbs and poultices. She spoke English but preferred her own language. Come on," she said, tugging on Cash's hand and leading him to the stairs. "Let's get upstairs while the coast is clear. I don't want to wait until midnight. Not tonight."

He followed, because he didn't want to wait, either.

Eleven

After Fiona's dramatic return, Nadine's days in Rock Creek fell into a comfortable pattern. She saw Hannah, and anyone else who had a complaint. In less than a week she acquired several patients who seemed delighted to have a doctor, real or not, in their town. Nate Lang, the preacher, had done his best, but his training had come in time of war. When it came to a rash or a stomachache, he didn't have much experience.

JD took to spending a few minutes with his mother every afternoon, before he and the older Sullivan boys jumped into their furtive treasure hunt they still seemed to think was a secret. She took her meals in the dining room, usually sharing a table with one or more of the Sullivans.

When darkness fell and the town went to sleep, Cash came to her. She didn't mind that their relationship remained secret. All that mattered was that when no one else was around, he became her lover. Tender and fierce, he taught her what pleasure was all about. He took her to the edge of something so brilliant and wonderful, she was in utter awe of what she'd discovered.

Cash never mentioned love, and Nadine was afraid if

she did, he'd run far and fast. Most nights they talked, but they kept the conversation safe. They talked about a lot of things, but never about *them*. The past was too painful, and to hear Cash tell it, they had no future. Sometimes, she thought they did. The future was there, and all she had to do was reach out and grab it. Maybe if she took a chance and told him again how she felt, that she loved him, that she was willing to risk anything to be with him, that future would become real.

They did talk about JD. She was distressed that he showed no inclinations of giving up his dreams of becoming a gunfighter, but Cash told her to be patient. She tried, and some days she actually succeeded. In spite of the man Cash had become, she did trust him with their son.

Tonight she waited, as she did every night. The bedside lamp burned low. The coverlet was turned back, but she did not crawl into the bed. Not alone. She'd made a special purchase that afternoon at the sole dress shop in town. Two pretty girls ran the shop, and their work was quite nice.

The nightgown was simple white satin, and it fit her snugly here and there. No shapeless linen for her tonight. The neckline was a low V that didn't quite cover the swell of her breasts. It would do Cash in, she was quite sure.

Where was he? He usually arrived not long after the hotel settled into a complete quiet, sneaking through the front door and climbing the stairs quietly, then coming through her unlocked door. He always left long before sunrise.

A noise outside her open window startled her. A

scrape, a muttered curse. She ran to the window and leaned out, to see Cash scaling the wall by moonlight.

"What on earth are you doing?" she asked with a wide smile.

"Someone locked the front door," he said as he grabbed onto what appeared to be an insubstantial hold and hauled himself up. "And the back," he added softly. "I can't believe I'm climbing up the wall of the Paradise Hotel just to get laid."

He was trying to be crude, of course, but she didn't let his attitude mar the sweetness of the moment. He could have turned away from the locked door and waited until tomorrow. But no, in his fine suit and ruffled shirt and diamond stickpin, he scaled a wall to come to her.

She offered a hand when he reached the window, but he ordered her back and climbed in under his own power. He stood there for a moment, leaning forward, hands on knees, taking a few deep breaths.

"You wanted to know the real me?" he said breathlessly. "Well, I do not work up a sweat if I can find a way around it."

She hummed beneath her breath. "I have seen you work up quite a sweat a time or two," she teased.

He lifted his dark eyes, and when he got a good look at her, his eyebrows rose, his spine straightened. "Good Lord, what are you wearing?"

She smiled. "I bought it just for you."

"You're trying to kill me."

"Actually, it was seduction I had in mind."

"Not a difficult task." He came toward her, reached

out, and brushed the back of his hand over a satin-covered breast.

"You never cease to amaze me," he whispered, his eyes on the slow movement of his dark hand against white satin that shimmered under his touch.

"I'm glad I have the power to amaze you." Her body was ready for his. All he had to do was touch her once, look at her this way, as if he were starving. "You certainly amaze me."

He smiled and stepped back. One step only. "Take it off," he ordered.

Nadine smiled and reached down to grab the nightgown in both hands. Cash stopped her with his strong hands over hers. "Slowly," he whispered. "Very, very slowly."

How many days had he been riding? Danny looked at the unfamiliar landscape surrounding him. He couldn't remember how many days it had been since he'd been shot. Sometimes he blacked out and when he woke he didn't know where he was.

The bleeding had stopped, though every now and then the wound in his side would start to seep again. It hurt. It hurt so much he wanted to fall out of the saddle and cry, but he didn't. He had to get to Nadine. She would make everything right somehow. Melvin was dead, Danny had been forced to shoot a woman, something he'd never intended or expected to be a part of his war, and he hurt.

Nadine would make everything better.

Finally he saw it. Marianna, familiar in so many

ways. He rode and he rode and he rode, and the town got no closer. It was always just out of reach. Always too far away.

And then suddenly he was there, among familiar buildings. Nadine would be in school, unless it was a Saturday or a Sunday. He couldn't be sure of the day, but he was sure she would be in town, in the schoolhouse, studying and assisting the teacher with the little ones. She'd always been good at that, taking care of the little ones.

He left his stolen horse and slipped through an alley, one hand over the wound at his side. He glanced down and saw himself clearly for the first time in days. So much blood. Nadine would be scared at the sight of so much blood, but he didn't have time to clean himself up and find new clothes. After he saw her, he would take care of such inconsequential matters.

The church was in plain view from the alley as he stopped to rest with his back against the wall. The doors burst open and he squinted at the sight before him. This couldn't be right. He must be hallucinating.

Nadine walked down the steps. She wore a white satin wedding dress and carried a bouquet of pink flowers. Her father was there, and Joseph Ellington, dressed in his best suit, had his arm hooked through Nadine's. She smiled so bright.

No, he realized with a shake of his head. She wasn't smiling, she was crying. Big fat tears ran down her face, and her father ordered her to hush.

And then she smiled again, and Danny sank to the ground with his back against the wall. Bleeding. Hurting. Understanding that everything he'd thought he knew was wrong. One woman had bushwhacked him and Melvin, and Nadine had lied. She'd said she loved him but she didn't. She was another man's wife.

He could still see them, but Nadine wasn't wearing her wedding dress anymore. She still wore white satin, but this was a flimsy slip of a thing. She wasn't a girl anymore, she was a woman. She began to dance, to remove the slip of satin, but she stopped in the middle of the dance and began to cry again. She lifted her head and looked at the sky and screamed.

He tried to scream with her, but he couldn't.

"Danny," she cried. "Danny!" Finally she looked at him, seeing him past all the things and the people between them. Peering into the alley where he hid. "Cash?"

Cash shot up in bed, his breath gone, the dream still all too real. Nadine's hands were on him. She'd shaken him awake.

"Cash?" she said again. "Are you all right?"

He shook off the nightmare. "I'm fine," he said, his voice unsteady.

"You are not fine." Nadine sat beside him and ran her hand down his back and up again, her fingers easy against his spine. "You're trembling."

"It was just"—a memory, a nightmare—"hell, I don't know what to believe anymore."

He had never before questioned what was real and what was not. His world was black and white. There was no room for gray, for hazy nightmares that were part memory, part nightmarish fantasy.

Nadine laid her lips on his back, a brief, comforting kiss. "Believe that I love you."

He shook his head gently. No, that was too easy. Too impossible.

"Believe that I wasn't truly alive until I came here and fell in love with you all over again."

He turned and took her in his arms, pulled her around so she'd be forced to look him in the eye. The only light in the room was carried on pale moonbeams shining through the window, but it was enough. He saw her beautiful face and knew that she was telling the truth, or what she believed to be the truth. He could also see that this wasn't easy for her. She didn't know what to expect next, but he knew too well how he had to respond.

"I can't love you back."

She didn't flinch or cry or pull away from him. Instead, she laid a hand on his cheek and whispered, "I know you think you can't. I believe you're wrong."

He did love her. Deep down, he had no doubt that was true. But it didn't matter. She thought it would be so easy for him to change his name and his appearance and become someone else. Someone who didn't live his life waiting for a bullet. Someone who didn't put anyone he loved in danger.

But he couldn't, and wouldn't, deny who he was and what he'd become.

He felt too good when he was with Nadine, and that meant he'd let his guard down. If he let himself claim her, if he allowed himself to love her, one day a man like the one in Webberville would come to their door. He'd be sleeping deeply with Nadine in his arms, and he wouldn't be fast enough. Content, happy, he'd grow lazy and vulnerable.

And when the door burst open and a man with a pistol appeared there, he wouldn't be the only one who ended up dead.

It came to him, then, what he had to do. He'd hand the job of curing JD of his obsession over to Reese or Sullivan or Nate. Nate would know what to do. Any one of them would do a better job than he could, anyway. He'd tell Nadine that he had somewhere to be, and he'd ride away. She would stay in Rock Creek until Hannah delivered, and he wouldn't come back until she and JD had gone home to Marianna.

And he needed to go today, dammit. Before he came to depend on her any more than he already did.

He wanted to love her one more time before he left. He pulled her bare body tighter against his, lowered his mouth to hers. He didn't want to talk about the damned dream, or love, or leaving. He just wanted to be inside her. She melted against him as they kissed, knowing too well what he wanted. What he needed.

They both jumped back when a loud thud sounded at her door. The door shook as someone pounded a fist there.

Cash jumped from the bed and reached for his guns. The fact that he had to cross the room to reach his holster and the weapons there was proof that he'd already lost his edge. As he grabbed a weapon from the holster, a voice called out.

"Nadine?"

Cash relaxed and returned the six-shooter to its holster. Jed.

The big man didn't stop pounding. "Wake up, Nadine. It's Hannah. I think it's time."

"I'll be right there," Nadine called, stepping from the bed and grabbing her wrapper, slipping it on and pulling it snug at her waist.

And still Jed pounded. "Hurry. She—" The door gave way under his incessant pounding, swinging sharply inward and banging against the inner wall.

Jed stood there, wearing his trousers and nothing else, his fist raised and his eyes on a naked Cash.

"She doesn't look too good," Jed finished in a lowered voice.

"I'll be right there," Nadine promised, and Cash crossed the room to close the door.

Well, hell.

Jed was right, Nadine thought as she stepped away from her patient. Hannah didn't look good. Giving birth was never easy work, but she had a bad feeling about this one. As the hours of Hannah's labor wore on, her face went too pale. She didn't make enough noise. She should be screaming.

Mary and Eden were there to assist, had been in and out of the room all morning. Jed refused to leave. He hovered over Hannah and got in Nadine's way at every turn, and was almost as pale as the pregnant woman on the bed.

A number of towels lined a laundry basket awaiting the arrival of the Rourke baby or babies. Midday sunlight streamed into the room, marking the hours that had passed.

Jed Rourke left his wife's side and stalked across the room to stand before Nadine. "Do something," he hissed.

"There's nothing more I can do," Nadine said, feeling helpless as she waited.

"You have to be able to do something!" Jed's hands balled into fists as he glared down at her.

Hannah screamed. It wasn't a strong cry, but she definitely drew Nadine's attention away from the impatient husband.

Again Jed got in the way. It was almost as if he were trying to be in the wrong place at the wrong time.

"Come on, Jedidiah," Eden said softly. "You need to go wait downstairs."

He shook off the suggestion.

Mary stepped in. "The boys are in the lobby. You kept a couple of them company while they went through this. Let them do the same for you."

Again, he dismissed the suggestion and bent over Hannah, almost as if he were willing her to be strong, to have the baby *now*.

Nadine shoved him aside. "Get out," she said firmly, not bothering to be as nice as the other ladies.

"I will not."

Nadine threw open the door. All morning, whenever Mary or Eden had opened that door, Cash had been there. Peeking in, pacing in the hallway. In the dark hours of the morning he'd pulled on his trousers and shirt and boots, but the rest of his clothing and his weapons were still in her room, just across the hall.

She kept expecting the door to open on an empty hallway, but he was always there.

"Cash," she said sharply. "Get your friend out of this room. Now."

Cash stepped to the doorway. Judging by the expression on his face, he knew making Jed Rourke do anything he didn't want to do was going to be impossible. "Come on," he said gently. "Let's go make some coffee."

"I'm not leaving," Jed insisted.

"Jedidiah," Eden began.

The big man spun on his sister. "I am *not* leaving!"

Cash stepped into the already crowded room and laid a hand on Jed's arm. While everything else was falling apart, Cash remained calm. "Come on," he said again. "Let Nadine do her job."

Jed looked down at a pale, sweating Hannah. "Go with Cash," she whispered. She tried to give him a smile, but it didn't quite work. "We'll be fine here. This is woman's work, Jed. No place for a man."

"I don't want to leave," he said softly.

"We won't go far," Cash said calmly. "We'll sit in the hall so we'll be right here, close by." He turned Jed around, and the big man actually allowed that to happen. "We'll be right here, and when the baby is born, Nadine will tell us, won't you, Nadine?"

"Yes. The minute the baby is born, I'll let you know."

"If Hannah asks for me, you'll holler for me, right?" Jed asked anxiously.

"Of course," Nadine said as Cash led Jed into the

hallway. Hannah screamed, and she closed the door on two very helpless-looking men.

Cash sat on the floor, his back to the wall, his eyes on Jed.

Jed sat, too, after a couple of hours of ceaseless pacing. Cash had tried to keep the expectant father downstairs, where the others guys came and went with words of encouragement and lighthearted teasing that didn't go over well. Jed wanted to be as close to Hannah as he could be. His head hung between his knees, and whenever there was a cry from the room at his back he cringed. Hell, except for those flinches, he hadn't moved for the past half hour. And he hadn't asked once what the hell Cash had been doing in Nadine's room.

Like he needed to ask.

"Do me a favor," Cash said softly.

Jed lifted his head, moving slowly. He looked like he hadn't slept in a month. "What do you want, runt?"

"Don't tell anyone that I was in Nadine's room last night."

Jed planted cold blue eyes on Cash's face. "What's the matter?" he snapped. "Afraid people around here will start expecting you to behave like a decent sort just because you took up with an honest woman?"

"There is that," Cash said with a half-smile, trying to be flippant. The smile didn't last. "Mainly I don't want JD to hear that his mother has taken up with the town scoundrel. He's a good kid. I don't want him . . . doubting his mother."

Jed's eyes widened just a little. "You're worried about what the kid will think?"

"And about what the people in town will think of Nadine," he added. "She's a good person. She doesn't need to have her name whispered in connection to mine."

"Then you shoulda left her alone," Jed growled.

"I know," Cash sighed. "I wish I had." *I wish I could.*

Jed leaned his head against the wall and looked up at the ceiling. "Don't worry. I won't tell a soul."

"Thank you."

"Of course, everyone that matters already knows."

Cash sighed. Of course they did. He'd known that all along. Trying to keep a secret around here was damn near impossible. Still, he knew his friends and their wives wouldn't spread malicious gossip. They were like family, and family secrets stayed close.

Jed looked like he was being tortured, and Cash knew exactly how the big guy felt. Battle was easy compared to this. Helplessness was damn hard for men who were accustomed to taking charge.

What Jed needed was something to think about besides what was happening on the other side of that wall. "The plans for the wedding are going well," he said softly.

"I shoulda told you to forget it, once Nadine ordered Hannah to bed."

"I thought you might want to have the ceremony anyway, after the baby is born. A celebration of sorts."

Jed actually smiled. "That might be a good idea."

"Down by the river," Cash continued. Hannah

screamed, and Jed flinched. "At sunrise," he continued. "You know, down there by that big flat rock that juts out over the water. The ceremony will be followed by a picnic. White cake and champagne, with lemonade for the little ones."

Jed closed his eyes as if he were picturing the scene in his mind.

"Nate will perform the ceremony, of course," Cash continued. "And I assume Millie and Fiona will expect to be flower girls. Matching pink dresses for those two, I imagine."

Jed actually smiled, until Hannah screamed. Loud, this time.

"Son of a bitch!" Jed said, jumping to his feet. Cash was right behind him. "I am not going to sit here while . . ."

The door opened briefly, and a wanly smiling Eden glanced out. "It's a boy," she said. Jed stepped forward, and Eden slammed the door in his face.

Jed, shut out of the room once again, turned around with a crooked smile on his pale, stubbled face. "A boy," he said. "That's good."

"Yeah," Cash said with a grin of his own. "Congratulations."

"They'll let me in soon, right?" Jed asked, glancing nervously at the door.

Hannah screamed again, making it clear she was not done. There was a pause, and the baby's cry sounded again.

The door opened and Mary stuck her head out. "Another boy," she said quickly, and then she slammed the door.

Jed went impossibly white. "Two boys. Well, Nadine said it might be twins."

"Two at a time," Cash said with a smile. "I'm impressed."

"Damn right," Jed said, sounding tough even though he swayed on his feet.

The minutes passed, and Jed paced with an increasing turbulence. "What's taking so long? Shouldn't they be done by now?" He laid horrified eyes on Cash. "Something's wrong with Hannah."

Nothing could stop Jed from opening the door, but Cash did try. The door swung open, and in a matter of seconds they took it all in. Mary on the floor by the laundry basket, Eden at the head of the bed, holding Hannah's hand, and a bloody Nadine bent over her task at the end of the bed.

"That's too much blood," Jed whispered.

"Get out," Nadine snapped without lifting her head from her duty.

Cash grabbed Jed's arm and pulled him into the hallway, closing the door behind him.

"Everything's fine," he said calmly.

"That was not fine," Jed whispered. "What I just saw wasn't anything close to *fine!*"

"Nadine knows what she's doing," Cash said, trying to keep his voice low and easy.

"Don't talk to me like I'm a nitwit!" Jed shouted. "Hannah is in there bleeding to death, and I can't do a damn thing to help her." He looked like he wanted to hit something. Hard. "I don't need you to pat me on the back and tell me everything's going to be fine when I can see for myself that—"

The door opened again, and Eden stuck her head out. She wasn't smiling this time. "It's a girl," she said before retreating into the room again.

"I thought they said two boys," Jed said, his voice a croak.

"They did."

"Two boys *and* a girl?" The big man slumped to the floor, his back to the wall, his knees drawn up. *"Three?* Good God, three babies. That can't be right. We must've misunderstood."

A moment later the door opened. Jed could not see from his position on the floor, but Cash had, for a few seconds, a clear view of Nadine bent over a very still Hannah.

Eden stepped into the hallway, the laundry basket in her hands. Inside the laundry basket, three very tiny babies were nestled in blankets and lying on a bed of soft towels.

She placed the basket on the floor beside Jed and sat beside him. Eden, who was always so full of energy, looked dead on her feet.

Jed stared into the basket. "There *are* three," he said in wonder. "And they're so small," he whispered.

"Small, yes," Eden said. "But Nadine says they're perfectly well formed and healthy. We'll have to keep them warm, and—"

Jed's head snapped up. "How's Hannah? You haven't said a word about Hannah."

Eden looked suddenly uncomfortable. "It was a long labor, and there were a few complications. Nadine thinks Hannah will be fine."

"She thinks?" Jed glanced down at the babies,

reached out an incredibly large finger and touched the cheek of each baby. Then he stood up and looked over at Cash. "Try to stop me and I'll break your arm."

"I won't try to stop you." Like he could!

Jed opened the door and stepped inside, and this time when Nadine lifted her head, she did not order him out.

It had been touch and go for hours, but Hannah was finally looking good. Jed had been an angel through it all, holding Hannah's hand, telling her he loved her and that the babies were beautiful. Remaining calm through it all.

The day had come and gone and the sky was dark again, and Nadine was so tired, she could barely think straight. She sat in a chair at the end of the bed. The sheets had been changed, the patient cleaned and dressed in a fresh nightgown, and the three babies, wrapped in little blankets, were currently nestled in their father's arms as he sat at his wife's bedside. Hannah was sound asleep.

"Do you know how rare triplets are?" she whispered.

Jed nodded.

"The fact that Hannah is thirty-two and that twins run in her family make her more likely to have a multiple birth, but . . . I never expected this."

Jed smiled tiredly. "Neither did we."

Time to get down to business. Oh, she hated this part. "There were some complications."

"I know," Jed breathed.

"And I have to tell you"—she took a deep breath.

Heavens, she did not want to do this—"Hannah can't have any more babies."

Jed lifted his head and laid frightened eyes on her. "You mean, if she tries to have another baby it'll be dangerous?"

"No," Nadine said tiredly, realizing she'd chosen her words poorly. "Hannah will be unable to conceive again. There was some damage . . ."

"Thank God," Jed said, closing his eyes in evident relief. "I couldn't go through this again; I swear I couldn't bear it." He glanced down at the babies in his arms. "Three kids will be plenty for us." He barely lifted one baby with a shift of his arm. "This is Vincent," he said, "the name we agreed on for a boy. Since he was the first born, he's Vincent. This little guy," he said with another shift of his arm, "will have to wait on his name. Hannah would never forgive me if I named him while she was asleep." With a soft smile he leaned over and kissed the third baby's forehead. "And this is Annabelle. Annabelle Nadine Rourke."

Nadine smiled, relieved that he had taken the news so well. Some men would not have. "Thank you."

Jed lifted his head and laid very serious, very blue eyes on her. "No," he said softly. "Thank *you*. If you ever need anything, anything at all, you ask and it's yours."

Can you make Cash love me? She kept that question to herself.

Cash paced in the lobby. Damn, this place was quiet. Had it ever been like this before? Dark and silent, echoing like a tomb.

He spun around when he heard footsteps on the stairs, expecting, hoping it was Nadine. But Eden, with Alex in her arms, walked gently down the stairs, her husband behind her.

"Is everybody all right?" he snapped.

Eden smiled. It was an exhausted smile, but an Eden grin all the same. "Yes, everyone's fine."

"God, this place is quiet," Cash said, running a hand through his hair. "Doesn't seem natural."

"I know what you mean," Sullivan said. Eden sat on the couch and Sullivan lowered himself to sit beside her. "It was such a long day, we farmed all the kids but Alex out for the night."

Eden laid her head on Sullivan's shoulder, and Alex managed to cuddle with both parents. "Fiona is spending the night with Georgie, and the boys, including JD, are all staying with Nate and Jo and baby Angelo. Millie is sleeping over with Carrie, so everyone's happy."

Cash leaned against the front desk. Most of the day he'd paced the hallway unarmed, but before he'd come downstairs he'd strapped on his guns. He never went far without them. Sheriff Sullivan was unarmed at the moment, he noticed.

There had been a time when Sinclair Sullivan had been a loner, an outcast even more so than Cash. Half Comanche, half Irish, he hadn't fit in anywhere, except with the other five of the men who had fought together in the war and then banded together again to become what some called the Rock Creek Six.

Eden had changed that, and now Sullivan was a family man. A sheriff. He seemed . . . content. Cash shook his head. Hadn't he warned Sullivan, years earlier, to steer clear of Eden Rourke? Good thing he had ignored that advice. God, they looked so perfect, husband and wife and child. Something he would never know. Something he had missed.

Eden lifted sleepy eyes to him, head on Sullivan's shoulder, baby rubbing his nose against her shoulder. "Is she here because of you?" she whispered.

"I don't know what you're talking about," Cash said coolly.

"Nadine," Eden said with a knowing smile, not at all fooled. "Is she here because of you?"

Cash fidgeted. "Yes," he finally answered. "I suppose she is."

"Then, thank you. I never could've done what she did today. The babies, Hannah's difficulties . . ." Eden shuddered, and Sullivan tightened his arm around her. "We could have lost them all. Nadine saved four lives today, and if she hadn't been here . . ." Tears sprang to Eden's blue eyes.

"Make her stay," Sullivan, a man of few words, said. "We need her here."

Of course they needed Nadine here. And Nadine needed them; he saw that too clearly. But if she stayed, he would have to go and not come back. Not ever.

"I'll try."

Sullivan smiled widely. "Eden's pregnant again."

Cash lifted his eyebrows. "Really?"

"We haven't told anyone yet," Eden confided in a low voice. "It took me so long to get pregnant with Alex after Fiona was born, I wondered if I'd ever have another baby."

"Are you happy?"

Her smile told it all. "Of course."

Of course.

Sullivan's face sobered. "I want Nadine here when Eden delivers."

Like Jed, Sullivan worried for his wife. That's all a family was, Cash thought sullenly. More people to worry about. Heartache waiting to happen. He didn't need that. Hell, no one needed that kind of obligation. That kind of incessant dread.

But it was too late for him. Marriage or no marriage, Nadine and JD were his. He would worry about them until the day he died; he just wouldn't be around to watch life happen to them. He wouldn't know when they were sick, or hurt, or sad. Would it hurt less that way? Or would it hurt all the goddamned time?

"Cash?" His head popped up when Nadine spoke his name. She stood on the stairway, so exhausted she looked like she needed someone to hold her up. *Him,* he thought glumly, she needed him to hold her up. "Come to bed."

She asked right in front of Sullivan and Eden. After what she'd been through today, she was probably delirious. So much for discretion.

"I don't know what you're—"

"I'm too tired to pretend right now," she whispered. "I just need to sleep. I won't sleep at all if you're not there."

Hell, Eden and Sullivan knew, Jed knew. Every one of the handful of men Cash called friend—and their nosy wives—knew that Nadine Ellington had no sense at all where men were concerned. If she did, she never would have taken up with him.

Giving in, he pushed away from the front counter and walked to the stairway. "Good night," he called softly, his eyes on Nadine.

" 'Night," Eden said sleepily. "Pancakes for breakfast."

"Great," Cash said as he placed his arm around Nadine and they took the last few steps together.

Twelve

Nadine rolled over and snuggled more securely in Cash's arms. Goodness, it felt good here, warm and right. She opened one eye, surprised to see that the room was flooded with sunlight. It was surely mid-morning. She never slept this long!

She lifted her head to find Cash watching her with a soft smile on his face. "You've been awake awhile," she whispered.

"Yes, I have."

"Why didn't you get up and go down for Eden's pancakes?"

"I'd rather watch you."

They'd dropped into bed exhausted last night. She'd surely fallen asleep the moment her head hit the pillow. With Cash beside her, she slept so well.

His expression grew serious, his eyes dark. "You amaze me," he whispered.

"How?"

"In more ways than I expected," he admitted. "You saved four lives yesterday. Everyone else was in a panic, and you knew what to do. Because of you those babies and Hannah are alive today." He placed a brief kiss on her forehead. "No, you saved five lives. Jed wouldn't be worth a nickel without Hannah."

"I kinda sensed that," she whispered, snuggling tighter against Cash's chest.

His hands rocked at her back, and he sighed long and low. "You should stay," he said softly.

Nadine closed her eyes and smiled widely. Oh, she had so hoped for this. She hadn't expected that he would come around so soon, but she could only be glad. "I would love to stay here."

"The town needs you," he said.

Nadine lifted her head. Her unbound hair fell over Cash's chest, and he grabbed a strand to finger. "What about you?" she said softly. "Do you need me?"

Brave, he pinned his eyes to hers. "Daniel Cash doesn't *need* anyone, and if he did, he would never admit it."

She didn't believe him, and still the words stung.

"Nadine," he said, his tone turning serious. "You're a doctor. You know how to prevent a pregnancy, right?"

"Of course. There are several ways. . . ."

"Have you been practicing any of those . . . ways?"

"No."

He fell onto his back and stared at the ceiling. "Sometimes it takes a while for a woman to get pregnant, I know, but since you ended up carrying JD after our first time, I'm a little worried that all I have to do is breathe on you."

Nadine rolled over and draped herself across his chest. "Breathing has nothing to do with it, I assure you," she teased. "Maybe I should give you a lesson on how babies are made."

His hand settled possessively in her hair. His heart beat steadily beneath her ear. "What if you are pregnant?" he asked, no note of teasing in his voice.

"You could always make an honest woman of me."

"No," he said softly. "I can't."

Nadine lifted her head and stared down at Cash. "Why not?"

"I can't ever marry."

"Are you already married?"

"No."

"Did you enter the priesthood while I wasn't looking?"

He almost smiled. "Not hardly."

"Then why can you never get married?"

A lazy finger rocked down her cheek, and he shifted his gaze so he no longer looked her in the eye. "If I loved a woman enough to marry her, she'd be marked the moment she took my name. If I . . . had a child, that child would live in constant danger, just because he was cursed with my name." His finger drifted down to her neck. "And that's why you're going to stay here in Rock Creek." His eyes snapped back up to hers, and all hint of warmth was gone. "And I'm not."

Cash walked into the dim saloon and found Evan polishing the long bar. The man lifted his head, gave him a knowing grin, and nodded once before silently returning to his chore.

There had been moments, days, sometimes weeks when he'd loved this saloon. It was the only place he'd ever called home, and even though he came and went and sometimes stayed away for months at a time, this plain, dim, rustic saloon was the closest thing to home he'd known in a very long time. Everything he'd thought he needed could be found in this simple place. A game of cards, a soft bed, a steady supply of whiskey.

Taking a seat at his usual table, Cash propped his feet on the table and stared at Evan. "You're fired."

"What?" Evan placed his meaty hands on the bar and leaned forward. "I didn't say anything. I didn't say a word to nobody. . . ."

Cash reached into the deep pocket of his jacket and withdrew a wad of cash. He tossed it, money clip and all, toward the bar, where it landed directly before Evan. "A little something to see you over until you find another job." The wad of money was more than enough to see Evan through the year. "I hear Henry Loring is looking for a new cook. That's what you did before you came here, right?"

Evan nodded his head and scooped up the wad of cash.

"You never liked living in town, anyway," Cash said.

"You leaving again?" Evan stuffed the money in his trouser pocket, pushing it deep in case Cash changed his mind.

"For good this time." Cash glanced around the room.

"When are you closing up?"

"Now."

Nadine had convinced him to stay until the Fourth of July celebration. Since they had both been naked, he'd been easy to . . . convince. But once that day had passed, he was gone. There would be no more giving in, no endless line of "Stay until JD's birthday." "Stay until Christmas." "Stay until spring." He could so easily get caught up in something so simple and treacherous. A week here, a month or two there. Until it became "Stay until the baby's born."

No, once the Fourth of July passed, he'd ride out of Rock Creek for the last time. He'd have to go far this time, so in a moment of weakness he wouldn't be tempted to ride into Rock Creek in the dead of night and sneak into Nadine's room just to look at her.

He'd have two weeks to talk JD out of his ambition. Two weeks to make love to Nadine like there was no tomorrow. Two weeks to convince her that he didn't love her and never had.

Two weeks to say good-bye.

"This room is empty at the moment," Eden said brightly, throwing open the door of an unoccupied room on the third floor. "We can clean it up and bring in whatever you need, until you find a permanent place to practice."

Nadine surveyed the room with skeptical eyes. It was too small, and even those who were truly ill would have to climb two flights of stairs. But it would do. And if she had a patient who was too ill to make the climb, she'd go to them. That's how she'd operated in Marianna. From a small room in her house, traveling on horseback to visit most of her patients.

"I wish I had all my books and equipment," she said. "JD and I came here with no more than we could carry, since we traveled on horseback."

She'd had no idea she might stay, that she might find the man she'd always loved in the gunslinger Daniel Cash, and they'd end up together again. "All I brought with me was my medical bag and the few supplies I always carry in it."

"You can wire home and ask them to pack up and ship all your things. That way you won't have to take the time to ride back and see to it yourself." Eden glanced around the dusty room, her eyes wide and deceptively innocent. "Unless, of course, there's someone there you need to see. A special friend, perhaps, or a beau."

"No," Nadine said softly. "There's no one in Marianna I need to see. My friends will understand."

"You mean there's no—"

"I mean I love Cash," she said, placing her steady eyes on Eden. "Is that what you're trying to find out?"

Eden blushed prettily. "Daniel doesn't exactly need anyone to look out for him, and if he thought I'd even suggested such a thing, he'd be furious with me. But I swear, sometimes that man needs a keeper more than any one of my children."

Nadine smiled. "I know what you mean."

"The fact that he actually asked you to stay gives me hope. I so want him to be happy."

Nadine stared at Eden. She was a beautiful woman, sweet and kind, and obviously madly in love with her husband. But there was something between Eden and Cash that made Nadine feel a surge of jealousy. That something Eden and Cash had was not love, she knew, and it was nothing sexual. But they shared a friendship that was dear and true and real, the kind of friendship that lasts forever.

"He lets you call him Daniel," she said softly.

"He saved my life and I made him soup," Eden said simply. The explanation obviously made some sense to her, but it made none to Nadine.

"I can't cook," she said simply. "The last time I made soup, JD said it tasted like I'd boiled an old shoe and added a few vegetables."

"You have your own talents," Eden said with a smile. "And they are much more marvelous than the ability to make a tasty soup. Why are you worried? I'm sure Daniel adores you. I have never seen him look at a woman the way he looks at you. Besides, he asked you to stay, didn't he?"

Nadine stared at the mattress on the bed in the room that would become her office for a while. "Yes," she whispered. "But he also told me that he's leaving. I convinced him to stay until the Fourth of July celebration you and the other ladies have been talking about, but once that's done . . . he's leaving."

She shifted her head to see that Eden's smile was gone. A doctor for a friend was a lousy trade, Nadine knew that. But Eden didn't look angry, she looked determined.

"We'll see about that," she said softly.

Cash sat on the green sofa in the lobby of the Paradise Hotel, a fabulous dinner sitting well on his stomach, a dread he tried to ignore making his heart heavy. Teddy and JD came through, headed for the stairs, their heads together as they conspired, no doubt about women and buried treasure. JD saw Cash sitting there, smiled, and waved without slowing his step. God, he looked so much like a child.

When JD's and Teddy's lowered voices had faded completely, Cash forced himself to his feet. He'd be back later, but he wouldn't climb the stairs now. When the place was quiet, when JD was asleep, then it would be safe to return. Who was he kidding? These nights with Nadine were anything but safe.

Before he reached the doorway, Reese filled it. When he saw Cash, he came to a stop there, blocking the exit. Why did he have the feeling Reese had come here looking for him?

"I saw that your place is shut down," Reese said casually. A tad too casually for Cash's liking.

"You're still an observant man, I see," Cash answered.

"Going somewhere?"

Cash shook his head. "Eventually."

"I thought you loved that place."

"I used to. Now it bores me."

"What are you going to do with yourself?" Reese finally stepped inside. "Are you any good at carpentry?"

"Good God, no," Cash said, horrified.

"That's too bad. The school needs some work. I just thought that maybe . . ."

Cash closed the distance between himself and his former captain. "If you're trying to save me from myself," he said caustically, "you're going to have to get in line."

The expression on Reese's face changed, subtly and tellingly. Schoolteacher or not, he was not a man to be trifled with. "You can't live like this forever."

"Why not?" Cash gave the man a wide smile. "I like living the way I do. No apron strings, no roots, no boundaries."

"You can't possibly—"

"We can't all be schoolmarms," Cash interrupted.

Reese didn't take the bait; he remained calm. "If you need anything, you know where I am."

"Thank you," Cash said, brushing past. "But I have everything I need." It was an empty lie and they both knew it, but Reese remained silent as Cash turned toward his dark, shut-down saloon.

Nadine looked content, lying on her back in the bed they shared, staring at the ceiling with a smile on her face. "You have no idea what a relief it is to have JD sleeping above my head," she whispered.

"You didn't trust me to keep him safe at the saloon?"

"It's not that I didn't trust you, it's just . . ." She couldn't find the right words, so her delicate hand gestured helplessly.

"He's not a child, Nadine," Cash said, his hands behind his head as he stared at the same ceiling. "You're going to have to stop treating him like one."

She rolled onto her side and laid her eyes on him. "He's all I have. He's been all I have for so long that I can't clearly recall living any other way."

"He is going to grow up."

Nadine laid her head on his chest, nuzzled her soft

cheek against his chest. "When he quits sneaking around trying to find buried treasure," she whispered with a smile, "I might start to worry about him growing up."

Cash laid his hand in her hair. He liked this, their time lying in the dark and talking, almost as much as he liked the sex. He'd never done this with any other woman, laid awake and just talked for hours. "He did like the idea of bunking with Teddy well enough," he said. "They probably hatched all kinds of plans before they went to sleep."

The saloon was closed, though he and JD had done a little work in the building that afternoon. There was still more work to be done before he left. His own room above the saloon was empty, and as far as most people knew, he slept there still. The room JD had been sleeping in most nights was perfectly serviceable. But he hadn't liked the idea of leaving JD there all alone. Eden's suggestion that JD move above stairs with the other children had been the perfect solution. It certainly made Nadine happy.

Her hand grazed over his ribs, and came to rest over the scar at his side. The first, oldest, and worst scar. "This was a bad wound," she said softly.

"Yes, it was."

"Want to tell me what happened?"

"Not especially."

She sighed, and he felt her hot breath on his skin. "I hope you had someone to take care of you."

Cash laughed bitterly. "Four someones," he whispered.

Nadine lifted her head and looked down at him, her

face soft and deeply shadowed by broken moonlight. "Four someones?"

What difference did it make? Two weeks from now he'd be gone. But what part of the story did he dare to tell? He would not tell her a sad story that would bring tears to her eyes, and he would not hurt her with the entire truth.

He had ridden away from Marianna expecting to die. Not caring that he would soon be dead. Hurting so much death would be a relief. But he'd awakened in a soft bed, surrounded by four beautiful, half-clothed women. They'd undressed him, cleaned him, bandaged the wound, and watched over him with an intensity, demanding that he heal.

"I was separated from my unit," he said simply. "When I awoke I was in a . . . large house outside the city limits of a small town."

"What town?" she asked, naively curious.

Cash sighed. Damn, he didn't want to tell all, but he would not lie to her. Not now, not like this. "A little town close to the Texas-Louisiana border."

Her eyes went wide. "You were so close to home," she whispered, placing her hands on his cheeks and leaning in to place her nose on his. "If you had traveled a little farther, I might've been able to—"

"I had already been to Marianna," he said sharply. "I was on my way back to my unit when they found me."

Nadine didn't move. For a few seconds the room was so still and quiet, he felt and heard her heart beating against his. "When did this happen?"

"March 1862," he whispered.

Nadine didn't say a word, she didn't even breathe.

A tear dropped from her eye and landed on his face. "Is that when you saw me? My wedding day?"

"Yes."

"And you thought . . ." She swallowed hard. "You thought I was happy?" she asked, remembering an older conversation.

"It doesn't matter now."

"It does," she breathed. "You were there, and you were hurt." Her hand skimmed tenderly over the scar. Another tear dropped onto his cheek, and another. "I hate that," she whispered hoarsely. "So much."

He felt her gain control. She stiffened a little, her tears stopped, and she ran a slightly trembling hand through his hair. "But someone found you and took care of you, thank God. Four women? Were they sisters?"

"Business associates," he said.

Nadine's head came up slowly. "Business associates? You recuperated in a . . . in a . . ."

"Cathouse," he said, supplying the word she could not bring herself to say.

It hadn't taken him long to figure out what kind of establishment he was in. The women . . . he couldn't remember their names or their faces, but he certainly did remember their bodies . . . had always been clothed in sheer nightgowns or low-cut dresses not completely fastened. A young man with a broken heart, he had been utterly fascinated.

"I thought I was dead," he whispered. "But they took care of me and I did heal."

They'd done their best to heal more than his body. They'd set about to mend his heart as soon as he found himself able. He must have mentioned Nadine's name in his fevered state, because they knew what had happened. And they all did their best to make him feel better the only way they knew how. It had been his first experience with sex for pure pleasure, and they had taught him well. Some nights he'd come awake to find one of the women already in his bed. Hands and mouths on him, bodies pressed against his.

One of them, the blond one, had told him he was young and pretty, and they didn't have many young and pretty men left in the area. Everyone had gone off to war. He didn't care why they came to his bed, only that they did. And by the time he left he'd convinced himself that what he'd had with Nadine was no different from what he'd had with four women whose names he wouldn't remember.

"When I was able to travel, they gave me the clothes that used to belong to a gambler who had died in someone's bed. A black suit, a ruffled shirt." He smiled. "I hated that shirt at first. What kind of a man wears ruffles? But it turned out to be a lucky shirt. Nothing touched me after that."

"The scar on your thigh," she said softly.

"That came much later," he said, offering no further explanation. The protection had lasted through the war. Later . . . he had always been lucky, but he had not remained untouched.

Nadine settled her head against his chest. "After you healed, you went back to war."

And eventually joined Reese and the elite band Colonel Mosby assembled. Six men who were fearless, talented, deadly. Men who didn't care if they lived or not. "Yes."

More silent tears touched his chest. "It's so unfair," Nadine whispered. "All I wanted was you. You and our baby. They told me you were dead, and while I was marrying Joseph, you were wounded and watching and . . . so close."

"It doesn't do either of us any good to cry about it now," Cash said. "Maybe it was fate. Maybe we just weren't meant to be."

Nadine didn't lift her head, but something in her body changed. It softened, it raked against his like a cat's. Her hand snaked lower to touch him. His response was quick and undeniable. "How can you say we weren't meant to be? We're together now. We can be together always if you'll just dismiss this ridiculous notion that love and family are for everyone in the world but Daniel Cash."

She lifted her leg over his, very slowly snaked over and across until she straddled him. "Maybe we had to wait, and maybe we had to go through hell to get here. But that doesn't mean we don't belong together."

He didn't want to argue with her, not now, but she had to know. "I'm not staying," he whispered.

"I have two weeks to change your mind," she whispered, and then she laid her mouth over his, took him into her slick, hot body, and did her best to do just that.

Thirteen

For the past three days, they had worked in what had once been Rogue's Palace in the morning, and come down to the river for target practice in the afternoon, before JD sneaked off to tap on walls and tug at floorboards with Teddy and Rafe.

The kid was good. He had adjusted quickly to Cash's efforts to rattle him, learning to ignore the crisply barked orders and distractions that were thrown his way. He didn't miss often, and he remained calm as he fired. JD had the kind of confidence that could get him killed.

It was one of those hot summer days that sent most people scurrying for shade, but Cash and JD stood bravely in the sun. Jacket and vest long ago discarded, Cash had rolled the sleeves of his shirt up in concession to the heat. He sweated profusely while he watched his son kill whiskey bottles and empty cans with ease.

Yeah, the kid was too good.

None of Cash's subtle warnings about the life of a gunslinger were getting through the boy's thick skull. Danger meant nothing to him, and he didn't quite seem to grasp the concept that his life would be on the line every day. He thought he was untouchable. Invincible. Cash remembered that feeling too well.

Cash knew he could always hand this chore over to one of the other guys, or to all of them. That wasn't enough. He wanted to know, before he left Rock Creek, that JD had come to his senses.

A scruffy-looking yellow dog had been hanging around the last two days. The dumb creature didn't even have the sense to run from gunfire, but watched the proceedings curiously from what he no doubt considered a safe distance.

Cash glanced at JD's straight, proud back, the smoking gun in the kid's hand, and the mutt.

"Shoot the dog," he ordered.

JD turned around and looked past Cash to the hill where the dog stood. The mutt's tongue was hanging out, his tail wagged.

"I can't shoot that dog," he said, shaking his head to reaffirm his position on the subject. "Carrie and Millie feed him. They'd be really pissed if I killed their dog."

Cash would not back down. "You've proven to me that you can shoot objects that don't shoot back and don't bleed. If you're going to be a gunfighter—"

"That dog can't shoot back," JD interrupted.

"But it will bleed."

"Millie and Carrie—"

"Every man you will face as a gunfighter has someone who *feeds* them," Cash snapped. "A wife, a mother, a sister. If you hesitate, if you think of the man before you as a living being who is cared for by someone, you're dead, because he's going to get off the first shot while you're standing there wondering if you're doing the right thing." He knew his son, he knew there was no way the kid would ever shoot that mutt. He just wasn't sure JD knew that yet.

"Shoot the dog."

The kid got a gleam in his eye and he smiled. "This is just one of your tests. You don't really want me to shoot the dog. *You* wouldn't shoot it."

Cash drew his six-shooter, spun, and fired. The bullet hit the ground a good foot away from the stupid dog. Dirt and grass went flying, and the mutt finally got smart and made his escape at a run.

He turned around to see that JD had gone deathly white. "You missed," he said, sounding relieved.

I never miss. "Yeah," Cash said as he holstered his gun. "Maybe I should be getting in some target practice myself."

JD's nostrils flared. "I can't believe you'd shoot a *dog,*" he said as he holstered his own weapon easily.

"A gunslinger with a conscience is a dead gunslinger."

With a youthful, arrogant gait, JD walked toward him. "You know, I don't think I want to be a gunfighter anymore," he said sullenly.

Cash withheld a grin. "Oh, really?"

"So far it hasn't been much fun."

"I never said it was fun, kid."

"I'm thinking maybe when Teddy goes to work for his uncle Jed, maybe I'll see if I can get a job there, too."

Rourke Detective Agency. Cash wasn't sure that

Nadine would like that idea, either, but at least JD knew he'd have to wait a few years before beginning that career.

"I don't know if Mr. Rourke will hire me or not," JD admitted. "He still calls me a little woodpecker whenever he sees me, and that kinda rankles."

"I imagine it does."

"But if I show him that I can shoot, and that I'd make a good detective, maybe he'd hire me anyway."

"I imagine he would," Cash said, trying not to sound as relieved as he felt. He really wouldn't mind leaving his son in Jed's hands. "And since your mother's going to stay here in Rock Creek, you could go to school when it starts up again."

"Yeah. Teddy said Mr. Reese is a pretty good teacher." He gave Cash a half-smile. "But he doesn't look much like any teacher I ever had in Marianna."

"I'm sure he doesn't."

"I probably won't be able to get away with much foolishness in his classroom."

Cash tried not to smile. "I don't imagine so."

The kid looked directly at him, eyes wide and naive and so much like his mother's. "Are you disappointed?" he asked. "That I changed my mind?"

"Not at all," Cash said calmly. "The last thing I need out there is more competition."

The grin JD flashed was genuine and so very young. "Can I tell Ma what we're doing to your saloon? We'll be done in just a few days."

"Not yet," Cash said. "I want it to be a surprise. Let's wait until we're finished."

As they walked away from the river, JD added a

little swagger to his walk. Cash could tell the kid was doing some serious thinking, the way his eyes narrowed and his lips hardened. He might have looked quite tough for thirteen, if not for the way his face paled and his voice trembled as he said, "I feel I have to warn you, Cash. If you ever shoot that dog, you'll have to answer to me."

Cash smiled. "I'll bear that in mind."

Nadine hurried down the stairs with a bounce in her step and a wide smile on her face. Eden was alone in the lobby of the Paradise Hotel, dusting the long front desk. "Do you know where Cash is?" Nadine asked, almost whispering.

"He's taking a bath," Eden said, nodding toward the room on the ground floor where the tub was located.

Nadine glanced into the dining room. "Where are the boys?"

Eden smiled. "They're digging up the garden, trying to stay out of my line of vision so I'll have no idea what they're up to."

Nadine paced in the lobby until Eden excused herself to check on how her kitchen help was proceeding with supper. When there was no one around to see, Nadine slipped past the stairs to the doorway of the small room where Cash bathed. She pushed against the door, but it was bolted on the inside.

She heard the brush of metal against leather as Cash drew his gun. Good heavens, he couldn't even take a bath without keeping his weapons close at hand!

"It's me," she said softly. "Let me in."

She heard the splash of water, a soft footstep, and then the bolt was lifted and the door swung open. A naked, dripping-wet Cash grabbed her arm and pulled her inside before closing and rebolting the door.

She threw her arms around his neck and held on tight, burying her face against his wet shoulder. Laughing and crying at the same time, she held him close. "You did it," she whispered against his skin. "I knew you could."

"I see you've talked with JD."

She nodded her head. "He wants to go to work for Jed. A week ago he couldn't stand the man!"

"I think Teddy has been working on him there," Cash said casually. "And Teddy probably has as much to do with his decision to give up his notion of being a gunfighter as I do."

"I don't want to thank Teddy," she whispered, taking her head from Cash's shoulder so she could look up at him. "I want to thank you."

A window set high in the wall allowed light to spill into the small room, bathing them in warm sunshine. Cash looked so vulnerable—naked, wet, his arms around her and his dark eyes boring into hers. He didn't look like a gunfighter, he looked like a man. Her man. The years that had passed since she'd first fallen in love with him showed in the scars he wore and the small lines around his eyes. The darkness in those eyes told of the things he had seen and borne, and the dusting of dark hair on his hard chest and lean legs reminded her that he was no longer a boy.

"I love you," she whispered. "I would give my soul to keep you here with us."

"Don't say that," he commanded.

"It's the truth." She unbuttoned her blouse and then whipped it over her head. "Don't ask me to lie to you, Cash. Don't ask me to pretend I don't love you."

"You're kidding yourself—"

"Don't ruin this moment for me," she interrupted, touching a finger to Cash's lips. "JD is safe, I have you, for the moment everything is perfect. I haven't had many perfect moments in my life. Don't take this one away."

He didn't try to tell her again that she didn't, couldn't, love him.

She removed her clothing, which was damp from coming in contact with Cash's wet body, and tossed it to the floor. She walked into his arms again and lifted her face to look him in the eye. That little beard, in conjunction with his dark eyes, made him look slightly devilish. A fact of which he was surely aware. But she saw so much more than a devil. More than a soldier, a gunfighter, a killer. She saw the father of her son, her lover, a tender man hiding behind a façade he'd constructed so carefully, he probably didn't know who he was anymore. She knew, though. She knew.

She laid her lips on the side of his neck and sucked softly. Heavens, she loved the feel of his skin against hers, the taste of his flesh on her tongue. The way he responded when she touched him.

When she'd come to Rock Creek looking for help, she hadn't expected to love Cash the way she did, and she had certainly never expected to find pleasure in an act she had always thought a woman's duty and nothing more. There was pleasure here because she loved him. Why couldn't he see and accept that?

Feeling bold, she reached between their bodies and touched him, wrapping her fingers around his arousal. "I want to love you. I want to make love with you as often as possible before you go."

He mumbled something she couldn't understand. It sounded like an assent. He cupped her breast and trailed one lazy hand down her back.

"Because once you're gone, no one will ever touch me this way."

His hand pressed along her body, dipping down from her breast to her stomach to delve between her thighs. He touched her gently, but with passion and urgency.

"It doesn't matter who's doing the touching," he said darkly. "As long as it's done correctly."

Was he trying to remind her that she was replaceable? Or that he was?

She lifted her head and looked him in the eye as she stroked his length and he aroused her with his fingers. "It does matter," she whispered. "It matters very much."

Cash didn't argue with her again, but lowered her to the floor and settled himself between her spread legs. He pushed inside her with a low growl and a sense of surrender she tasted as he laid his mouth over hers. He made love to her hard, without tenderness, his body pounding over and into hers with an urgency she felt to her bones.

She wrapped her legs around his lean hips and raked her fingers through his black-as-night hair. "I love you," she whispered. He only loved her harder, his hips driving and his mouth devouring. He pushed deep, fast and grinding, and she lost the will to speak as she got completely lost in the sensations of his body in hers.

He loved her with a savage fierceness, but she felt the passion in his soul, the tenderness he tried to hide. Her release came with the same kind of fierceness, tempered with true love and the knowledge that this was her man. She started to cry out, but he caught her cry with his mouth, kissing her deep and finding his own release as she trembled around him.

She threaded her fingers through his hair and hooked one leg over his to keep him in place. She wanted him to stay inside her just a while longer.

"I never had a lover until I came here," she whispered. "If you leave me, I will never have another."

"I am going to leave, and trust me," he said coolly. "Eventually you will find yourself another lover."

She looked deep into his eyes and ran a finger along the edge of his well-trimmed beard. "Do you think you will be so easy to replace?"

"Yes."

"Do you think I will be so easy to replace?"

"Yes." Ah, the answer sounded cruel and cold and suitably carefree, but his eyes said something completely different. His eyes spoke of years of heartache, pain she could not begin to understand, and hopelessness.

"You're wrong," she said calmly, not taking the bait he offered. "No one will ever love you the way I do."

Cash slowly separated his body from hers. "I swear, if you keep telling me you love me, there's no way I'll wait around until next week's Fourth of July celebration. It's getting tiresome, Nadine."

He tried so hard to make her mad, to force her to be the one to send him away. So much for her perfect moment.

"Can I tell you how much I want you? How much I adore the way I feel when you're inside me?"

With a half-smile he lifted her from the floor and placed her in the bathtub, where she landed with a splash. He stepped in and sat down facing her, his legs drawn up and entangled with her own.

"You're turning into a shameless hussy," he teased. "I like it."

"Is that what you look for in a woman?" She splashed him, sending a handful of cool water across his chest. "Is that all you want? Shamelessness?"

"The more brazen the better," he said, splashing her as she had him, so water ran down her chest.

She reached across and draped her arms around his neck. "You make me feel brazen," she whispered. *And I love you.* She couldn't say that, not again. Not yet. What would it take to make him see that without each other they were nothing? Alone they were lost. Together they were perfect. The thought of going back to a life without Cash in it terrified her.

Jed Rourke sat on the green sofa in the hotel lobby, a baby in each arm. The babies were small anyway, JD thought, but in their father's big arms they looked extra tiny.

Rourke lifted his head and grinned. "Hey, little woodpecker. Find any gold yet?"

JD still didn't like the name Rourke had pinned on him, but he didn't argue. If he wanted to work for this man one day, he'd have to put up with stuff like that. Teddy said his uncle liked to tease all the kids, and he shouldn't take the "little woodpecker" handle as an insult.

"Not yet," he said, stepping closer to take a good look at the babies. They were bundled up so tight and snug, all he could see was their little faces. Little, wrinkled, pink faces. "Which one is which?"

Rourke barely lifted the baby in his left arm. "This is Vincent Byron. I think we're going to call him Vin, though. Suits him. This little boy," he said with a smile, "is William Lee. Will for short."

"You can tell them apart?" JD asked, narrowing his eyes to look for minor differences, finding none.

"Sure I can," Rourke said confidently.

"Where's the other one?" Three babies at once! He had never known of such a thing happening to anyone he knew. He'd already heard that if not for his mother, they wouldn't have survived.

"Annabelle Nadine is upstairs with her mother," Rourke said with a grin. "Have you seen her yet? She's a doll, a real, beautiful doll."

If Annabelle Nadine looked anything like her brothers, she was wrinkled and pink and not at all beautiful. Not that he would dare point that out to the man he wanted to be his employer one day. "Are you going to call her Ann or Anna?" He'd shortened the boys names, after all.

"Annie," Rourke said. "I took one look at her and knew she was an Annie."

The big man's expression softened. "I owe your mother the world," he said. "She saved my family. My whole damn family. She's a remarkable woman."

He'd never thought of her as anything more than his mother. The woman who fed and clothed him, who made him study and had once washed his mouth out with soap. He had known, for years, that she took care of people, but he had never seen anything like this. "Yeah, I guess she is."

"I'm glad y'all are staying with us."

"Me, too," JD admitted softly. Heck, small or not, he liked Rock Creek. He liked all the kids and most of the adults. Even Rico had seemed all right the last time he'd seen him, here in this hotel lobby, offering Rourke his congratulations.

Besides, he wasn't completely stupid. He was no *niño tonto*. Rico's visit, the knife to the throat, had probably been one of Cash's tests.

He'd had nightmares about that knife at his throat, not that he'd admit it to anyone. If that exercise had been conducted to point out that being scared was unpleasant, then it had succeeded.

JD sat down on the sofa and leaned over Will. Or was it Vin? If he was going to stay here, there was no reason not to state his case and get it out in the open.

"I'm a great shootist," he said, his eyes on the baby. "Fast *and* accurate."

"That's what Teddy tells me," Rourke said with a nod of his head.

"I was going to be a gunfighter like Cash, but I've changed my mind."

"Do tell."

"But a man who's good with a gun shouldn't waste his time keeping a shop or raising cattle or cotton," JD said, horrified that his voice squeaked once.

"You're right about that," Rourke said. "You know, Teddy is planning on going to work for me when he's a bit older. I don't know if he's mentioned it or not, but I'm opening my own detective agency."

"He mentioned it." JD's heart started beating too hard. This was better than finding gold! He wasn't going to have to ask. Jed Rourke, one of the Rock Creek Six, was going to offer him a job!

"If you're interested in working for me when you're a little bit older—"

"Yeah!" JD said, the pitch of his voice higher than he'd planned it to be. "That would be great."

"You have to finish your schoolin' first," Rourke said seriously. "I won't have any idiots working for me." He leaned back on the sofa, a sleeping baby boy in each arm. "Shoot, that's years away, little woodpecker. You'll probably change your mind by the time you get out of school."

He didn't mind so much when Rourke called him little woodpecker in that friendly tone. So long as he didn't use that nickname in front of the girls! If Carrie and Millie ever found out . . .

"I won't change my mind, Mr. Rourke."

The big man closed his eyes and smiled. "Call me Uncle Jed."

Fourteen

Eden was more determined than ever to feed him this morning. She kept bringing food to his table, when all he really wanted was a cup of coffee and maybe a biscuit. It didn't take him long to begin to suspect that something was up.

When Eden sat down beside him and smiled too brightly, he knew he was about to find out exactly what that something was.

"How are you this morning?" she asked, folding her hands on the table.

"Fine and dandy. And you?"

She nodded. "Wonderful. I just wanted to thank you again for helping out so much when Fiona was lost." She shuddered visibly as she remembered.

But that wasn't the reason for her mood. She'd thanked him, and everyone else, many times after that horrifying incident. Since then she'd been diligently trying to forget what had happened that day. So, why was she bringing it up now?

"I just don't know what we'd do without you around here," she said.

Cash took a deep, stilling breath. At least he knew

why Eden had been so jumpy lately, and why she was so damned and determined to feed him. "She told you, didn't she?"

"I don't . . . whatever are you . . ." she stammered, and then she took a deep breath of her own and looked him square in the eye.

"You'd make a lousy poker player, Eden," he said with a smile. "You're the worst liar I ever met."

"You're not really going to leave, are you?" she asked.

"Yep."

"It's not right."

He thought about telling her that Rock Creek needed Nadine more than it had ever needed Daniel Cash, but he didn't. That kind of confession would be more telling than was acceptable. "Rock Creek just isn't the place it used to be. There are too damn many kids, for one thing. I can't take two steps without tripping over one."

"Oh, you love the children," Eden countered.

"I most certainly do not." He tried to sound properly mortified at the very idea. "And they are only part of the problem. All my friends have turned into old women who would rather knit booties than go off looking for a good fight."

Eden pursed her lips. "Is that what you're looking for? A good fight?"

"Always." He gave his cuff more attention than it needed. "I don't imagine we need to discuss the lack of suitable female companionship in this fine town."

"I don't imagine we do," she said primly.

He set emotionless eyes on her face. "So why on earth should I stay here?"

"Because we need you," Eden said simply, and without hesitation.

"I disagree."

"You don't get a vote," she snapped.

He couldn't help but smile. Eden rarely lost her temper, but on occasion it was very clear that she and Jed were related by blood. Her response to his smile was a teary-eyed pursing of her lips. "I don't want you to be like Isatekwa," she said softly.

"The Comanche?"

"He used to be a warrior, but alone he was just . . . just . . ."

Pathetic. Lonely. Forever lost. He wasn't about to agree with her. "You think I can't make it without someone around to watch my back?"

She nodded her head. "Yes."

"I've been on my own for the past year."

"But things are different now. I have a bad feeling, Daniel." She twisted her hands slightly. "I think if you leave here, we'll have word of your death within six months."

"Nice of you to give me so long to live," he growled.

"Stay," she insisted. She wagged a finger at him like a scolding mother might. "What you really need is a wife and a few babies."

"Bite your tongue. Babies?"

"Oh, you love babies."

"They're toothless parasites."

"Bite *your* tongue."

Eden pursed her lips as Fiona ran to the table to join them. "Uncle Cash!" she cried, heading for his lap.

"Scram, kid," he said in his coldest voice, determined to prove his point to Eden.

Fiona was not deterred. She never was. Undaunted, she climbed into his lap and gave him a sloppy kiss on the cheek.

"You're wrinkling my jacket."

"Sorry." Fiona sat and ran her little palms over his lapel, smoothing the wrinkles. "There now, all better."

Eden looked on with a too-knowing smile.

It was impossible to look into those wide hazel eyes and remain angry. Or cold. Or distant. And when Fiona reached up and laid her little hands on his cheeks, he quit trying.

"My daddy has one gray hair." She pointed a finger at Cash's temple. "Right there. It's brand new. He says it's his Fiona lightning."

"I don't doubt that." Cash smiled, but looking at Fiona his heart broke a little. It was a sentimental reaction he could not afford. "You'd better run along," he said, lifting her off his lap and setting her on her feet.

"Okay, but I won't go far, right, Mommy?"

"Right," Eden said as she watched Fiona run into the lobby and then up the stairs.

"That's what you need," Eden said softly.

"God above, one Fiona in this world is enough."

Eden smiled. "A daughter," she said, turning her eyes back to him. "A little girl. That's what you need."

Cash wanted to tell her that would never happen, but the words stuck in his throat. "How could you wish that on me? I thought you liked me, at least part of the time. If I had a daughter, I would be forever protecting her from men like her father."

"It's what fathers do," she said gently.

He knew that. He saw it every day, in the men around him. "Is the lecture over, Mommy?" he asked caustically.

"For now." She bit her bottom lip. "Just promise you won't leave without talking to me first."

He could lie to just about anyone else, but not Eden. Some of her disgustingly open qualities rubbed off on him when he spent too much time with her. Just another reason to leave.

"Promise," she said again as he remained silent.

Cash pushed his chair back, finished with this conversation even if Eden was not. "Sorry. I can't do that."

Blindfolded, the men in her life on either side of her holding her hands and guiding her, Nadine smiled widely. Just moments earlier they had run across the street, dashing through the soft summer rain, but once they'd reached the safety of the boardwalk with its wide overhang, Cash and JD had tied a silk scarf over her eyes and slowed their step.

"What's the big surprise?" she asked softly.

"If we told you, it wouldn't be a surprise," JD said. She heard the excitement in his voice, and smiled wider.

Finally they came to a stop and Cash released her hand. His hands on her shoulders turned her around, and before her a door opened. Shoving gently, Cash guided her into a room and began to untie the blindfold.

For a moment she didn't recognize Rogue's Palace. Only the long bar and the empty shelves behind it gave the place away.

Everything else had changed. The rickety chairs and tables had been cleared away, and in their place was a desk and swivel chair, a long, sturdy table, and two narrow beds head to head in the far corner. An empty bookcase had been placed near the desk.

"It'll look a lot better when your things arrive from Marianna," Cash said in a low voice. "And if there's anything else you need to make the place complete . . ."

"What have you done?"

He removed a folded sheet of paper from his pocket and handed it to her. She took the paper with trembling fingers. "The place is yours. Rock Creek doesn't need another saloon, but it does need a decent clinic."

She was alternately thrilled and terrified. As exciting as this was, as wonderful, it only proved to her that Cash hadn't lied. Good heavens, he really was leaving and he wasn't coming back. Giving her this place was proof of that fact.

"And the upstairs is great," JD said, bounding up to the top step before turning around to look down at her. "There are four rooms. One for you, one for me, and two that can be converted into rooms for patients. And the storeroom!" he said, rushing back down to open the door at the back of the room. "It's still full of whiskey right now, but once it's cleaned out you can store your supplies here."

"What supplies?" she mumbled.

Cash leaned down and placed his mouth close to her ear. "I ordered you a few things from New York. A stethoscope, a set of surgical knives, a selection of the most common drugs, and—"

She spun on him and looked up. If JD wasn't here she'd throw her arms around Cash's neck and hold on tight. She'd laugh and cry, thank him and beg him to stay. "Why?" she whispered.

"Because you are an incredible woman who deserves to have everything she wants."

"Everything?"

"Almost everything."

JD was oblivious. He went around the room checking every detail. "I told Cash you'd need a big bookcase for all your books," he said. "We built this ourselves."

"You did?"

"Yeah. Show her your thumb, Cash," JD said brightly.

"That's really not necessary," he said in a voice that held a hint of dire warning.

"So," JD said, coming to stand with them. "Do you like it?" It struck Nadine, with a tug of her heart, how tall JD was getting. Had he grown since they'd been here? Or was it just seeing Cash and his son together that reminded her of the time that had passed? JD would soon be a man. A couple more inches, and he'd be as tall as Cash.

"I love it," she said, glancing around the room. Her own office, her own clinic. Tears stung her eyes.

"Great. I'm going back to the hotel," he said, his part of the job done. "I told Teddy I wouldn't be away long." Like a whirlwind he was gone, leaving Nadine alone with Cash.

"You shouldn't have done this," she said softly.

"It'll be good for the town, and for you."

She took his hands in hers and lifted them both, and immediately spotted the bruised thumb on his left hand. "Why didn't you tell me about this?" she said, raising the thumb to her mouth for a kiss.

"If I had known a kiss was your prescribed medicine, I would have shown you my wound right away."

She hadn't seen the bruise last night, since he came to her long after dark and left before the sun came up. He was determined that JD never know about them. He was right, of course, but in keeping their relationship secret she missed so many little things. Walking up the stairs with him at night, going down to breakfast together. Strolling down the street arm in arm, sitting on the lobby sofa with her head on his shoulder at the end of a long day.

She turned away from Cash and walked to the desk, running her fingers along the edge. "You ordered me a stethoscope?"

"JD said the one you had was rather old," he said sheepishly.

"And surgical instruments?"

"Only the best, and they should be here soon. I sent a telegram to the company in New York and offered to pay double if they'd get the order here quickly."

He no doubt wanted to see her settled before he rode away. Nadine turned and lifted herself to sit on the edge of her desk. Her calico skirt swished as she rocked her feet. "I never dreamed I'd have a place like this," she said. "But, dammit"—she felt her face turn warm, and no doubt quite pink, as she cursed—"I don't want to trade you for it."

He forced a crooked smile. "Trust me, it's a pretty good trade."

She wanted to keep him and she didn't know how. "I don't think so," she whispered.

The rain forced them to take their search indoors. Drops pattered against the hotel walls and on the roof far above, and the place was crowded, since no one could stay outdoors.

Uncle Jed and Aunt Hannah and all their babies were in the lobby, and just about everyone in town came to see the triplets and wish the new parents good luck.

They could take the day off, but JD was impatient. The gold was here somewhere, he knew it! Rafe and Teddy were searching for hidden crevices under the lobby stairs, and JD opened the door of the small room where the bathtub was located.

It didn't seem like a logical place to hide a treasure, but since they'd looked everywhere else . . .

He knocked on walls, trying to be quiet so the people in the lobby wouldn't hear. Nothing. Teddy joined him, leaving Rafe to continue the search of the section under the stairs, and together they began to examine floorboards.

The treasure was probably hidden somewhere in the garden, JD thought, and it might take years to find it! He got down on his stomach and squinted to study the boards beneath the heavy tub. Some of the boards had been warped from getting constantly soaked with splashed bathwater, and a couple of them were darker in color than the others. One plank was loose, the end very clearly sticking up above the rest.

His heart skipped a beat. "Teddy, help me move this tub."

Teddy didn't complain about the weight, but took the opposite end and hefted. They moved the tub over so it blocked the doorway, and dropped to their knees. JD's mouth went dry as he reached out and grabbed the end of the loosened board.

The floorboard came up easily, as did the one next to it. Teddy helped him clear away loose boards until a good-sized opening was there for them to peek into.

Gold. Not just coins, but *bars* of gold. Quite a few of them.

Teddy stared at the bars, wide-eyed, for a long while, and then he scurried to the door. "Rafe," he whispered. "Get in here."

Rafe was able to squeeze through the small space. With the tub blocking the door, it could swing open only a few inches. It was quicker to scramble into the tub than around it, and that's what the kid did.

"Look," Teddy said, pointing into the hole.

It was a special moment, one he would surely remember for the rest of his life. A hushed silence filled the room, and then Rafe let out a holler that rang in JD's ears.

"We did it!" Rafe shouted, hopping up and down. "We found the gold!"

JD looked at Teddy and raised his eyebrows. The kid hadn't found anything. Teddy just shrugged his shoulders. He had learned to live with the annoyances of a little brother, JD supposed.

Soon the doorway was jammed with people. People who couldn't get in. "What are you boys doing in there?" Sheriff Sullivan asked, sounding not at all excited.

"We found the gold, Pa," Rafe said, scrambling to the doorway.

"It's not nice to tease your old man," the sheriff joked.

"We're not teasing," Teddy said in a low voice.

JD and Teddy moved the tub aside, just far enough for the door to swing in. Just about everyone was behind Sheriff Sullivan, since they'd all gathered to coo over the new babies. Jed was there, and the schoolteacher Mr. Reese, and Rico. Even the preacher. Cash brought up the rear, and he had a satisfied smile on his face. His eyes landed on JD, and JD smiled back. If he didn't know any better, he'd think Cash was proud of him.

They lifted the bars of gold out of the hole in the floor and handed them along the line and out of the small room, until JD heard a feminine voice, Teddy's ma by the sounds of it, exclaim and then laugh. Then all the women laughed, and the little girls squealed.

One of the babies, disturbed by all the excitement,

started to cry. Another one joined in, and soon the place was in chaos.

When the treasure had been removed from the place where it had been hidden for so long, JD and Teddy joined the others in the lobby to stare at the impressive pile of gold.

JD and Teddy stood side by side, and Uncle Jed came up behind them to place a weighty arm over each one's shoulder. "One day, these two are going to be my best men," he said proudly.

JD smiled.

"Rafe!" Jed called. The kid was on the floor, his eyes riveted to the gold. "You going to come to work for your Uncle Jed one of these days?"

"Sure," he said halfheartedly. "If Ma will let me." The kid looked up and grinned. "We're rich! JD gets half, and Teddy gets half, and I get half of Teddy's half—"

"Not so fast," Cash interrupted in a low voice. All eyes turned to him, and everyone grew silent. "When Eden got this place from that old grump, what was his name?"

"Grady," Eden whispered.

"That's it. When that old grump Grady left Eden this hotel, he said this building and *everything in it* was hers. That includes the gold."

"That is true," Rico said with a curt nod. "I was there, and I remember well."

Mrs. Sullivan looked a little embarrassed. "Well, the boys did find it."

Looking at all the gold, JD wondered what he'd do with half of that pile. He didn't need a big house anymore. And he had a job lined up when he was older and ready. He glanced at Teddy, and Teddy nodded silently.

"Cash is right," JD said evenly. "It's not ours."

Mrs. Sullivan stared down at the gold. After a moment, she cocked her head to one side and smiled. "I have been talking about replacing this sofa for years."

"A sofa?" Hannah Rourke said with a smile. "You can do better than that, Eden."

"Well, we could use an addition to the hotel. I'm afraid we're about to outgrow this place." She laid a hand over her stomach. The sheriff smiled. Uncle Jed cursed. "And a new church!" she said, looking at the preacher and his wife. "Oh, we could build a new church, couldn't we?" She shifted her eyes to the schoolteacher, a tall man who looked nothing like a professor, even holding his youngest daughter in his arms. "And a new school," she added. "A grand school with lots of new books." She looked up at her husband. "Is there enough here to do all that?"

"Twice and then some," the sheriff answered.

"Then we'll set aside money for the boys to go to college," she said with a nod of her head.

Teddy grunted and JD winced. "College?" JD muttered. "I don't need to go to college." What would a detective need extra schooling for?

"What if *I* want to go to college?" Millie asked.

"And the girls, too," Mrs. Sullivan added.

That decided, chaos reigned once again. Everyone talked at once, about plans for the school and the church and the addition to the hotel.

"Add a billiards table to your list of things this town desperately needs," Cash suggested.

"Daniel!" Mrs. Sullivan said, laughing.

The gunman smiled, turned away, and nodded to JD in what seemed to be silent approval.

The next day was the Fourth of July, and Cash dreaded the coming of the celebration and the inevitable leaving. What had possessed him to stay this long? How the hell was he going to leave?

Tonight Nadine had dressed in her fancy white nightgown. She had no idea that the sight of her in white satin sometimes gave him nightmares, and he would never tell her. Besides, she was so beautiful in that nightgown, she took his breath away. It was enough to make him consider changing his name, shaving his beard, dressing in denim and leather, and putting away his holster.

But he would never do that. Inside, he would be the same man, and he would not hide from who he had become. He would not run from who he was. Besides, a change of name and clothes was no guarantee that he wouldn't be found, that his family would be safe.

He stood by the window, and Nadine came to him. "When will you leave?"

"The morning of the fifth," he said. It was the only lie he would ever tell her. Tomorrow night, while she slept, he'd slip away without saying good-bye. It would be easiest, he knew, to leave that way. Like a coward, escaping in the dark of night.

She wrapped her arms around his waist and held on

tight, looking up bravely into his eyes. "I wish I could convince you to stay," she whispered.

He spun Nadine around, unable to look her in the eye any longer, and snaked his arms around her, pulling her back snugly against his chest. "It's been great," he said, trying to sound indifferent. "But I can't stay."

Nadine sighed, melted into his chest and his arms. "I know why you won't stay, but I don't agree. You can protect us."

"What if I can't?"

"Maybe that's a risk I'm willing to take."

"With your life and with JD's?"

She sighed. "Is it such a bad trade? A father who loves you against the possibility of danger. Besides, you're right. JD is almost grown. I can't . . . smother him forever. If you gave him the choice . . ."

Cash's hand dipped down to lay flat over her belly. "And this one? What kind of a choice will this one have?"

She held her breath for a silent moment. "How long have you known?"

"We've been lovers over a month, Nadine." Cash didn't tell her that he'd known about the baby for weeks.

He couldn't explain how he knew, so he kept that information to himself. She wouldn't understand if he told her the understanding had come to him in the same way he knew when a poker player was bluffing, or when a gun was pointed at his back. "Uninterrupted lovers." The hand that didn't press against her belly rose to her breasts and cupped one. "And as of last week, your breasts are fuller. More sensitive." He laid his mouth against her neck. "Were you going to tell me?"

"No," she whispered.

"Why not?"

"I don't want to keep you that way. I don't want to beg you to stay for the sake of the child, and then have you resent us days or months or years from now."

It hurt more than he had imagined it could to know another child would grow up and he wouldn't be around to see it. He hated to leave Rock Creek, but he was grateful to be leaving his family here, where the people would love and care for them, protect them when he could not.

"If I thought you would be safe with me—"

"Ask me if I care about living my life safe," she interrupted, frustrated and close to tears. "Ask me what I want."

He didn't dare.

Fifteen

The day was bright and hot, but the lump in her throat was cold and the celebration was dimmed by the knowledge that come tomorrow, Cash would be gone.

And she would be left alone with a stubborn, almost-grown child and a baby on the way.

She hadn't wanted to tell Cash about the baby for all the reasons she'd told him last night, but she was glad he knew. He deserved to know. He deserved the chance to make the choice to be a part of his child's life this time.

But he was still planning to leave. She had felt it in the desperation and sadness that had tinged his love-making the previous night and that morning. Cash didn't want to go, but he would. And he wouldn't come back.

She had too much pride to beg. She was a woman who could take care of herself no matter what the circumstances. But her life would never be the same. How could he ride away from what they had? It wasn't fair, not to her or to him.

Kids played games in the street, and tables laden with food and drink had been set up along the boardwalk. Flags flew, and red, white, and blue banners hung from many of the businesses, including the Paradise Hotel.

JD and Teddy and Rafe, along with a number of the other boys from town and the surrounding area, played football at the far end of town. She heard them shouting, and they sounded like little boys, not treasure hunters, not budding detectives.

Three Queens had been turned into a family place for the day, and the only drinks the bartender served were lemonade and coffee. Accompanied by Johnny on piano, Lily sang patriotic songs, throwing in a good number of favorite Confederate tunes. Those old war songs were probably not fitting for the occasion, but the crowd loved them. The music and merriment from Three Queens spilled onto the street.

Eden had prepared a number of pies, and she was not the only one. There was to be a pie-eating contest in the afternoon, Nadine had heard, as well as sack races and a number of other games.

Cash was here. She had seen him more than once, mingling sullenly in the crowd. But he didn't join her. He didn't stand beside her with his arm around her shoulder or her waist, the way his friends stood with their wives. He was determined to protect her, still.

She didn't want to be protected. Not from Cash.

Nadine let the sunshine warm her, she listened with an open heart to the beautiful music, but she couldn't make herself truly join in the festivities. Today she didn't feel at all like celebrating.

* * *

"Are you lost?"

Cash turned around to find a smiling Nate descending on him, a baby in his arms, a lightness in his gait.

"Do I look lost, Rev?" Cash asked coolly.

"A little. I don't recall you ever attending one of the town shindigs before."

"I do usually make plans to be far away," he said, squinting at the joyful crowd. "The Fourth of July slipped up on me this year."

Cash laid his eyes on the squirming baby, Angelo, in Nate's arms. He still had a difficult time seeing Nate as a father. "What have you done to your hair?" he asked. "It looks like shit."

"I'm letting it grow. And it doesn't look like shit; you're just not accustomed to it yet."

"I see a little bit of dark hair there," Cash gestured casually to Nate's head as he exaggerated a bit, "but I also see a helluva lot of gray. No wonder you kept your head shaved for so many years."

Nate just laughed. Laughed! The man Cash had fought, drank, and caroused with was still there. He saw the man he remembered, but he also saw more. A man who was content after a lifetime of discontent. A man who was comfortable with who and where he was. It was downright unnatural.

He wouldn't be here long enough to get accustomed to the reformed Nate. Just as well.

"How come you're not escorting Nadine around today?" Nate asked casually. "You're not going to leave her to fend for herself all day, are you?"

Disheartened, Cash sighed. Was there no one in this town who did not see how he felt? "For God's sake, the woman is not my responsibility. I'm sure she can fend for herself quite well."

Nate scoffed. "Don't give me that line of bull. I know you too well, Cash."

That was the problem. Everyone here knew him too well. And he had never been able to fool Nate. "She's too good for me."

"They usually are," Nate confided in a low voice.

He had ridden away without a word before, but this was different. This time he was leaving for good. If anyone deserved to know that, it was Nate. "I'm leaving tonight."

He managed to surprise the Rev. "Leaving? Why? For how long?"

Nate was surprised. At least Eden hadn't spread the news all over town. "I'm not coming back." It hurt to say the words, so he turned his eyes away from the man who saw too much.

Nate didn't argue, at least not right away. Cash felt quite sure there was an argument coming. Drunk, Nate had always managed to have his say. Sober, he was unrelenting.

"Here," Nate said, shifting the baby and deftly depositing Angelo into Cash's arms.

"What the hell . . ." Cash said as he tightened his grip on the squirming kid. "What are you thinking? What if I drop him?"

Nate grinned. "You've never dropped anything in your life unless you planned it. I have every confidence that you will not drop my son." The preacher turned away. "I have to find Jo. Stay right here."

"But . . ." Cash began, but it was too late. Nate was gone.

Cash stared at the baby. Just like he'd told Eden, a toothless parasite. Useless. Ugly. Much too fragile. Angelo looked at the man who held him with complete and total trust, so Cash could add half-witted to the list of infant qualities.

Fiona was one thing; she was like a train and could not be stopped. But Cash had studiously avoided being put in this position with any of the babies who sprouted constantly around town. Hands under Angelo's arms, Cash held it away from him and looked the kid in the eye.

Angelo looked back, kicked his little legs, and smiled. Hmmm. He hadn't known they smiled when they were this little. Maybe babies weren't altogether ugly, Cash decided as he pulled Angelo in a little closer. The big eyes and the fat cheeks were almost endearing.

Angelo gurgled and grabbed his own ear. Moments later, he reached out and grabbed Cash's nose.

"You look just like your father used to," Cash said softly. "Hardly any hair at all, arms and legs a little wobbly, a great deal of drool on your chin." In spite of himself, Cash grinned, and the baby reacted by smiling again and kicking his legs. A few blubbering words of nonsense escaped from the kid's mouth. "And there were many times when he made no more sense to me than you do now."

Angelo was heavy, solid and warm and utterly trusting. Nate knew Cash would never drop his kid, but how did the baby know? What made him trust so easily? Hefted there at Cash's shoulder, Angelo grabbed Cash's ear and tugged gently, gurgling all the while.

Cash's heart constricted. Who would his baby trust? Would it be a boy or girl? Hair on the head or bald? Fat-faced or wrinkled? God in heaven, he wanted to know. And he wanted to hold his own child just like this.

He wanted to marry Nadine, tell JD he was his real father, and be there to raise the baby Nadine carried beneath her heart. For the first time in years, Cash wished he were someone else.

"If you continue to tug on my ear," he said coolly, "I *will* have to call you out." The baby continued to tug. "I see you have no more sense than your father. Did you inherit no good qualities from your mother? Except for her poor choice of husband, she's always seemed to be a fine woman."

Angelo stuck out his tongue and blew bubbles and drool. A disgustingly large glob of the drool landed on Cash's shoulder. It seemed to be the baby's only available method of revenge.

"Sorry," Cash said softly. "I should know better than to insult a man's mother. I'm sure she knew exactly what she was doing when she married Nate."

Jo had married Nate because she loved him. Was that love enough? For them, apparently so. For him . . . it couldn't be that simple.

Could it?

He searched the crowd and found Nadine easily. She looked every bit as miserable as he felt. Like it or not, his life wasn't that simple. What he wanted, what she wanted, wasn't strong enough to make up for what he'd done. But he wished more than anything that fourteen years ago he'd stepped out of that alley, shown himself, and carried Nadine away.

But wishing was a waste of time.

Nate came back to reclaim his child. "See?" the preacher said as he swung his son into his arms again. "Not so bad, was it?"

"I dropped him twice," Cash said without a smile. "You just can't see because I brushed off the dirt." He grimaced at the wet spot on his shoulder. "Disgusting," he muttered.

Nate smiled. "Hell, Cash, I was watching you the whole time. What did you two talk about?"

"The weather."

Nate swung his son about easily. "I want to talk to you before you leave," he said, his expression turning serious. "Come by the church tonight."

"Sure," Cash said. "I'll stop by on my way out of town."

They both knew he was lying.

Music had been playing on the street for some time now as two fine guitarists from a nearby ranch played waltzes and lively Spanish tunes. Nadine had danced with several cowboys, Jed and the sheriff, and a fumble-footed shopkeeper. She caught Cash watching more than once, but he never asked her to dance.

The sun was going down, and soon they would begin their last night together. It broke her heart all over again.

Feeling brave, she walked past partygoers and made her way to Cash on her own. If he was going to reject her, he would have to reject her to her face. He was talking with the teacher, and their conversation centered around plans for the new school.

Nadine tapped Cash on the shoulder. He turned his head and looked down at her, almost as if he were surprised to see her standing there.

"Dance with me," she said quietly.

"I don't . . ."

She took his hand and dragged him away from a grinning Reese. "Don't tell me you don't dance," she said. "I won't believe you."

She stopped in the center of the area that had been set aside for dancing, and tilted her head back to look at Cash as he took her in his arms. A waltz began, an unexpectedly beautiful tune performed by the two guitarists. She had never heard anything like it.

Cash danced beautifully. They moved together in their own rhythm, so accustomed to each other, the dance came to them second nature. Nights spent making love, touching and caressing, had attuned their bodies in a special way. She knew the strength of his arms and he knew the curve of her hip. They moved to the music the way they made love, without a single misstep.

"I knew you could dance," she said.

"I wasn't going to say I don't dance," he said nonchalantly. "I was going to say I don't think it's a good idea."

"Why not?"

His eyes were dark and serious, the tension in the length of his body there for her to see and feel. "Too many people already know about us."

"I'm tired of keeping secrets," she whispered as he swung her around.

Cash apparently was not. He was accustomed to living with secrets; he was used to living his life alone. Solitary. No one to worry about but himself.

"I've been thinking about the baby," he said.

"So have I."

He ignored her. "When the times comes, you can tell everyone that the father is someone from Marianna. Tell them he died, so there will be no reason for anyone to track him down with the news."

She gathered all her strength to argue with him. "I plan to tell everyone this is your child."

Cash paled. "You will not," he insisted.

"And I'm going to tell JD that he's your son."

"I forbid it," he said.

"Well, you won't be here to stop me, will you?" she said angrily.

Cash stopped dancing and dragged her off the makeshift dance floor. Walking faster than was comfortable for her shorter legs, he hauled her down the boardwalk and into an alley far away from the prying eyes of the crowd. He had made love to her here once. He had taken her against the wall at her back.

Right now he was not thinking of that night, or love, or how they came together. He was so angry. His eyes had gone midnight-black, a muscle in his jaw twitched. "If you let the world know that JD and this baby are mine, they will be in danger and so will you."

"Then stay here and protect us," she whispered.

He shook his head. "If I thought I could, I would. But—"

"What are you so afraid of?" she interrupted. "Are you really afraid of putting us in danger? Or are you scared that loving us will change your life?"

"Both," he admitted readily. "I'm a selfish bastard, Nadine. I won't change my life for anyone. I could try, but I'd fail miserably."

"I don't think so." She took his face in her hands. "A selfish man doesn't take the time to guide his son onto the right path. He doesn't turn his favorite place in the world into a clinic. He doesn't hide from what he wants for himself in order to protect a child. And I know you want me, you can't tell me that's not true."

Cash took a deep breath and rested his forehead against hers. "All right, dammit, I'll admit it. I want to stay here. I want to marry you and hold that baby and watch it grow and tell JD that I'm his father. Does that make you happy?"

"Yes."

"Well, it doesn't make me happy. You don't know what my life is like, Nadine. You think we can wash away the last fourteen years like they never happened, but it won't work. Too much has happened, and there are some parts of my life that I can't . . . shake off. I can't start over, it's too damn late. Promise me you won't tell anyone that baby is mine."

"I can't do that," she whispered. "I love you too much to deny your child."

"You don't want to be a part of my life. I've done things, Nadine," he said darkly, trying to be cold, trying to scare her. "Terrible things that keep me up at night."

"I know," she whispered.

"You don't know," he insisted through clenched teeth.

"I know," she said again, so softly her words were no more than a breath of air.

Cash closed his eyes and groaned. One hand raked roughly through her hair, while the other reached down to grasp her hip and pull her tightly against him. "It will never work," he whispered. "No matter how much I want it to, this will *never* work."

"We can make it work," Nadine said confidently.

"Why are you doing this to me now? You know I won't leave you here to fend for yourself, dammit, not if you insist on being so foolish as to tell the world that JD is my child, that the baby you carry is mine."

"I insist."

Cash didn't stalk away from her, release his hold, or curse at her. She expected any one of those reactions, but no matter what he said or did, she would not back down. She loved him. She would not deny that any longer.

Cash placed his mouth close to hers. It seemed that he held his breath, that he waited for the sun to set and night to begin to fall, with gray shadows and a softening of the sky. The night was theirs. They had made it theirs.

"You ask for too much."

"I know."

He took a deep breath, brushed a steady finger down her cheek. "All I want is for you and JD to be safe and happy. To be protected from the mess I've made of my life."

"I don't need to be protected from you, Cash," she insisted. "I love you. Please, please don't go."

They stood there for what seemed like a long time. Silent, barely touching. Nadine was caught up in the way Cash leaned into her, in the scent of his body close to hers, in the strength he had relied on for so long and the love he tried to deny.

His breath caught in his throat. "Marry me," he whispered.

Nadine smiled and raked her lips against his. "Yes."

"Good God, what am I doing," Cash said, lifting her off her feet. "Have I actually let you make an honest man out of me?"

"I certainly hope so."

He kissed her, deep and desperate. He held her tight and made silent promises with his mouth. He did love her; he would not leave her.

"It won't be easy," he said as he placed her on her feet.

"Truly worthwhile things rarely are," she answered.

Cash kissed her again, he very gently touched the side of her breast, and as he lowered his mouth to her neck he whispered in a voice so low and dark she almost didn't hear, "I love you, Nadine. Dammit, I didn't know I could ever love anyone so much."

Her heart felt so light, she was sure it would fly out of her body.

JD made his way into the nearest vacant building, trying to catch his breath. He'd gone looking for his mother to tell her about the football game and the way he'd scored, and he'd found her. He'd found her in an alley with Daniel Cash!

Cash had his hands all over her, and they'd been kissing . . . not a friendly peck on the cheek, but a long mouth-to-mouth kiss. They'd been holding each other so tight, they looked like one person, not two.

No wonder Cash had been so nice to him. No wonder the gunslinger had spent so much time trying to talk him out of following in his footsteps. All so he could make Nadine Ellington happy, so she'd kiss him like that whenever he wanted.

His mother had had no time for men in Marianna. JD had thought one marriage, one love, had been enough for her. But here she was, throwing herself at a gambler and a gunslinger. All so he'd do as she asked? So he'd scare JD out of what he had once wanted?

The tears in his eyes made him angry. He wouldn't cry. Not because his mother was whoring herself to get what she wanted, not because Cash had only pretended to like him to make a woman happy. Men didn't cry when they got mad, JD thought as he threw open the door to the back room of what had once been Rogue's Place. They got drunk.

Sixteen

What had he done? Cash paced the boardwalk in front of the hotel, waiting for JD. Nadine was inside. The last time he'd seen the woman he was going to marry, she'd been talking to Eden, wearing a huge grin on her face. Looking so happy it was as if a light radiated from her.

Beautiful as the sight of a truly happy Nadine was, Cash suffered fleeting doubts. Was he about to make the worst mistake of his life? Or the best decision? He wanted so much to have Nadine and JD and that baby, but he was still terrified of what might happen. He was still afraid they might have to one day pay for his mistakes.

The first step was to tell everyone the news. His friends would not be surprised, he thought. As for those who were not his friends . . . who cared? But JD would be told first. They had decided that for sure. How would the kid take the news that kind, ordinary Joseph Ellington was not his father? That Daniel Cash was?

He wanted it to work so much; if wishing alone could make it so, they would never have another worry.

Movement across the street caught his eye. Lily, dressed in her finest as always, headed toward the hotel, a swing all her own in her step. As she neared Cash and the hotel entrance, she smiled.

"Ah," she said softly. *"Canaille."*

Not even Lily could darken his mood tonight. He shook a finger in her direction. "Speak English, woman. This is Texas, not France."

"I simply called you a scoundrel."

"Oh." He grinned as she stepped onto the boardwalk. "And all this time I thought you were insulting me." He leaned against the post. "The woman who stole my saloon should show the proper respect."

"For the thousandth time, I didn't steal that saloon. It was never yours. You were just a squatter."

"A squatter? Now, that's an insult."

She narrowed her eyes at him as she stepped toward the hotel door. "You are in a very good mood this evening, *canaille*. Why do I get the feeling that means trouble is coming to Rock Creek?"

Lily didn't wait for an answer but sauntered into the hotel with a wide smile on her face. Well, she had a point. For the past several years, the only thing that had made him really happy was . . . trouble. Trouble of the worst possible kind. Could he really change so much, all for a woman and a boy and a baby?

Yeah.

A few minutes later he caught sight of Teddy and Rafe hurrying toward home. Unfortunately JD was not with them.

Teddy nodded as he approached.

"Where's JD?" Cash asked.

Teddy shrugged, and Rafe supplied a more telling answer. "We were playing football, and he just left. I thought he'd come back to play another game, but he didn't. I don't know where he is." He added his own shrug, a belated imitation of his older brother.

Cash wasn't worried as he stepped into the street. JD was thirteen years old, not a child like Fiona. He hadn't gone missing, he just wasn't home yet. Walking down the middle of the deserted street by moonlight, he kept his eyes peeled for a familiar head of dark hair. All was eerily quiet tonight, and a chill ran down his spine. It had been a long day, and it looked and sounded as if the entire town had gone to bed early. Few lights shone from the windows of the homes he passed, no children ran and shouted at this time of night.

JD was bound to turn up soon, Cash thought as he turned around and headed back toward the hotel. He could wait in the lobby. For all he knew, the kid had gone in through the back door and was in his room, asleep after the day's strenuous activities.

Cash was walking back toward the hotel, intending to search and then wait there, when he saw the figure on the street. At first he thought it was a stranger, an armed gunman on the opposite side of the street walking away from Rogue's Palace . . . Nadine's clinic. With the eye of a soldier, he took it all in quickly. Long black duster that disappeared into the night, hat worn low over the eyes, gun belt low on the hips.

It was the swagger that gave JD away, the same swagger he'd fallen into walking away from the river after their last target practice. What the hell . . . He opened his mouth to call out to the boy, but before he could say a word, JD's posture changed in a way that made Cash's heart jump into his throat.

The kid drew and fired, the report explosively loud on the quiet street, the gun aimed high and to the side. Cash took off at a slow run. Down the street, the kid stumbled and righted himself quickly.

Sullivan ran from the hotel, his hand over his weapon, his eyes on JD. But Sullivan wouldn't know it was JD, not in the dark, not with the kid wearing that getup.

"Drop it," Sullivan ordered.

JD ignored the order and fired again, twice in rapid succession, and before Cash's eyes Sullivan took a stance he knew too well. The sheriff drew his gun, he took aim . . . at JD.

Cash was almost alongside Sullivan, still at a run. His heart caught in his throat; his pulse pounded so hard he could hear it and nothing else. He opened his mouth to shout a warning, but it was too late to warn Sullivan that JD was the one walking down the street. It was too late to make him stop.

Without conscious thought, without stopping his run toward JD, Cash drew his gun and fired. Sullivan's gun went flying, and he dropped to his knees, left hand coming up slowly to touch the bloody wound at his shoulder.

Cash continued running toward JD, but he holstered his six-shooter. "Put that down!" he ordered when he was close enough for the kid to hear.

JD stopped, planted his feet and grinned, and swayed drunkenly as he lifted his gun.

Behind him, Sullivan shouted, "The babies are up there!"

Cash threw himself at JD and knocked the gun aside. It went off, the bullet firing harmlessly into the air. "What the hell are you thinking?" he shouted, his hand manacling JD's wrist. Cash looked the kid up and down, noting his own duster, his own hat, a pair of old boots with one-inch heels that were too big for JD's feet.

"I was jus' tryin' to dot the 'i' in Paradise," JD said, slurring his words. If the stench of whiskey hadn't told the story, those words would have.

Cash looked over his shoulder. The "i" in Paradise was positioned between the second and third floors. The upward trajectory would carry the bullets JD fired into the third-floor bedroom Millie and Fiona shared. "Goddammit," he said, dragging JD along with him as he rushed toward the hotel. Sullivan, slowed by the wound to his shoulder, rose to his feet and followed. Jed passed JD and Cash and went to assist his wounded brother-in-law.

Cash dragged JD into the lobby and up the stairs. Dear God, he didn't want his son to be responsible for harming or maybe even *killing* one of the kids in that room. He would do anything to prevent it. Anything. What if he was too late?

As they reached the third floor, he heard Eden crying from that room. Nadine was calmly soothing an unharmed Millie, and Hannah held one of her own babies as if she couldn't ever hold that child close enough.

Fiona.

Cash pushed past the women and dragged JD into the girls' room. Fiona sat on the floor, crying, her head bent over a doll, while Eden soothed her. He saw no blood, though he would breathe easier when he got a closer look at Sullivan's daughter. Just to be certain.

Assured that Fiona was all right, his eyes flicked over the signs of violence in the room. A bullet had slammed into the wall by the door, another had torn into a pillow on the bed. And Fiona lifted her doll for her mother to examine. A bullet had torn through the doll's midsection.

"Do you see what you did?" Cash seethed. "What did you think was behind the Paradise Hotel sign? Did you think the bullets would stop when they hit what you wanted them to hit?"

"JD did this?" Nadine asked, paling as she lifted her head from a weepy-eyed Millie.

JD went even whiter than his mother. "I didn't think . . . I was just aiming for the 'i.' " He glanced around the room, and when he saw where the bullet had torn into the bed, he swayed and lifted a hand to his mouth.

"Nadine," Cash snapped. "Get downstairs. Sullivan's been shot."

"What?" Eden jumped up and followed.

"It's a shoulder wound, nothing serious." He did know enough to aim for a place where minimal damage would be done.

"JD shot the sheriff?" Nadine asked, her voice low and trembling.

"No," Cash said, dragging JD down the stairs and into the lobby where Jed was examining Sullivan on the sofa. "I did."

Before anyone could respond, he dragged JD into

the night, where his son promptly rushed to the edge of the boardwalk and vomited the whiskey he had ingested onto the street. Cash had a very strong urge to join his son, to stand at the edge of the boardwalk and spew his guts. He pushed down the urge and stood there, waiting until the kid was finished retching and gagging, and was so weak he could hardly stand up.

"What got into you?" he asked softly. "What the hell were you thinking?"

JD turned around and lifted his eyes, pinning them to Cash's. Hell, the kid was fearless. "What do you care? I figured you'd be off somewhere poking my mother and wouldn't give a shit what I did." The kid sounded tough, but tears came to his eyes, catching the light that poured from the hotel lobby. "We came to Rock Creek to ask for your help, and you turned my mother into your own personal whore."

Cash grabbed his son by the collar and pulled him up on his toes so they were eye to eye. "If any other man said those things about your mother, he'd be dead now."

"Go ahead," JD said, only the telltale tears marring his tough act. "Shoot me."

His rage dwindled to a simmer, his heart slowed to something close to a normal rhythm. He didn't know how JD had found out, but once the kid knew there was going to be a wedding, that the three of them . . . the four of them . . . were going to be a family, he'd think differently.

"Listen to me, JD," Cash began calmly. Hell, there was so much to say, he didn't know where to start. "Your mother and I . . ."

"You keep your goddamn hands off my mother," JD said, his voice rising slightly.

"JD . . ."

"I hate you," the boy added in a lower voice.

The words, so heartfelt, cut to the core.

"I hate you," JD said again, and Cash had no doubt that the words were true.

Nadine wished she had the instruments Cash had ordered as she worked on the man laid out on his own bed. Sullivan had insisted the climb to the third floor would not be too arduous, but by the time he'd reached his bed, he was about to pass out.

"I'm going to have to remove the bullet," she said calmly.

He simply nodded.

She wanted to talk to Cash and JD, but there was no time. The sooner she got this done and the bleeding stopped, the better off Sullivan would be. She had to force her hands to stop trembling. Thinking about how close JD had come to accidentally taking the life of a child terrified her.

Everyone wanted to watch and to help, but Nadine forced them all, even Eden, from the room. The people surrounding the bed were agitated, weeping and angry. She needed peace and quiet to accomplish her chore.

Once they were alone, Sullivan spoke in a low voice. "I can't believe Cash actually shot me."

"What happened?" Nadine asked as she cleaned the area around the wound.

"I didn't know it was JD out there. All I knew was

that someone was shooting at the hotel, and when I saw where he was aiming, I drew. I panicked. He was aiming right for the girls' room."

"Cash thought you were going to shoot JD."

"I guess so."

Nadine closed her eyes.

"We shouldn't have let the girls have a room on the street side," Sullivan said weakly. "We've been safe for so long we . . . we forgot what it's like to be on guard all the time." He smiled weakly. "Millie likes that room because it gets the morning sun."

Nadine opened her bag and removed a scalpel. She had done this only twice before. Once she'd removed a bullet from the leg of a man who had accidentally shot himself, and another time she'd removed a bullet from the Marianna sheriff's arm. She had never delved into shoulder muscle.

A soft knock on the door interrupted her as she was about to begin. The preacher, Nate, opened the door. "Need some help?" he asked. He had rolled up his sleeves and looked ready to get to work. "I've done this before," he added.

Nadine gratefully waved him in.

What was taking so long? How long did it take to dig out a damn bullet?

Sullivan was tough, Cash reminded himself as he paced in the empty lobby. There was nothing to worry about. Nothing at all.

JD had finally climbed the stairs and into the bed in Nadine's room. The kid was sick, and in the morning he wouldn't feel any better. His head would be pounding and he'd realize what he'd done. That's when the real pain would start.

The babies were finally in bed, and everyone else, *everyone,* waited in the third-floor hallway for the surgery to be finished.

He didn't dare go up there, not now. He couldn't look any one of them in the eye. Especially Eden. He played the shooting over and over in his mind, wondering what he could have done differently. If he'd seen what was happening a split second sooner, would a shout have stopped Sullivan in time? If he'd aimed over Sullivan's head and fired a warning shot, would it have done the trick?

If he'd done anything differently, would Nadine and Nate be upstairs right now, trying to save JD?

He heard a footstep on the stair and turned, hoping to see Nadine with a smile on her face and good news about Sullivan's condition. But it was Eden, all alone and red-eyed.

"Why?" she asked, a hard edge to her voice he was not accustomed to. "Why did you *shoot* him?"

Cash watched as Eden finished walking down the stairs, hanging on to the banister as if she needed the support. Once she reached the lobby, she headed straight for him.

"I had no choice," he whispered. "He was going to shoot JD."

She shook her head. "You could have shouted to him that it was JD. He never would've shot that child."

"It was too late."

"Too late to yell but not too late to shoot?" Eden countered accusingly.

It was his instinct, he had to admit, to shoot first and talk later. So much a part of who he was that he had drawn his gun and shot Sullivan without a single second thought.

"I couldn't let him shoot JD," he said again. The sight of that weapon aimed at the boy had brought out a protective instinct he was unaccustomed to, that he didn't know how to handle. But he wanted Eden to realize why he'd done what he'd done. She was a mother, surely she would understand. "He's my son."

Her red-rimmed eyes went wide. "JD is your . . ."

Cash nodded. "I didn't know about him until they came here, but yeah. He's mine."

Eden's expression softened. "I should have seen it," she whispered. "He does look like you, now that I think about it. He even . . . acts like you sometimes."

How could everything change so quickly? All his plans, everything he wanted, gone. Cash knew it even if no one else did.

"JD might look like me, but he has his mother's eyes," Cash said, feeling a bit dizzy all of a sudden. "Thank God for that." His vision swam, and he tried to blink the fuzziness away. His knees wobbled in a way they never had before. "I'm so glad he has his mother's eyes," he said hoarsely. "I don't want him to see what I've seen."

Eden laid a hand on his arm. "This changes everything for you, doesn't it?" she asked softly.

Cash nodded his head, then shook it. He couldn't stay here, not now. It didn't matter what he wanted, it didn't matter what Nadine wanted. He couldn't stay and he couldn't take Nadine and JD with him when he left. He'd stick around until Sullivan was on his feet again, a few days at most, and then he'd leave.

"Daniel," Eden said.

He looked down into wide blue eyes.

"If Sin dies," she continued once she had his full attention, "I'll kill you."

"He's not going to die," he assured her, something inside him breaking. He hadn't been lying when he'd told Nadine that Eden was like the sister he'd never had. She was gentle and good, but he had no doubt that this woman who would shoo a fly outside rather than swat it would kill him if her husband died.

The surgery was over, and it had gone as well as could be expected. Sullivan's shoulder was bandaged, and he slept deeply. Nate had been a tremendous help, but she'd removed the bullet and stitched the wound herself. Oh, she hoped she was not in for a regular round of this kind of doctoring by opening her clinic in Rock Creek.

She left a much-relieved Eden sitting at her husband's bedside, and walked down the stairs to her room, ready for rest, wondering if she would be able to sleep with the day's events whirling around in her mind.

Everyone else had gone home or to bed, but Cash stood outside her door, back to the wall and head down, those damned six-shooters resting comfortably against his thighs. He lifted his head and laid his eyes on her as she descended from the third floor.

"JD's sleeping in there," he said, nodding toward her door. "He's pretty much spread all over the bed."

"You checked on him?" she whispered.

He nodded. "The room next door is empty and prepared for a guest, so you can sleep there tonight."

You, he said. Not *we.* "Cash . . ."

"I'm going back to my room above the . . . above your clinic," he said before she could question him. "It's for the best, Nadine."

She knew he wasn't talking about one night. Could see in his dark eyes that he was on the verge of running. They'd come so close to starting over, and now . . . she didn't know what to expect next.

"And in the morning?" she asked calmly.

"I'll be here until Sullivan is on his feet, and then I have to go."

She shook her head. "No."

He placed his hands on her face, tender and sweet and trembling. "It was nice to pretend for a little while that we could make it work. But that's all it was, Nadine. Pretend. I can count my true friends on one hand, and tonight I shot one of them."

"Everyone understands . . ."

"That's what my life is like, Nadine. It's not going to change."

"If we want something bad enough, we can make it true."

Cash shook his head in denial. "JD hates me, and with good reason. He's ordered me to leave you alone, and whether or not I like it, the kid's right. I have no business pretending I can stay with you." His thumbs rocked on her cheeks.

"I have to go," he whispered.

"You think you can protect us by leaving, but I won't make it easy for you." She would fight if she had to. She fought now, reaching out to touch Cash tenderly, to lay her hand over his heart.

He ignored her gentle hand on his chest. "I know how you fight, Nadine. I'm prepared to fight back. If you tell anyone that child is mine, I'll deny it," he said harshly. "If you tell anyone I told you I love you, I'll deny it. As far as the world is concerned, I have no son, I have no woman, I have nothing." He dropped his hands from her face and backed away.

Seventeen

Cash had never been plagued with attacks of conscience before. When he couldn't sleep, it was because his mind was going in too many different directions, or because his instincts were telling him it wasn't safe to rest.

But he lay in the bed above what had once been Rogue's Palace, unable to close his eyes. Sullivan was wounded, JD hated him, and Nadine was going to have a child on her own, after he left. A child he could never claim, a child born out of wedlock.

For years he had despised Joseph Ellington for marrying Nadine. He'd cursed the man on nights he'd joined Nate in draining a bottle; he'd blamed Ellington for ruining his life . . . and then, sober again, he would silently and bitterly thank Nadine's husband for saving him from a life of domestic hell.

Knowing what he knew now, that Ellington and Nadine had believed him dead and she'd been carrying his child, he found a kind of respect for Joseph Ellington. There was a quiet nobility in taking in and protecting another man's child.

Cash's heart pounded. Who would protect Nadine

now? Who would look after JD and the baby? He'd gone into battle more times than he could count, during the war and after. He'd hired his gun out to protect those who could not protect themselves. But this was different. A family needed more than a gun. So much more.

Cash left his bed long before sunrise, slipped on one of his lucky shirts, a vest, and his best black suit, and strapped on his guns before stepping onto a quiet Rock Creek street.

It was peaceful, with no sign of last night's bloodshed. All was quiet. This place had been a shithole when he'd first seen it. The people scared, the town dying. Today it flourished, in part because of what he and the other five had done. Bringing this town back to life was one of the few truly good things he'd accomplished in his life. When he looked back, he couldn't find nearly enough good things in his memory.

Nate was a light sleeper, just as Cash was, and it didn't take much of a knock on the rectory door to wake the preacher.

Bleary-eyed with lack of sleep and dressed in nothing but a pair of trousers, Nate opened the door. "What's wrong?"

He and Nate had been through a lot together. They had ridden to hell and back and survived. They'd fought side by side and with each other, kicked ass, celebrated, commiserated . . .

"I need a favor," he said softly.

Without asking what the favor was, Nate nodded his head.

* * *

Nadine was so tired, she didn't want to wake up, not even to that familiar hand shaking her shoulder. It was barely light outside, gray and quiet. The perfect time for sleeping.

"Nadine," Cash called, shaking her shoulder again.

She was so accustomed to waking with him at her side, it took her a moment to remember that he hadn't stayed with her last night. She opened her eyes to find him hovering over her, dressed and somber.

"What's wrong?" Someone must be hurt, or very ill, for him to come to her this way.

"You said you would marry me."

"I did."

"Then let's do it now."

She smiled softly. "Right now? Oh, I'm so glad you changed your mind—"

"I didn't change my mind," he interrupted. "I'm still leaving, but . . . for the sake of the baby, I want us to be married. When he's older you can let him know that . . . that I did do the right thing. By then no one will care about Daniel Cash."

Because he'd be dead. The words were unspoken, but she knew what he meant. He was going to leave Rock Creek and go out there and get himself killed.

"You're doing this just for the baby?" she whispered.

"Yes."

She should tell him to go to hell, that she didn't want him this way. He looked so miserable, she didn't have the heart. "All right."

Nadine dressed while Cash paced, not bothering to root through her things to search for something special.

A green calico skirt and linen blouse would do just fine. She tied a ribbon at the nape of her neck, capturing the thickness of her hair instead of taking the time to twist it up.

When she was ready, Cash took her arm and led her down the stairs, onto the street, and toward the church. His steps were too long, too fast, and she hurried to keep up. Outside the church doors, he stopped, took a deep breath, and muttered a foul word. Then he threw the doors open and walked inside, where Nate and his wife waited.

Cash closed the doors behind them, then glared accusingly at Jo, who held a sleeping baby in her arms. "I said no one," he muttered.

"We need a witness," Nate said. "Jo won't tell anyone."

"So this is a secret, too?" Nadine asked as they walked toward the altar.

"Yes. Eventually the people who count will know. That's all that matters."

She had always heard that weddings were supposed to be happy occasions. Neither of her weddings could be called happy. The first wedding had been horrendous. Her father demanding, her heart breaking. Had she stopped crying for even five minutes that day? Not that she could remember. She'd thought Danny dead, and the only reason she'd had for going on was the baby she carried.

And now . . . their marriage would be a secret, her baby would never know his father, and in a matter of days Cash would leave her again. This time she wouldn't be able to naively fool herself into thinking he would be coming back one day.

The solemn words Nate spoke didn't mean a lot to her. This ceremony was a legality, nothing more. A way for Cash to soothe his conscience a little. A wedding should be the beginning of a wonderful life, but all throughout her secret wedding she kept thinking that *this* ceremony marked the end.

Married. It was a circumstance he had avoided, ridiculed, frowned upon, and now entered. Like fatherhood, the condition required more than Cash had ever been able to give. Lucky for him, this marriage wasn't real. Yeah, he was a real lucky guy. So why did he have a boulder sitting in his stomach?

Holding Nadine's hand, all but hauling her behind him in the early morning light, he headed for Rogue's Palace. More specifically, he headed for the bed above stairs, where he had not been able to sleep last night. He wasn't planning on sleeping now.

"Where are we going?" Nadine asked as he led her into the dim clinic that had once been his saloon.

"Where all newlyweds go, darlin'. To bed."

"Cash . . ."

"Satin sheets," he said, not bothering to turn around and look at Nadine. If he did, how could he continue to convince himself that he didn't care about losing her? "Whiskey, if you need it." God only knows, he might need a swig or two to get through the next few days.

As soon as he stepped into the room, Cash released Nadine's hand and shrugged off his coat. With his back to her, he began to undress. The vest and shirt went first, and then he turned around to find Nadine standing in the doorway, staring at him as if he were a stranger.

It would be best if she turned and walked away right now. Clean break, no tender feelings left, no annoying hope that things might work out. "What are you waiting for?" he asked coolly. "Lose the clothes."

Nadine cocked her head and studied him with eyes that saw too much.

"Hurry up," he said. "Don't we have to consummate the marriage for it to be legal?"

"Is that why we're here?" she asked softly.

"Yes." He waited for his bride to turn and run, as she should, but instead she stepped into the room and closed the door behind her, unbuttoning her blouse as she walked toward him.

"That took a long time to heal, didn't it?" she asked, nodding to the scar on his side.

He glanced down. "I guess it did."

Nadine whipped the blouse over her head and began to unbutton her skirt. "Turn around."

He did as she asked, stiffening as she laid her hand over the scar on his back. "What's this one?"

"Knife. The only time I never saw it coming. If Nate hadn't been there—" He stopped in midsentence as Nadine ran her fingers down the old scar.

"They look different by daylight," she said. "Meaner. Harsher."

"So do I," he said as he turned to face her.

They finished the job of undressing, not assisting each other as they usually did, but circling around restlessly and dropping one piece of clothing at a time until they were both naked.

Nadine didn't look harsher by daylight. She looked as beautiful as ever, perfection in his very imperfect world.

"This one," she said, laying her hand over the scar on his thigh.

"Shot by a whore," he said, keeping the complicated story simple, making it ugly.

She didn't recoil in horror but caressed the scar. "Do you know much I hurt for each and every one of these scars? The big ones, the small ones." She traced the fingers of her other hand over a very thin, tiny mark on his forearm. He couldn't even remember how he got that one. "I can heal just about anything, but I can't do a damn thing about your scars." She lifted his arm and laid her lips over the insignificant mark, tenderly, eyes closed and lips slightly parted.

She took her time, kissing each scar, tracing every mark with gentle fingers and then tasting, caressing, healing. Circling around him slowly, constantly moving, she kissed and traced the small scars on his back. She even knelt before him and kissed the puckered mark on his thigh. While she kissed him there, one hand rested on his erection, the fingers deftly stroking while she ran her tongue from the scar to his inner thigh and back again.

When she rose to her feet, she wrapped her arms around him and kissed him one more time, there above his heart, her soft lips lingering where the flesh was unmarked, as if she tasted every beat.

He laid her on red satin sheets, parted her thighs

with his hand, and entered her quickly. She was ready. Wet and welcoming, she lifted her hips and took him in. He made love to her fast and hard, eyes on the tantalizing sight of pale flesh on red satin, of perfect flesh against his own imperfect body, her gentle curves against his hard planes.

Eyes closed, she openly savored every stroke, welcomed every thrust, until she parted her lips and shuddered, her inner muscles grabbing him, squeezing as she climaxed with a hoarse cry. Cash drove deep one last time, came hard and fierce while Nadine still quivered beneath and around him.

And when he drifted down to cover her sweating body with his, she smiled and hummed in contentment. But then, she didn't know this was the last time they would ever be together this way.

His head pounded, and he didn't want to open his eyes. The bit of light that shot through his closed eyelids hurt badly enough. Oh, he would never drink another drop of whiskey, he swore it.

"Come on, JD," a gruff voice commanded. "Wake up."

He opened one eye to find Cash glaring down at him. JD swallowed hard. Had he really threatened to kill Cash last night? Had his mother really taken up with the gunslinger who had once been his hero?

"We need to talk."

JD sat up, trying to hide the fact that it *hurt* to move. "I don't have anything to say to you," he mumbled.

"Well, I have plenty to say to you." Cash tossed him his trousers and shirt, leaving the borrowed duster and hat on the chair by the window, where he'd placed them the night before.

Delving into Cash's trunk, stealing the gunslinger's things, had made JD feel big for a few minutes. Now he just felt like a thief.

But since it was impossible to argue in his underwear, he dressed quickly. "I don't need you to tell me I made a big mistake."

"I don't imagine I do," Cash said, staring out the window while JD dressed.

"And I don't plan to make drinking a regular diversion."

"I certainly hope not."

That could mean only one thing. Cash intended to talk about his mother. It was a discussion JD wasn't looking forward to. He tried to remember exactly what he'd said last night, but he couldn't. It hadn't been pretty, he knew that much.

"All right," JD said, straightening his spine. "What do you have to say?"

Cash turned around, his eyes raking over every corner of the room as he moved. "Not here," he said softly. He stalked from the room, and JD followed.

He knew almost as soon as they left the hotel where they were headed. The river. JD's dread grew with every step. For all he knew, Cash planned to beat the tar out of him. For taking his things, for shooting into Millie and Fiona's bedroom. For ordering Cash to stay away from his mother. JD took a deep breath and fought back the nausea and pain. Hell, maybe Cash should beat the tar out of him. Not for warning him away from Nadine, not for something so small as borrowing his clothes. But for shooting into the hotel . . . maybe he'd feel better if someone did make him pay.

Cash went to the rock that jutted over the water and sat, looking toward the east, relaxing. He didn't look like he was about to beat anyone up. "Have a seat," he said.

JD sat beside the gunslinger, who continued to stare out over the water as if there were something special there. Something besides sun on flowing water, wildflowers, and a scraggly collection of birds.

Something about the harshness of the morning sunlight made Cash look older. There were lines around his dark eyes, lines bracketing his stern mouth. It was almost as if he'd aged overnight. Maybe he had. Maybe they all had.

"I don't want you to think that I, or anyone, would ever disrespect your mother," Cash said. He turned and planted his black, narrowed eyes on JD. "I've loved her since I was not much older than you are now. She's a fine woman. If I made a few mistakes, it was because I loved her too much. You were right to defend her," he added darkly. "I respect that."

"I didn't think you loved her. I just thought—"

"Not that I want you to tell her I said that," Cash interrupted curtly. "That's just between us. A little secret."

"Sure," JD said, feeling confused. Why was something like that a secret?

"I'm leaving town soon," Cash said. "I'm sure you'll take good care of your mother after I'm gone."

"Yeah," JD said, his heart sinking. Was Cash leaving

because he'd warned the gunslinger to leave his mother alone? "But you don't have to—"

"She's a good woman," Cash interrupted again. "Remember that, no matter what. If anyone made any mistakes here, it was me."

He actually looked sad, which made JD feel guilty all over again.

Cash stared out over the water again, squinting against the sun. "About your father," he began. And then he became silent for so long, JD began to get anxious.

"What about him?" JD finally urged.

"Joseph Ellington was a good man," Cash said. "The finest. I hate that he died before you had a chance to really know him."

"Everybody says that about him," JD said, leaning slightly forward to look at Cash's stony face.

Cash nodded. "That's it. Go home, JD."

JD ran, leaving the gunfighter sitting by the river.

Cash made his way slowly into town, taking his time, thinking about the days to come. That stupid yellow dog was soon right beside him.

"Get lost, mutt," he mumbled.

The mutt didn't have the sense to obey, but continued to lope along with his tongue hanging out and his tail wagging.

In the days ahead, he would do everything in his power to make sure that Nadine and JD and the baby were taken care of. He had never asked much of his friends, not since the end of the war. But he was going to ask now. He would beg if he had to.

The dog danced in his path, making Cash come up short again and again. He cursed mightily under his breath, but before long he got used to the mutt.

"My kid likes you, you stupid dog," Cash said as he approached town. "He'd call out a gunslinger to keep you safe." JD was almost a man, and in spite of the mistakes he'd made . . . and he'd made plenty of them . . . he had a good heart. The boy had his mother's heart and his mother's eyes. Thank God.

Reese's house came into view, and he headed in that direction. The dog headed for Lily's place, where a meal no doubt awaited him.

A man might become a teacher, Cash thought as he approached Reese's house, he might put aside his soldiering to settle down, but deep down he was still the same man who had led them into battle and kept them all alive. And he had brought them here.

He knocked on the door soundly since he heard a baby's cry from inside the house. Reese answered the door, dressed in perfectly ordinary clothes for a perfectly ordinary day. His youngest daughter, a sniffling Virginia, clung to his shoulder.

"Sullivan?" Reese inquired crisply.

"Doing well as of an hour ago," Cash said.

Reese nodded, and when Mary came to the door he handed the baby over and stepped onto the porch, closing the door behind him.

Cash put all his pride aside. "I need your help."

Nadine examined Sullivan's wound, happy with its appearance.

Just a couple of hours earlier she had come awake,

alone in Cash's bed, wondering if she'd just woken from a dream. The wedding, the way he'd made love to her afterward . . . a mixture of emotions and sensations, so beautiful and sad at the same time, could not be real. Could they?

But coming awake wrapped in red satin sheets, finding her clothes tossed around the room . . . she knew what had happened was all too real. She also knew that if she didn't do something soon, she was going to lose Cash forever.

"You should rest for a few more days," she instructed as she rebandaged Sullivan's wound. "If you need help during your convalescence, I'm sure Cash would be happy to take on some of your duties, maybe act as deputy until you're on your feet." She knew Cash wanted badly to do something to make amends.

Sullivan shook his head. "Daniel Cash? The law in this town? Not even for one day."

"That's hardly fair," Nadine said softly.

"Fair? If word got out that Cash was acting deputy, this place would be overrun with ambitious gunfighters. I don't need that. None of us do. I have a deputy. If Marlon needs help, Jed and Rico will fill in until I'm able. I don't expect that will be more than a couple of days."

"Don't hold a grudge—" she began.

"I'm not rejecting the offer because Cash shot me," Sullivan interrupted. "Eden explained everything," he added in a low voice.

"She did?"

"She also said Cash doesn't want anyone to know."

Nadine shook her head. "I don't understand why he's so determined to keep it a secret."

"I do," Sullivan said kindly in spite of his current predicament. "Cash shot me without thinking twice, to protect that boy. I can't blame him. I'd do the same thing to protect any one of my kids."

"You should tell him that," Nadine suggested. "He's so sure this has ruined . . . everything. All he wants is to start over. You did that, and so did the others. Why is Cash so certain he can't do the same thing?"

"When you have a name like Cash does, it's not so easy," Sullivan said, his voice low and understanding. "He's like a brother to me, and if I could make things right for him, I would. But his life is catching up with him, and I don't think he's got any place left to hide."

Nadine closed her eyes. So many secrets. A son, a marriage, a baby. And no place to hide for any of them.

Eighteen

It would be so easy to indulge in one wedding night. One last night in Nadine's bed, one night where everything in his life was as right as it was ever going to be. She was his wife, they were together, to hell with tomorrow.

But that was impossible. He wanted more than anything to cross the street and walk up the stairs to Nadine's room, but he wouldn't for three very good reasons. First of all, leaving was already going to hurt too much. Best to make a clean break, and sooner was always better than later. He also had to consider the possibility that if he indulged in one more night with Nadine, she would talk him into staying. For another week, for another month. Forever. He had a feeling he would not put up much of a fight in the right circumstances.

But it was the third reason that kept him in his chair in Three Queens. If he went to Nadine now, she would know how he felt. She would romanticize their time together and after he left she would wait for him to come back. The faithful wife, waiting for her vagabond husband. He couldn't do that to her, give her hope where there was none.

He shouldn't have taken her to his room after the solemn, hellish wedding that morning. He'd meant the episode to be cold physical pleasure and nothing else, a distant and heartless good-bye. But with a touch and a word, Nadine had come too close to making their last joining something more, a meeting of the heart as well as the body.

She had such hope, such foolish optimism. Hell, not going to her tonight would not be enough. He'd have to make her understand that she meant nothing to him. That once he left Rock Creek, he would never come back.

Lily was onstage singing. Usually such entertainment in an otherwise perfectly good saloon annoyed him, but tonight he liked it. Rico's wife had never cut Cash any slack, and there were times when the very sight of her got his hackles up. But, he had to admit, the sound of her voice was oddly soothing tonight. It made him forget for a few minutes what he'd done and what he still had to do.

Rico joined him at the table. The kid wasn't wearing his usual easy grin as he pulled out a chair and sat. They didn't have much to smile about tonight.

"Jed said Sullivan is doing well. Complaining that the doctor will not let him out of bed, but that is to be expected."

Cash just nodded.

"He is *robusto*. He will be on his feet in no time."

"English, kid," Cash said without any real fire in his voice or his heart. He took a deep breath and stared not at the man across the table but at the whiskey before him. "If it had been daylight, I would have shot the gun out of his hand. But it was too dark, and I was running, and Sullivan was moving. I didn't want to shoot his gun hand, maybe blow off a finger or damage the muscle so that he'd have to learn to shoot with his left. He was never very good with his left hand, you remember?"

"*Sí.*"

"I could've winged him in the leg and that would've dropped him, but it wouldn't have made him drop his gun, and he still would've fired at JD." Cash finally lifted his eyes from the whiskey. Did they all look at him differently now? Would they forever look at him differently? They fought, they argued . . . but they didn't shoot one another.

"It is not your fault," Rico said softly.

"How could it possibly not be my fault?" Cash asked, his voice sharp. "I shot him."

"To save a child," Rico said. "Your child," he added softly.

Cash almost laughed. "Eden told you?"

"No one told me, *amigo.*" Rico gave in to a weak smile. "JD walks like you, with that I-dare-the-world-to-stop-me swagger."

Cash lifted his eyebrows slightly.

"He has your mouth," Rico continued.

"No, he has his mother's—"

"Not the shape," Rico interrupted. "The tendency to say that which should not be said in a way that is sure to offend everyone." His quick smile faded. "He stands like you, he squints at the sun like you . . . he eats a biscuit like you do."

"There's only one goddamn way to eat a biscuit," Cash said through clenched teeth.

Rico didn't argue.

"So everyone knows," Cash said, fiddling with his glass.

"I do not think so," Rico said in a low voice. "Remember, Sullivan taught me to watch, to look for the small things that might give a man away. If anyone else has noticed, they have not mentioned it to me."

Cash shook his head. One more reason to leave town. The less often he and JD stood side by side, the less likely it was anyone else would notice the similarities. "It doesn't matter that JD is . . . mine. There should've been another way."

"If there had been another way, you would have found it."

Cash sighed and pushed his whiskey away. He might not have his wedding night with Nadine ahead of him, but he did need to speak to her. The whiskey didn't give him courage for the confrontation to come, it made him weak.

"That kid has such a temper," he said beneath his breath. "And pride, more than is healthy. He's too young to back up that smart mouth of his." Cash lifted his eyes to Rico. "Would you do something for me?"

"Of course."

"Don't tell anyone he's mine. The name Cash isn't exactly a fine gift to lay on a young man."

"He might not agree."

Cash shook his head. "It's what I want."

Rico nodded solemnly.

"And after I'm gone, teach the kid how to handle a knife," Cash added. "I swear, he's going to need all the help he can get." His insides twisted at the thought.

"I will do what I can."

"Don't tell anyone that I asked you to teach him. Make it look like it's your idea."

"If you wish." Rico looked only slightly puzzled. "When are you leaving?"

"When I know Sullivan is going to be all right."

"And when are you coming back?"

To hell with this. Cash pulled his whiskey toward him and finished the glass. Lily finished her song to a lively round of applause that made his head ache.

"I'm not," he said as he pushed his chair back, and stood slowly.

Nadine fidgeted as she walked down the stairs and into the hotel lobby. Sullivan didn't look quite as good as she wanted him to, and she hadn't seen Cash since she'd awakened alone in his bed. All in all, it had been a distressingly horrible wedding day.

What had she expected? That Cash would tell the world that he loved her and they were married? No, he had never promised her anything like that. He'd married her for the sake of the child. Had he finally had an attack of conscience? Unlikely. The man who had made love to her that morning apparently had none.

He was waiting for her in the lobby. At least, she assumed he waited for her. Stony-faced and rigid, he paced before the green sofa. When he caught sight of her, he stopped pacing and lifted his head. If there was any tenderness for her in his heart, he didn't show it.

"Sullivan's all right?" he snapped.

"Considering what he's been through . . ."

"Considering that I shot him, you mean."

Nadine ran her fingers through hair that had come

undone hours before. "No one blames you . . ." she began.

"I blame myself," he said softly. "Is he going to recover completely?"

"I'll know in a day or two." She walked toward him. "Come on. Let's grab a bite to eat and get to bed. Eden said there are biscuits and ham in the kitchen." She gave Cash a wan smile. "She's sitting with Sullivan now. If sheer will can save him, he'll be completely recovered by morning."

Cash looked her dead in the eye, and she saw . . . nothing. No love, no regret. Nothing. "I'm not hungry. You go ahead." He didn't move from his position, or even relax.

What she really wanted was for him to love her. She wanted to sleep in his arms, and forget all that had happened in the past day. Looking at him standing there, she felt certain no love existed in his mind or in his heart. "And you'll be waiting for me upstairs when I'm finished?"

"I think not," he said coolly.

She was too tired to fight with him, too weary to wrestle through his stubbornness and his worries to get to the truth. "We're married."

"Good God, don't remind me," he said with disdain. "I never thought the day would come. After all these years of so carefully avoiding the trap of marriage, I was finally done in. Should have known it would be you to do it."

Nadine shook her head. "I know you still plan to leave," she said softly. "I want to change your mind, but you've made it quite clear that I don't have the power to do that. I promise I won't even try if it'll make you feel better." She needed him tonight. She'd make whatever promises were necessary.

"It's not that," he said, flicking at a piece of dust on his cuff. "I'm just"—he shrugged his shoulders— "done with you."

"Done?" she whispered, horrified.

"It was fun while it lasted, and I do regret the fact that I knocked you up, but—"

"Fun while it lasted?" she interrupted. "What's gotten into you?"

"Nothing." He planted those cold dark eyes on her again, and she didn't dare take a single step closer. "Don't tell me you believed all the things I said." He sounded only slightly horrified. "I was lonely, you came along . . ." He shrugged his shoulders again. "Hellfire, Eden and the other fine ladies of Rock Creek manage to reform or run off every hooker who finds her way to town. What's an unmarried man to do?"

Nadine felt her heart turn into stone and sink heavily. "I don't believe you," she whispered. Oh, but he didn't look like he was lying. He looked completely, deadly serious. "You said you couldn't stay with us because of your reputation, because you'd put us in danger."

"A convenient excuse I've used before," he said distantly.

"But—"

"Oh, for God's sake, Nadine," Cash interrupted curtly. "Do you have no pride? I just told you that I don't—want—you." He snapped out each word so she'd be certain to understand.

And she did understand, all too well. "I don't know you."

"You never did."

"I was just . . ."

"A convenient woman," he finished for her.

So tired and taken aback that she could not think straight, Nadine cocked her head and looked at Cash with new eyes. "You said you loved me," she whispered. She had waited so long to hear him say those words, and now . . . he was taking them back. He was taking it all back.

"I've said those very same words to more women than I can count. They're pretty, powerful words that will usually get a man where he wants to go."

He had used her the way a man like him used any woman who was foolish enough to allow herself to see only what she wanted to see. To fabricate love where there was none.

She imagined there had been women who threw themselves at his feet when he sent them packing. When he was *done* with them. But she would not beg. She had too much pride to throw away what was left of her dignity.

"I've tried so hard to get through to you," she said tiredly, the events of the day catching up with her in a way that made her dizzy. "But I can't do this alone. When two people are together, truly *together,* they both have to give some of themselves. You don't do that, Cash. No matter how hard I try . . ." She shook her head. "I can't struggle like this every day just to get through to you. Loving someone shouldn't be a constant battle."

"It seems I'm leaving just in time," he said, not at all moved by her frustrated plea. "Already tired of patching up my messes, are you? Can't say that I blame you."

"I do hope you'll tell JD good-bye before you leave," she said in a low, almost calm voice.

"Why? The kid hates me."

"He does not," she said quickly. "Don't break his heart by riding out of town without a word." She took a deep breath and headed for the kitchen. "I'm going to eat something. I imagine you'll be gone when I get back."

"I imagine I will."

She held back the silent tears until there was no way he could see her face. As she entered the kitchen, she heard the hotel door slam.

He'd finished off last night in Three Queens before they'd closed up and thrown him out. Not interested in sleeping, he'd spent the rest of the night roaming the town, even walking down by the river. He'd spent part of the night in the Paradise Hotel garden, standing in shadows and looking up at the dark window of Nadine's room.

He was a bastard in every sense of the word and had always been, but what choice did he have? None. No choice. For once in his life he could do something right. He could make a clean break of this so Nadine could get on with her life. And so she wouldn't mourn too hard or long when he finally got himself killed.

Not long after the sun came up, he found himself knocking on the door to Three Queens. Eventually Lily came to the door and opened it.

"Merde! We are not open, *canaille."* She looked sleepy, straight from the bed. "I am beginning to wish that *salle terrible* of yours was still in operation. Do you not have any whiskey left. . . ."

"Can't you insult me in English?" he snapped.

She smiled. "If you wish."

He took a deep breath and lifted a hand, silently offering a truce. "Rico adores you," he admitted grudgingly.

Lily relaxed, her face softening as she leaned against the doorjamb. "And I him."

"I'm guessing he told you about JD."

She nodded.

"It would really be best if as few people as possible knew. I don't have any reason to suspect that you would give a shit what I want, but—"

"It is your secret to keep or tell," she interrupted.

Cash breathed a sigh of relief. "Thank you," he said softly.

Lily lifted her eyebrows in surprise.

"No reason to look shocked," Cash said indignantly. "I do have a few good manners left."

"Go to bed, *canaille,"* Lily said as she started to turn away. "You look very tired. No reason to fret. Your secret is safe here."

"Wait," Cash said, interrupting her departure. "I just need to ask you one more favor."

Nadine didn't like the way Sullivan lay back in his bed, unnaturally content to be there. He was too pale, a pallor to his normally dark skin.

Fiona had crawled onto the edge of the bed. Nadine had tried to gently move the little girl, knowing a simple shaking of the bed would be painful for Sullivan. But the sheriff had waved Nadine off and wrapped his good arm around his daughter.

Nadine was stitching the hole in Fiona's doll, mending the damage done by a bullet JD had fired, while father and daughter visited.

"What happened, Daddy?" Fiona asked, leaning over him to look at his bandaged shoulder.

"Nothing."

"Who hurt you?" She pouted. "Nobody will tell me anything. They think I'm still a baby,"

"Nobody hurt me, Fiona. It was just an accident."

Nadine kept her head down and listened. Cash thought he was on his own, always, when he had friends who would protect him this way.

"Does it hurt?" Fiona asked.

"No."

"Then why are in you bed?"

"It doesn't hurt, but it does make me a little tired."

"Oh."

Nadine looked up just in time to see Fiona lay her head down on her father, using his chest as a pillow.

It broke her heart to think that Cash didn't want this. A home, a family, the friends who would do anything for him. She still wanted to fight for what she wanted, but like Sullivan, she was tired. Tired of being the only one who cared enough to fight. Tired of watching Cash do his best to destroy himself.

"All better," Nadine said, holding the mended doll up for Fiona to see.

Fiona bounded off the bed, and Sullivan winced. Not much, but Nadine noticed. It was her job to notice.

"Did it hurt?" Fiona asked as she took the doll, poking one little finger at the stitched midsection of the soft toy.

"Not a bit."

"Good. I'm going to go show Mommy." Fiona skipped from the room, and Nadine moved to Sullivan's bedside.

"You look beat," the sheriff said, attempting a smile. "If you don't watch it, you'll end up somebody's patient."

"I'm fine," she said, reaching out to lay a hand on his forehead. He was too warm, dammit. "Let's change that bandage and see what we've got."

Eden sat down slowly, taking the closest chair to the kitchen door. The dining room was empty. She needed rest but wished for chaos to take her mind off the events of the past two days. She had prepared an early supper for everyone, and all she wanted to do now was climb the stairs, slip into the bed with her husband, and hold him close while she slept.

She had never thought to see Sin shot. She had certainly never thought it might be Daniel who would do the shooting. Throughout the previous day she had remained at Sin's side, and most of that day, too. Nadine had been in a horrid mood all that day. Eden only hoped the healer's bad disposition was not caused by something she saw in her patient.

Her wish for chaos was answered in a way when

Daniel appeared in the doorway between the dining room and the lobby. She hadn't spoken to him since threatening to kill him if Sin died. She had meant it at the time, but knowing JD was his son, she did understand why he'd done what he'd done. A little.

"How is he?" Daniel asked.

"Nadine is with him now."

Daniel walked into the room, taking in everything as he always did. Something in him had changed since the shooting. This was the man she'd first met on arriving in Rock Creek. There was something dark about him, something more animal than human. Oh, he could be civilized and charming, but he cared for nothing and no one and didn't care who knew it. He'd shed some of that darkness over the years. At least, she'd thought he had.

He sat down on the chair across the table from her and leaned forward. Her heart went out to him no matter what he'd done. Darkness or no, he was hurting. He looked like he hadn't eaten or slept since Sin had been shot. He might not admit it, but he did care. As deeply as anyone.

"Let me make you something to eat," she said, beginning to rise. It was a slow and easy effort. She hadn't slept much herself in the past two days.

"No," he said. "Sit down."

She gratefully did as Daniel asked, looking at him and wondering if she'd ever be able to see him as she once had. He had been her friend, a part of the family she'd made for herself.

"I have no right to ask you for anything," Daniel said. "I certainly have no right to ask you for a favor."

"What kind of favor?"

He glanced toward the kitchen, the windows, the doorway. "Nadine is going to have a baby," he whispered.

In spite of her exhaustion and worry, she managed to smile. Nothing but a baby could make her smile at a time like this, she imagined. "That's wonderful."

Daniel didn't smile. In fact, nothing in his sharp face so much as twitched. "I want you to be there for Nadine when she has the baby. You've taken care of all of us in one way or another. I want you to promise me that you'll take care of Nadine. Be her friend. Help her with the baby."

"You make it sound like you won't be here."

"I won't," he said softly.

Eden sighed. "You can't leave now! How could you?" She shook her head as she might have when one of her own children did something foolish. "I told you to stay away from her. I knew something like this would happen." She put on her most intimidating face. "You have to marry her, Daniel."

"I already did." Again, he looked toward all the entrances. "But no one can know that, and I don't want you to tell anyone about the baby or the wedding. Not yet."

"I don't understand."

"Of course you do," he snapped. "I can't . . ." He took a deep breath and ran a hand through his hair. "I can't stick around and become the family man. Settle down and change my ways and . . . and . . ."

"And let someone love you?" Eden finished.

He laid dark eyes on her. "She deserves better than to live her life waiting for a bullet to take me out, and she certainly deserves better than to get caught in the cross fire."

"You shouldn't be afraid," she said gently.

"I am not *afraid* of anything," he insisted.

"Of course you are. I saw the same fear in Sin when I fell in love with him. Being alone is easy," she whispered. "Loving someone is hard. It makes your life better, but it also opens your life to more heartache and pain than you're prepared for, because you have more than yourself to worry about. When Nadine hurts, you hurt. When JD is in danger, you feel it deep inside."

She could tell by the fleeting expression of horror on his face that she had hit the nail on the head. And she also knew there was nothing more she could say. "And, Daniel, I really wouldn't kill you. I'm sorry I lost my temper and said I would."

"If anything happens to Sullivan, I'll put a gun in your hand and you'll have my blessing to pull the trigger."

The very idea made her heart skip a beat. How could he say something like that so casually?

Fiona came running into the room, putting an end to their conversation. She carried that old rag doll with her, and when she reached the table, she climbed into Daniel's lap, uninvited.

"Look, Uncle Cash, Dr. Nadine fixed my doll." She lifted the doll's dress to show off a neatly stitched dolly tummy.

"That's great, sweetheart," Daniel said. He had his head turned down, and still Nadine could see the pain in his eyes. For the years he'd missed with JD, perhaps. For the years he'd miss with the new baby Nadine carried.

"She sewed her up just like she sewed Daddy."
Fiona turned wide, innocent eyes up to Cash. "Do you
think it hurt? Daddy said it didn't hurt, but he looked
like it hurt a little."

Daniel swallowed, his face went pale. "I'm sure if
he said it didn't hurt, it didn't. Your papa wouldn't lie
to you."

"No," Fiona said decisively. "Lying is *bad*. Mommy
said so. My daddy would never lie."

Daniel stood with Fiona still in his grasp, swinging
her around so that she giggled, before setting her on
her feet. "That's right, sugar," he said. "Your daddy
would never lie. He's a good fella. The best."

Eden's first real smile of the day came to her face.
Everything was going to be all right. When she looked
up, an obviously exhausted Nadine stood in the doorway.

"Fiona," Nadine said, her eyes very purposely staying away from Daniel. "Would you go upstairs and
see what Millie's up to?"

"She's reading," Fiona said, making a face. She was
still quite put out that she could not yet read herself,
even though Eden had assured her that at four years
old she wasn't expected to read.

Eden took her eyes from her willful daughter and put
them on Nadine. Something was wrong. She knew it,
felt it, saw it on Nadine's face. Her moment of optimism
hadn't lasted nearly long enough. "Fiona, please go
check on Millie. Have her read to you for a while."

Fiona left reluctantly, a grimace on her face. When
she was gone, Nadine stepped into the room. "I think
I missed something. Maybe a scrap of his shirt that

was blown into the wound, or there's a small sliver of bone I missed."

Eden went dizzy at the picture those possibilities presented.

"His fever is getting higher, and the wound is infected. I'm going to have to go back in."

Daniel reached the doorway in two long strides. "But you can fix it, right?"

"I think so," Nadine said weakly.

"You *think* so?"

Eden rushed past them and toward the stairs, catching the last of their conversation.

"Get Nate for me," Nadine ordered. "I'm going to need help."

Nate wasted no time rushing over to the hotel, leaving Cash standing in front of the church with his hands in his pockets. He had never felt so helpless in his life.

He looked to the church, quiet and deceptively divine in the last light of day.

None of this was fair, he thought with a rising surge of pure anger. Sullivan, Eden, Nadine, JD . . . they didn't deserve any of this.

He turned and ran up the stairs to the church doors, throwing them open, stepping inside with fury and frustration and despair in his heart. He slammed the doors behind him, looked heavenward to the rustic, weathered ceiling, and shouted.

"What the hell do you want from me?"

He didn't get an answer. Of course not. He hadn't

talked to God in a long time, and even then . . . no one had ever been listening.

Alone in the long room, he stalked down the aisle. His boots clipped loudly on the uncovered wooden floor as he approached the altar. "I screw up, and everyone else has to pay. Well, if you have something to take out on me, take it out on *me,* you cowardly son of a bitch."

The light from outdoors was dying, so he lit a candle. He wasn't finished, not by a long shot. "You can't take Sullivan," he said in a lowered voice. Even he could hear the fear there. "He and Eden . . . they have all those kids, and another one on the way, and I don't think they're done yet. I don't think they're *close* to done. Why would you even think of taking his life?"

He paced before the altar where Nadine had become his wife. "If you're trying to make me pay through them, through Sullivan and Eden, through Nadine and JD, well . . . you've made your point. They haven't done anything wrong. They're here every Sunday, they live like goddamn saints. What else do you want?"

Cash stopped before the altar. "You want me on my knees, is that it?" He dropped to his knees, eyes heavenward, arms open wide. "Well, here I am," he whispered.

He heard the door open, turned his head to see Jo stick her head inside, no doubt brought by the noise he'd been making.

"Get out," he said. She obeyed, never saying a word.

Alone again, in the echo of the closing doors he closed his eyes. "I'm begging you," he said softly. "Don't let Sullivan die, don't make Eden pay for my mistakes. The kids need them, this town needs them. I don't want to be responsible for making Eden a widow, for Fiona growing up without a father. I don't want to be the man who killed her daddy."

His eyes stung as he kneeled there, his heart beat too hard. "And while I'm here, I might as well ask you to take care of Nadine and JD after I'm gone. They shouldn't suffer just because I love them. It isn't fair."

Life wasn't fair, and he had never expected anything so simple as justice in his world. But he wanted it now; he actually prayed for it.

He stayed there for a long time, on his knees. Cursing God, begging for justice. The light outside faded away until the only illumination came from the single candle he'd lit. No one else came to the door to tell him Sullivan was alive or dead, recovering or on his deathbed. So he prayed awhile longer.

His head swam, he swayed on his knees. He hadn't slept for more than two days, he hadn't eaten either. It was all catching up with him.

He dragged himself up and stepped back to the front pew, sitting down hard.

"What else can I do?" he whispered. "What the hell else can I do?"

Nadine was glad to have Nate with her as she treated Sullivan. This seemed to be his area of expertise, and he was eerily efficient. She didn't want to know how he had come to know so much about treating such wounds.

It was a scrap of fabric that interfered with the healing, just as Nadine had suspected. Going back into the already nasty wound was not for the squeamish, so no one remained in the room. No one but Nadine and the preacher. Even Sullivan was no longer with them, since he'd passed out as soon as Nadine had cut into his shoulder.

From everything she'd heard, Nate and Cash had once been two of a kind. For a long time they'd hired out their guns and lived with nothing to lose. Why was it that Nate could start over and Cash couldn't?

"This has been hard on Cash," Nate said, as if he could read Nadine's mind.

"I know."

"You wouldn't think it to look at him, but he's really not a bad person. He's just made some . . . really bad decisions."

"You don't have to tell me that," she said, glancing up. "Might not hurt for you to tell him, though."

Nate almost smiled. "He doesn't listen to me much anymore."

"Does he listen to anyone?" she snapped, unable to hide her anger.

"You know, he talked about you once, years ago."

"He did?" She looked down, not wanting Nate to see the pain in her eyes.

"I don't remember everything about our time on the trail," Nate qualified. "I used to drink. A lot. This night I'm thinking of, Cash got rip-roaring drunk with me. I don't know what set him off. Something that didn't seem like much at the time. We sat around a campfire in the middle of nowhere. He talked about a girl he used to know, and I pretended not to listen."

Nadine swallowed hard. She didn't want to know that sometimes Cash revealed his tender side for the world. It gave her hope, and she should have none. "That was a long time ago."

"Yes, it was," Nate said as together they finished bandaging Sullivan's wound. "But he loved you then, and I truly believe he loves you now."

"He has a funny way of showing his love."

Nate was silent for a moment, so Nadine looked up to study a suddenly solemn face. "Yeah," he finally said. "He does."

Nineteen

The world was his kingdom, and he ruled with the ruthlessness of a nineteen-year-old king who has no heart. He showed no mercy and he no longer feared death, and soon they called him a hero.

The soldiers he fought with called him fearless, a hero, but they were afraid of him, too. They were afraid of the deadness of his eyes and the accuracy of his aim and the way he stood tall before the enemy, as if daring them to shoot him. Bullets whizzed around him but never found their mark.

And so they sent him here. Cash studied the men in the secluded camp. The half-breed long-haired Sullivan, who hadn't said ten words in two days, and the Mex kid who tagged along with him, a boy surely too young to go to war, stayed close together much of the time. The kid, Rico, was damned good with a knife, no matter how young he was. The rough and vulgar Jed Rourke swaggered around the camp carrying his rifle like it was a part of him, another limb. Or a woman. The big man looked like he hadn't had a shave or a haircut or a bath in a while. A long while.

Nate Lang stayed drunk, and was given to quoting

the Bible when he was so intoxicated he couldn't stand up straight. Rourke had made the mistake of trying to stick Nate with the nickname Preacher. Nate had not taken it well, but in the days to come he would let Cash call him Rev. He didn't seem to mind that irreverent tag so much. Reese had quickly become their leader, not because he wanted to be but because he was the only man fit for the job. Determined and serious, he was a man who would brook no nonsense.

They were all heroes of a sort. Not a one of them was over twenty-five, and not a one of them was afraid to die.

Nate plopped himself down beside Cash and offered to share his flask. Cash refused.

The drunk looked up and down Cash's crisp uniform. Of the six, he was the only one wearing anything that remotely resembled a uniform. The jacket was open, offering him access to the double six-shooters he wore, and revealing a strictly nonregulation shirt.

"Nice shirt," Nate said, slurring the words just slightly. "No holes, no blood . . . It isn't even dirty. And ruffles on a soldier. I swear, it just doesn't look right." He squinted at the elaborate garment as if it pained him to look upon such a thing.

"This is my lucky shirt," Cash explained. The first of many, though he didn't know it yet.

"How lucky?" The drunk wobbled uncertainly as he took another sip from his flask.

"I haven't been shot since I put it on."

"Where does one obtain such a lucky shirt."

"I got mine from four grateful women."

Nate's eyebrows went up. "Four? At the same time?"

Cash nodded.

"I'm in awe," Nate mumbled, not sounding at all impressed.

So far nothing about this bunch had impressed Cash. Of course, they hadn't seen action yet. That would come soon enough. He might eventually respect them, but they would never be friends. Friends got their faces blown off or stabbed you in the back.

Nate continued to study Cash's getup curiously. "Are you as good with the left hand as with the right?"

"Almost." A little more practice, and he would be. Two guns meant twice as many bullets, twice as long to fight without having to stop and reload. Cash conducted an inspection of his own. His gaze finally ended up on Nate's head. There wasn't much to see. "What did you do to your hair? It looks like shit."

The drunk raised a hand to touch the very short stubble on his head. "I got tired of messing with it. It's not that bad. You'll get used to it."

Cash was quite sure he wouldn't be a part of this motley crew long enough to get used to anything.

Nate leaned too close, so close something in Cash went on alert. The hair on the back of his neck stood up as the drunk squinted at Cash's chin. "Kid, are you trying to grow a beard?"

"Yes," Cash answered in a low voice tinged with warning.

Nate didn't heed that warning. "Doesn't look like much of a beard to me."

"It will. I just started growing it." A month ago, he thought sourly, almost envying the hairy, older Rourke.

The drunk laid eyes that saw too much on Cash. "Why are you here?" he whispered.

"Because I'm good," Cash said proudly.

"Good at what?"

"Good at killing people."

Nate leaned in close. "So am I," he hissed. "So are we all."

Cash closed his eyes for a second, and when he opened them again, everything had changed. Sullivan was gone. A chill running up Cash's spine told him something was wrong. And then Eden walked from behind a wide tree, the gun in her hand aimed for his heart.

"You killed him," she said softly. "You killed him." In an instant she became the thief who had blown off Melvin's face, and then, an instant later, she was Eden again. She pulled the trigger.

Cash came up off the pew with a low cry. His heart pounded hard. His blood ran cold beneath his skin, and he still felt the explosion of gunfire from his nightmare. He laid a hand against his heart, checking for blood.

It took him a moment to remember where he was, what had happened. The candle on the altar had burned down to nothing and snuffed itself out. Early morning light shot through the windows.

They all knew he was here. If Jo knew, everyone knew. If Sullivan had survived the surgery, someone would have come to tell him. If he had died, someone would have come to tell him. Which meant Sullivan was still caught in between. Not dead, not alive.

Cash dropped his head into his hands. "You want a

life?" he whispered. "Take mine. It's a good trade, I promise you. I have more sins to atone for. Prove to me that you do know what justice is, and take my life in exchange for Sullivan's."

The doors behind him burst open, and JD ran to the front pew, wide-eyed and looking so damned young. The man within him was there, too, but he was still very much a child.

"There's a man here looking for you," JD said softly. "I couldn't sleep, so I went for a walk and there he was." The boy took a deep breath. "He said you killed his brother and he wants to call you out."

"Now?"

JD nodded. "What should I do? Should I get Uncle Jed?"

Cash laid a hand on JD's shoulder. "No. I can handle it. You run along and get into the hotel. Into one of the back rooms," he added. Just to be safe.

JD nodded again.

"How's Sullivan?"

"Better, I think," JD said.

"Good. Tell this man I'll be out in five minutes. I'll meet him in front of Rogue's Palace. The clinic," he amended. There was no more Rogue's Palace. "And then you go to the hotel, like I told you."

"Okay. Are you sure you don't want me to—"

"JD," Cash interrupted. If he thought about this too long, he'd change his mind. "Take care of your mother for me."

The kid's eyes went wide. "I will."

After JD had gone, Cash looked heavenward. "You work fast, I'll give you that."

* * *

JD delivered the message to the twitchy gunman and then ran back to the hotel, bounding up the stairs. Cash wouldn't have told him to take care of his mother unless . . . unless he didn't plan to survive this gunfight.

Last night he'd heard the preacher's wife telling her husband that Cash was in the church. He'd stayed there all night, apparently. Strange for a man who claimed to never set a foot in one.

He didn't like the way Cash had looked. Something about his eyes was . . . wrong. Deep in his gut, JD had a bad feeling about what was about to happen. He had to do something, didn't he? He couldn't just ignore this certainty that something really bad was about to happen.

JD burst into his mother's room. He wasn't going to hide in the back of the hotel like Cash had told him to, waiting to see what would happen next.

He should have known it would be a child, a freckle-faced kid not much older than JD, who came for him.

"Daniel Cash?" the kid asked, his voice squeaking uncertainly as Cash approached.

At just past dawn the streets of Rock Creek were deserted.

"Yep," Cash said calmly.

"I'm calling you out." The kid's voice was in the process of changing, either that or he was so scared, he couldn't manage to speak properly.

Cash gave the kid a cold, confident smile. "Are you putting me on?"

The kid shook his head. "You killed my brother in Webberville. He challenged you—"

"Webberville?" Cash asked with a slow, cold grin. "The only man I ever shot in Webberville tried to ambush me while I was unarmed and in bed with a woman. That was your brother?"

"He never woulda done that," the kid said softly.

Time's up. Cash knew that as he took a single step toward the frightened kid. He also knew that if he wanted to, he could take this boy out in the blink of an eye. The kid could draw first, but it wouldn't make any difference. *No more.* He was not about to shoot a freckle-faced kid whose voice hadn't changed yet. A child. A baby.

Cash spread his legs wide, took a firm and confident stance as he deftly unbuckled his gun belt and let it drop to the ground. The kid was too damned slow. The gun belt and the fancy six-shooters had already hit the ground before his own gun cleared the holster.

"You want to shoot me?" Cash asked calmly, spreading his arms wide.

"Cash."

Cash turned his head to see that JD watched from the boardwalk, just a few feet away. "Get out of here."

JD shook his head. Just as well, Cash thought as he returned his attention to the redheaded gunman. If JD ever decided again that he wanted to be a gunfighter, maybe this moment would be enough to scare some sense back into the kid.

With a yank he opened his ruffled shirt and presented the gun-wielding kid with an expanse of bare chest. "In the heart is best. Fast and clean. You don't want some wounded hombre coming back up on you, trust me."

He took a step forward. The kid's response was to shake. His legs trembled; his gun hand shook.

"Ever killed a man before?"

The boy shook his head quickly.

"Might as well get used to the sight of blood, then, the way a bullet tears into flesh. It's not pretty, but a gunfighter who retches over his victim is rarely feared and respected."

The boy's gaze was fixed to Cash's bare chest. "Aren't you going to pick up your guns?"

Cash shook his head. "No, I'm not. This is your lucky day, boy. You came calling on the morning I decided to retire for good. But before you become the man who shot Daniel Cash, let me give you a few pointers."

"Sh-sh-sure," the kid stuttered.

"You're about to become famous. A man needs to know what to expect when he enters a new profession, right? Otherwise you're just going to make yourself look stupid, and we can't have that."

He continued to bare his chest, his heart, for the kid as he walked slowly forward. "It's hardest in the beginning," he revealed. "The first time you see a man's guts spread across the ground, you want to run behind the nearest tree and spew your own guts up. But you don't," he added in a lowered voice. "You push it down, you squash it deep. It'll be that way for a while when you kill a man and you realize that a *thing* lies where a living human used to be. That a man's brains are gray, that he always manages to look . . . surprised right before he dies. But you don't give in. You push it deep."

The kid swallowed so hard, his Adam's apple bobbed.

"After a while it doesn't seem so horrible anymore."

The boy, wide-eyed, nodded.

"It gets worse," Cash whispered. "Pretty soon you find that you can't sleep, you can't . . . rest. Every rustle of a leaf might be the snick of a trigger. Every settling board in a house might be the creak of an intruder. Someone is coming for you, and he's faster, meaner, smarter than you are. Somebody's brother, son, father. You know he's coming, you just don't know when. Or where." Cash flicked his gaze to the boardwalk, where JD shadowed his every step. "Are you listening to me?"

"Yes, sir," JD said solemnly.

Cash fixed his gaze on the redheaded kid again. "So when is he going to arrive? While you're eating breakfast? Sleeping? Making love to a beautiful woman? You sit with your back to the wall, you keep an ear open at all times, and you never, never know a moment's peace."

The would-be gunfighter went pale, ghostly white.

"You trust no one," Cash whispered. "And true friends are rare. People cringe when they see you coming because they know you bring death with you. They smile and pretend to be your friend so you won't shoot them in the back. They smile and despise you.

"You watch while the people around you move on with their lives, take wives, have babies, make families, and you know you can never have what they've found, because if you mark a woman or a child with your name, you make them a target. You put them in danger simply because you . . . care for them. You can't tell a woman you love her. You can't even claim your own son." He looked at JD, and at that moment the kid knew. It showed on his paling face, in his sad eyes. The boy knew Daniel Cash was his father.

"And then the last phase hits you," Cash said softly, returning his attention to the redheaded gunman. "You don't care anymore, and it's much easier that way. You live by instinct alone. Something gets in your way, you shoot it. Your arm, your gun hand"—he offered his right hand for inspection—"takes on a life and a mind of its own. You become . . . a machine. A thing with no more heart than the bodies you've left scattered behind you. You become a man who would shoot a friend first and think later."

Cash had almost reached the trembling kid. When was the last time he'd cried? He knew exactly. Fourteen years ago. But right now tears filled and burned his eyes and he didn't care. "And then nothing matters anymore," he whispered. "Nothing."

He grabbed the barrel of the gun the kid held and pulled the muzzle against his chest so it touched his heart. "Go for the heart and make it fast. Do me one favor and don't make me lie in the street twitching and moaning and dying slow. That's so undignified. Not a pleasant way to go and not a pleasant thing to watch." He looked deep into the boy's pale eyes. "Pull the goddamn trigger and get on with it, kid."

"No!" JD shouted, lifting a hand that, Cash saw too late, held a six-shooter.

"Put that down," Cash ordered calmly.

"But you're . . ." JD began. "I can't let him . . ."

"JD, this kid is going to shoot me, and you're not

going to do a damn thing about it. Do you hear me? I won't have you taking up where I left off. I want better for you."

JD lowered his arm, and the redhead released the grip of the gun aimed at Cash's heart as if it had suddenly become hot. Cash caught the weapon by the barrel and easily tossed it aside. "Change your mind?"

"Did my brother really try to shoot you while you were in bed?"

Cash nodded once.

"So it was . . . self-defense when you shot him?"

Again Cash nodded.

The kid shook his head furiously. "They said . . . I thought you . . . Rollie wanted to make a name for himself, and he said . . . Aw, hell, I just want to get out of here."

"Not so fast."

Cash froze at the sound of that voice.

"I was just leaving, Sheriff," the boy said. "I swear."

Cash closed his eyes and wished the kid had shot him. Slowly he turned around, and saw that it wasn't just Sullivan behind him, but all of them. All five. Sullivan was pale but blessedly whole, his arm bandaged and in a sling, a six-shooter hanging from his left hand. Only someone who knew him well would realize that he was holding himself upright by leaning into Jed. That Nate, standing to the other side and just behind, added his support with a hand at Sullivan's back.

Sullivan looked suitably imposing, badge, bandage, and all. Rico held a Bowie knife in one hand, Jed had his Winchester, Reese was wearing both guns, and

Nate, in his preacher's collar, held a rifle as if he knew what to do with it. And he did.

"I want you to give a message to anyone you happen to meet who has the same kind of idea you had," Reese said calmly. "It's a simple message. If a man comes here to do battle with one of us, he takes on all six."

"All ten," a low voice said, and JD, Johnny, Teddy, and Rafe, youngsters no longer boys and not yet men, armed and stern-faced, joined the other five.

"Make that fifteen," a strident voice insisted, and Hannah stepped forward, a rifle in her hands. Lily had a knife, Jo and Mary each held six-shooters, and Eden was armed with a rolling pin. Most of them looked like they'd come straight from bed, hastily dressed and disheveled. They presented quite a picture.

"Sixteen," Nadine said softly, stepping into the street, unarmed, to stand beside Cash.

People began to come out, most of them armed in one way or another, to line up behind the six. The sixteen.

Reese managed a wan smile. "Let me amend that. Anyone who comes here to take on one of us takes on the entire Rock Creek Army."

The kid turned tail and ran for his horse. Within a matter of seconds the would-be gunfighter was high-tailing it out of town as though the Rock Creek Army was on his tail. Cash watched him go. The boy never so much as glanced over his shoulder.

Nadine moved so she stood directly before him. "Why didn't you tell me what your life was like?" she whispered.

"How much did you hear?"

"Enough," she said.

The emotions of the past fourteen years welled up inside him, choking him, threatening to send up everything he'd so diligently pushed down all these years. Two solitary tears ran down his cheeks. "Oh, God, don't let them see me like this. I'll never live it down," he whispered.

Nadine placed her hands on his cheeks, caressing him and at the same time wiping away the tears, and then she came up on her toes and laid her mouth over his.

"I love you," she whispered.

"That doesn't mean we can make this work," he answered softly. "I'm still . . ."

"Don't tell me you don't love me," she whispered. "I heard what you said, and besides . . . I had time for a few words with the ladies this morning while the guys were getting dressed and armed." She looked deep into his eyes. "You asked Eden to look out for me, Jo to make sure JD went to church. Lily to teach our baby to sing if it's a girl, Hannah . . ."

"Can't anyone in this town keep a secret?" Cash asked, turning around to glare at the Rock Creek Army.

"Families don't keep secrets," Eden said softly.

"I'm not—"

"Yes, you are," she interrupted.

"I can keep a secret, Uncle Cash," Fiona said, dancing away from the boardwalk and her sister Millie with her hand in the air. "I didn't tell anybody that Millie thinks JD is bery han'some."

"Fiona!" Millie shouted, horrified that her secret was out.

Fiona clapped a hand over her mouth. A moment

later, she lowered that hand slowly. "Whoops. I guess I can't keep a secret, either."

Cash turned to face them all—his friends, the people from town he had been so sure disdained him for who he had become, the women who had made these men and this town their own. What words were sufficient for a moment like this one? There were none.

His eyes landed on Rico's wife, properly formidable with a wicked knife in her hand. "I can't believe that even Lily came out to defend me," he said in a light-hearted voice.

The crowd began to break up as Lily stepped forward. "You might be a worthless rogue, Cash, but you are *our* worthless rogue."

"I knew you could insult me in English if you really wanted to."

Rico collected his wife, and they made their way arm in arm back to Three Queens.

Jed and Nate assisted Sullivan back into the hotel, and the Rock Creek Army dispersed, leaving Cash and Nadine and JD alone in the street.

The would-be gunfighter was gone; now things were going to get really scary.

"Are you really my . . ." JD began, turning pale.

No more secrets. "Yes," Cash said, offering a hand to the kid, inviting him into his arms and his life. "Are you horrified? Disgusted? Angry? I would be if I were in your shoes."

JD shook his head and walked slowly forward. "I don't know why, but it seems right to me."

In the middle of Rock Creek's main street, Cash took

his wife and son into a long, slow embrace. "I wish I could be certain I could keep you both safe forever."

"Nothing in life is certain," Nadine said calmly. "Give me a choice, and I'll take my chances with you."

"Me, too," JD whispered.

Nadine lifted her head and laid her lips briefly over his. "I love you, Danny."

He smiled.

It had been planned as a double wedding for the Cashes and the Rourkes, but at the last minute Jed and Hannah backed out. Jed declared he was about as married as a man could get, and besides . . . he wanted to stand back and watch Cash take his vows. A sight he didn't mind saying he'd thought never to see.

They were already married, but Cash had said he wanted to do this for Nadine . . . and for himself. It was a big step, the biggest, and he wanted to take it in front of the friends who had become his family.

Cash and Nadine were married, for the second time, beside the river at sunrise. Flowers from Eden's garden had been placed here and there, and everyone was in attendance. Even a healing Sullivan. Fiona and Georgie wore pink dresses that almost matched, and carried more flowers from Eden's garden. Fiona had been a little put out that Cash was not marrying her, since she insisted that she'd asked him first, but being a flower girl had mollified her. Nadine finally got her perfect wedding, her perfect wedding day.

The ceremony was performed by Nate, who did his best to keep a straight face. He managed to appear properly solemn most of the time. Nadine didn't mind, since the reverend's occasional smiles were as warm as the morning sun.

When Nate pronounced them man and wife, for the second time, his grin bloomed full and true.

After the ceremony, everyone gathered around to congratulate the bride and groom. There was lots of teasing in the grass by the river, a few happy tears.

In the past two days, Nadine had heard all about the favors Cash had asked of his friends. Everyone had been asked at least one favor, as Cash tried to hand the care of his family over to his friends. And he had almost convinced her that he didn't care.

Cash had asked everyone for something . . . everyone but Sullivan. He still insisted that he didn't have the right to ask anything of the man he'd shot. She wondered if Cash would ever completely forgive himself.

Sullivan was healing remarkably well, though he still didn't have all his strength back. Eden had as much to so with that healing as any medicine, Nadine knew.

The sheriff ambled over to Cash, his face stern and still paler than Nadine liked. He should have stayed in bed today, but nothing could keep him away from Daniel Cash's wedding, or so he said.

"Cash," he said in a low voice.

Nadine watched as her husband turned to face the man he'd shot. "Sullivan." He looked the sheriff up and down. "You're looking better."

"I'm feeling better."

"You do know I hated having to shoot you," Cash said, looking around to make sure Fiona was nowhere near.

Sullivan nodded. "Don't give it another thought. If you ever draw on one of my kids, I'll return the favor."

Cash patted his black-trousered thighs. "That'll be tough to do with no pistols."

"How does that feel?" Sullivan asked, nodding toward the place where holsters usually hung.

"Different," Cash admitted. "A little naked, but I think I can get used to it."

"Good." Sullivan smiled as Eden came up behind him and wrapped her arm around his waist.

"Time for us to go home," she said. "You boys okay?"

The men both nodded, and Eden and Sullivan left, walking slowly back toward town. Their brood followed behind them—and what a brood it was.

In a little while there would be a large celebratory breakfast in the hotel dining room. Since everyone was doing their part to put the special meal together, one by one the wedding attendees followed the Sullivans back to town, leaving the newlyweds and their son alone by the river.

JD, who had stoically accepted the news that Cash was his father, had been quieter than usual for the past couple of days. Cash had not pushed him and neither had Nadine. They'd let him have this time to accept everything he'd learned.

With the crowd scattered and nowhere left to hide, JD joined his parents with a solemn expression on his young face. He looked boldly up at Cash. Nadine didn't know what might come next; she was prepared for anything.

"Can I call you Dad?"

Cash smiled. Oh, he was beautiful when he smiled

this way, real and contented. "You'd better. Would you think I was being too weird if I told you I love you?"

"Yeah," JD said, but his smile was wide.

Nadine hadn't seen her son this happy in a very long time. This moment was better than gold.

JD ran off, telling them that he'd promised Teddy he'd help with the morning chores. When he was gone, everything was so still and quiet she could hear her own heartbeat.

Cash laid his hands on her face and looked her in the eye. "For better or for worse takes on a whole new meaning when you're marrying me."

"I know that," Nadine said softly.

"And yet here we are," he said, wonder in his voice. "I swear, I don't know whether to be relieved or terrified."

"I know exactly how I feel." She rose up on her toes and kissed him quickly. "Happy. Lucky. Blessed."

"I love you, Nadine Cash," he whispered.

"I love you, too."

He closed his eyes and took a deep breath. A half-smile flitted across his face. "Everything's going to be all right," he said. "I know it in my gut and in my heart." He opened his eyes and smiled wickedly at her, swung her up into his arms, and started walking toward town.

"I'm not really all that hungry," he said. "Let's go home, back to the clinic. Everybody else will be busy at the hotel. Maybe we can play a quick game of cards."

"Cards?"

"I know a game where no one loses." He kissed her quick and winked. "High card gets to be on top."

Epilogue

One year later

Luke Chandler slowed the pace of his horse as he neared Rock Creek. Not because he was nervous, of course. He just needed a few minutes to catch his breath, that's all. The little town looked different than he'd imagined it would. There was an awful lot of building going on, nice houses going up just beyond the main street, new buildings edging toward the boundary of the little town. Sure didn't look like anything to be afraid of.

This was where he'd make his name, once and for all. No more cowboying, no more wasting his time on stupid shooting competitions . . . By killing Daniel Cash, he'd finally make a name for himself.

The rumors he'd heard couldn't be true. A shudder, perhaps a small part of himself that wasn't so sure, shimmied down his spine. Stories, that's all they were. Tales to scare away anyone who might cause trouble. Of course, he'd heard the stories in more than one town, from more than one person.

They said that every now and then some really bad

men headed down this way, and they never came back. Just a few months ago, the Hargett gang had ridden to Rock Creek after hearing some silly tale about a bunch of gold. They hadn't been seen since.

Luke shook off the shiver in his spine. Jim Hargett was the meanest man he'd ever met, and the other members of his gang were almost as mean as he was. They'd probably just headed for Mexico, that's all. Yeah, that's it. Mexico.

It was after noon as he rode down the middle of the street. A kid playing in front of the hotel didn't mind telling him where he might find Daniel Cash. Luke flexed his fingers, worked a crick out of his neck, and headed in that direction.

The sign over the door he'd been directed to stopped him. THE ROCK CREEK CLINIC. Darn. What if someone had shot Daniel Cash before he got here!

Luke opened the door and pushed through, hand steady and resting over the butt of his gun, heart pounding as he wondered what he'd find here. He didn't feel bad about what he was going to do. From everything he'd heard, Daniel Cash was every bit as mean as Jim Hargett.

There were a couple of beds in the dim room, and what had once been a bar was lined with medicine and surgical equipment. In the center of the room, studiously bent over a young, dark-haired girl, sat a man in black. He had a small beard and mustache, the way Luke had heard Cash did, but this couldn't be the man he'd come looking for. There wasn't a gun to be seen.

Luke took his stance and rotated his neck, again

working out some of the stiffness. "I'm looking for a gunfighter named Cash."

The man lifted his head, met Luke's stare, then sighed and said, "Give me a minute, I'm almost done."

Ah, the doctor knew where Cash was. The gunslinger had been silent for so long, a lot of people were beginning to think Cash was dead. Luke didn't think so.

The doctor took his time with his patient. Removing a splinter, it looked like.

"Tell me again how you did this?" the doctor asked as he worked.

"I was climbing the post in front of the hotel."

"Why?"

"To get to the roof."

The doctor lifted his head and raised his eyebrows in obvious disapproval. "The roof? Why?"

The little girl shrugged. "Why not? I've never been up there before."

"No more climbing posts, or anything else, for a month," the doc said.

"A whole month!"

"Yes, a month, Fiona."

Fiona pouted but grudgingly agreed.

Finally, the doctor finished with his patient. The little girl looked at her finger and said, "Thanks, Uncle Cash."

"You're quite welcome, sweetheart," he answered with a smile.

Fiona left, barely slowing her step to look up as she passed. "You are in so much trouble," she whispered.

The doctor turned his full attention Luke's way. A

knot in his stomach, Luke looked into black eyes. "Did she call you . . . Uncle Cash?"

"Yep."

His mind worked. "So, the man I'm looking for is your brother or something?"

"Nope." Cash stood slowly. He spread his arms wide. "The man you're looking for is right here."

Luke didn't like the indecision that plagued him. Not only had he caught the man doctoring a little girl, Cash wasn't even wearing a gun. What kind of gunslinger was this?

"Strap on your guns and let's go," Luke ordered, setting his indecision aside.

Cash, *Uncle* Cash, the doctor . . . shook his head. "No. I don't do that anymore."

"What do you mean you don't do that anymore? You can't just . . . just *quit.*"

"Of course I can," Cash said calmly. "I don't shoot people anymore unless I really don't have any choice. In fact, I'm learning how to fix them instead."

"You mean to tell me you're really a *doctor?* " Luke holstered his gun in disgust.

"Learning to be." Cash smiled. "I'm learning to be a lot of things besides a gunfighter."

A woman with a baby in her arms, a tiny baby wrapped in a thin pink blanket, came walking down the stairs. "A new patient?"

"Not yet," Cash said with a small smile. "But if he doesn't change his ways, he's going to be somebody's patient one of these days."

He kissed the woman and took the baby from her. "How's my Caroline. Did she have a good nap?"